D1007381

MADDER CARMINE

MADDER CARMINE

or

A THRILLING ACCOUNT OF GUN
BATTLES, ROMANCE, HARROWING
ESCAPES, UNSHAVEN VILLAINS,
A SNAKEBITE, A DUBIOUS CIRCUS,
A MYSTERIOUS GIRL WITH A PALETTE
OF PAINTS AND A YOUNG MAN'S
EPIC JOURNEY TO FIND HER

TYLER ENFIELD

Copyright ©2015 Tyler Enfield
Enfield & Wizenty
(an imprint of Great Plains Publications)
233 Garfield Street
Winnipeg, MB R3G 2M1
www.greatplains.mb.ca

All rights reserved. No part of this publication may be reproduced or transmitted
in any form or in any means, or stored in a database and retrieval system,
without the prior written permission of Great Plains Publications, or, in the case
of photocopying or other reprographic copying, a license from Access Copyright
(Canadian Copyright Licensing Agency), 1 Yonge Street, Suite 1900, Toronto,
Ontario, Canada, M5E 1E5.

Great Plains Publications gratefully acknowledges the financial support provided
for its publishing program by the Government of Canada through the Canada
Book Fund; the Canada Council for the Arts; the Province of Manitoba through
the Book Publishing Tax Credit and the Book Publisher Marketing Assistance
Program; and the Manitoba Arts Council.

Design & Typography by Relish New Brand Experience
Printed in Canada by Friesens

LIBRARY AND ARCHIVES CANADA CATALOGUING IN PUBLICATION

Enfield, Tyler, author
    Madder Carmine / Tyler Enfield.

Issued in print and electronic formats.
ISBN 978-1-927855-30-0 (paperback).--ISBN 978-1-927855-31-7 (epub).--
ISBN 978-1-927855-32-4 (mobi)

    I. Title.

PS8609.N4M34 2015   JC813'.6   C2015-903704-2
                                         C2015-903705-0

ENVIRONMENTAL BENEFITS STATEMENT

Great Plains Publications saved the following
resources by printing the pages of this book on
chlorine free paper made with 100% post-consumer
waste.

TREES	WATER	ENERGY	SOLID WASTE	GREENHOUSE GASES
7	3,400	3	227	627
FULLY GROWN	GALLONS	MILLION BTUs	POUNDS	POUNDS

Environmental impact estimates were made using the Environmental Paper Network
Paper Calculator 3.2. For more information visit www.papercalculator.org.

Canadä

FSC
www.fsc.org
MIX
Paper from
responsible sources
FSC™ C016245

"MY GUIDE AND I ENTERED THAT HIDDEN TUNNEL
TO MAKE OUR WAY BACK UP TO THE SHINING WORLD...
WE CLIMBED, HE FIRST AND I BEHIND, UNTIL
THROUGH A SMALL ROUND OPENING AHEAD OF
US I SAW THE LOVELY THINGS THE HEAVENS HOLD,
AND WE CAME OUT TO SEE ONCE MORE THE STARS."

—Dante Alighieri, *Inferno*

PART I

STRANGE FOLK

I T IS AN INVINCIBLE FACT: WHEN A MAN FINDS HIMSELF outdoors without a pair of britches to his name, his whole world can be reduced to this lack. He has one thought only, like a giant magnet in his mind, forever tugging the iron of his will back to it. That thought is britches. And how can I get me some.

I myself can speak to this phenomenon for I have walked fifty-four miles through the Blue Honey Mountains, from Hickamaw to Nuckton without the benefit of a solitary sock. And let me tell you, until you feel the ice of wind across your hinterparts, you just don't know how lonesome a body can grow for a patch of cloth.

Need can be emboldening, and so can be the cold, so when I strode into my hometown that hapless day in late September of 1849 I did not slow my pace. A wagon driver saw me and whoa-whoa'd his horse. The sounds of hammering faltered. A mother shushed her child. A fella pulled the pipe from his mouth and followed me up the road with his eyes, but what can you do? You either got pants or you don't. The Lawsons' general store was near enough the edge of town and I bore the mixed hope that after six years gone they'd still remember me there, after which they'd summarily forget. I stamped up the porch and went directly in.

"Low there," I says, tipping what would have been my hat to the girl at the counter. She over-poured corn from the sack she was weighing, one side of the brass scale clanking against the counter and little kernels skittering across the floor like beads. The look on her face I found difficult to read, but I began to relax some, for it appeared nobody was going to reach for a rifle.

What's more, I believed I knew that clerk. It was Rachel Lawson, the storeman's daughter, standing there in her blue lace apron, looking sort of froze-like, staring, hands at her ears to hold back her curtain of locks. Rachel had one of those faces so pale, her eyelashes were practically invisible. That's Rachel Lawson. And quite a nice girl if I recall.

"How come you ain't got no britches on?"

None too delicate in her observations, though.

"Long story. Look here, how about setting me up with a pair of them overalls you got on the shelf back there." We'd never spoken that I could recall, but I knew of her good. Good old Rachel Lawson. "And while you're at it, might as well take down a couple of them licorice ropes for yourself. It's on me."

She let her hair fall back into her eyes. "And how you plan to pay for it all?"

Looking around, it seemed folks in the store were starting to take some notice of my situation.

"Pay?"

"Yeah. Pay."

"Welp," says I. "That is the thing of it. As I don't seem to got much on me right now."

"Now that's a fact."

Shrewd too, that girl. Though she failed to fathom that between money and britches, money was by far the lesser of my two predicaments. "Listen," I says. I tell her, "Listen here, I'm trusting you to see these are extra-ordinary circumstances. A fella does not choose to go thus clad, and on account of this fact you might be willing to forego all your little fancy conventions and allow me to—"

"My little—my—wait, what do I got?"

I tried to clarify with a vague wave of my hand. "Payment," I says. "You know, payment. Let me work for them denims. I ain't asking for charity, just a set of overalls and the labor to pay for it."

She just looked at me a while. A long while she looked. She seemed to be debating the seriousness of the affair, batting it around in her mind like she was watching someone in a clown suit trying to touch off a stick of dynamite. And I can tell you, there are a good deal more than sixty seconds to a minute when you're standing around, counting them naked.

By and by, old Rachel, she clucked her tongue in recognition. "Wait, I remember you! You're one of them Lereaux, aren't you! From up Blackwater Hollow? You're that Dannon one, that Dannon Lereaux."

It was the truth she spoke, and I told her so.

"You been gone long enough," she says. "So where you been?"

"Oh, you know."

"Huh," she says, laying her forearm on the counter and sweeping the corn back onto an open newspaper, then leaning forward on both hands all contemplative-like. "Dannon Lereaux. Isn't that something. So what are you, like eighteen now? So what you been up to? You're doing well?"

"Oh, well, you know," I says. Then recalling my manners, I added, "So how's your daddy been?"

"You know Daddy? Oh, what am I saying, course you do. Yeah, he's doing good."

"Good. That's good," I says. "Yeah, and your mama? She's doing fine?"

"Mama? Oh she's doing good. Yeah. Yeah she's doing real good."

"Good," I says. "That's real good. Listen, about them denims—"

"But wait! I just thought of a thing! Didn't you used to be the water-witch or something around here?"

"Dannon the Lereaux boy?" says an old fella in suspenders, one of the several onlookers now forming a crescent at my back. "He was a dowser all right. That you boy? You member me?"

I saw right off it was old man Willard. Old Willard Lee that's got the game eye from a horse-kick to the side of the head. Cocking his thumb at me, he says to Rachel, "I swear to you, this boy could locate a rain puddle in China. And if you had a drill could dig deep enough, I'd prove it to you, yes I would. He's the one that dowsed me my nigra well, and I ain't never seen nothing like it."

"Well I knew it!" cried Rachel, who's now all fired up. "Cause I remember good now! They used to say you dowse scientific-like. Like you never miss a well. That so?"

"More than less," I tell her, and then to expedite the matter I laid out how I needed willow switches to do it. A pair of them, and had to be willow. It had been a while, but I suspected I could still locate a spring of good water within ten feet of precision. Good water, mind you. "All goes fine, I can tell you how many gallons per minute you'll be getting too," I added, and old man Willard confirmed this with a 'Hyup' and a nod, that game eye of his rolling round in his head.

Now dowsing's one of those things I've been doing so long I can't remember if I was ever taught proper or just figured it out on my own during my days as a lonely youngin in the Blue Honeys. Either way, I was born to it I suppose. I have a skill in the matter, and as this girl tells me her daddy's looking to dig a second well prior to winter I agreed to the transaction. New clothing for water suited me fine.

Thing is, as she turned around to fetch me my overalls from the shelf, I saw the hem of her dress was tucked up into the back of her underdrawers, which gave me quite a sight of her backside. Course she didn't know this and I could have told her, but something about the irony of a pretty girl in such a sorry state can help a man, who is standing dumb and naked in the middle of a gawking crowd, to salvage the smallest fragment of dignity from what would otherwise be everlasting ruination.

⎯⎯⎯◈⎯⎯⎯

My Pa, he says when I was born I was big as a prize bass, and about as ugly too. His opinion of me never changed much either. I was the middle child of nine, and the only one still alive when Pa declared it wasn't all the loss that stole his faith in God, but our Lord choosing me for the living.

That's Phineas Lereaux for you. Good old Phinny, about as fixed in his path as the Shallewapre River and a heart the color of her mud. His back, too, was slouched as her undercut banks, and I could not walk that river without recalling my old man, hunched in his chestnut rocker, getting cornliquordrunk and ornery.

But I cannot complain, for the man was good enough to kill himself off early on in my days. I was approximately twelve the night his favorite hound dog got killed. By another hound, no less, and old Phinny, he was a fourth generation coon-hunting man who rightly believed God's sole plan, from Adam on down, was expressed in a man and his hound dog running varmints up a tree. Well old Phineas drank himself a fifth of whiskey in his grief and took a long walk down a short path to the river.

Mama said, "'Tis' to our good fortune," and complained only that old Phinny never buried a dime. But if my pa said one word of truth in his life it was on this very topic, that of fortune, the ruthlessly benevolent nature of which this story is really all about.

The day he drowned himself, old Phineas, he tied up all the hounds in the feedshed till the echoes of their baying came back off the mountains. Shoulders humped, he came back out carrying a bucket of corn slop, for reasons no one would ever divine, and chucked the whole of it against the south wall of our cabin. In shape, the spill took the likeness of a turkey, wattles and all, as it spangled the timbers of our log-built and my pa stared at it for the longest while as it dripped slowly to the earth. He was like a madman gazing at himself in the mirror. I could only guess what he saw.

"Fortune."

Then he spat. But even when he didn't spit he had a way of speaking made you think of it. "For-tune!" he says again and then sniffed back something big. I was scattering a pan of corn to the yard chickens, my eyes fixed on Pa, never once thinking to turn away. Somehow I knew, beyond the innocence of my young years, that I would never again encounter a man more generously disgusted with life than my pa was right then. "Mind yourself, Dannon," he says to me then, though his gaze never left the slop on the wall. "Mind yourself boy, because fortune'll abandon you. Like death and certain mules it knows no master, you hear? Death and mules." He turned and chucked the empty pail into the heap of chickens that scattered and arced across our muddy yard. "Even if a man should grab hold of fortune for a time and believe he tugs upon the reins, he is a fool for thinking it."

Slowly, deep in thought-like, he scraped the bottom of one bare foot clean and then the other against the sagging steps of our porch, leaving little crests of mud to dry with the others. "Death and mules…"

That night old Phinny found death all right. As to the mules part of it all, I wouldn't learn till later. For it wasn't long after Pa died they sent me away.

Old Rachel, the storeman's pale-face daughter, she was good as her word. She set me up with the overalls and a decent hat, and a plug of black tobacco near big as my fist. She gave me a new hankie for my pocket too, a nice pocket hankie, only it was red, which I cannot see on account my color blindness. Daltonism, they call it. Mixing up my reds and greens. They say it probably has to do with all the haywire in my head and would straighten itself out if I could only stop talking so crazy all the while.

Anyhow, while Rachel restocked the shelves and portioned up a barrel-shipment of glue into quart jars, I waited around on the porch of her daddy's store, just chawing and spitting and watching folks go by. It had been more than six years since I'd been back. Three at the one place, then the three more soldiering. That's a powerful long stretch to be gone from a place and it made me feel half a stranger.

Across the road I saw some McCotts with their youngins, who I recognized by their mama's straw-hair. Then some of those Dowleys, you know those folks that cluster their cabins like frogs' eggs around the base of Little Partridge, never conversing to nobody but kin? Saw a couple of them. They were trying to sell those speckled eggs they were always toting about in baskets, even when I was a youngin. I would have bought one myself, fresh speckled egg, just snap it right open and drink it down, but I was still considerably bald with respect to finances. So I made do watching a couple those Turner boys shoe a horse for an old fella with a wagon full of lumber. I knew they were Turners right off because every Turner you ever saw has legs bowed as a pair of sickles and little black eyes on either side of his head. Mama used to say that's because those folks live on the backside of Little Partridge where visitors were too few and church too far, which is a shame and blight respectively. But that was just Mama's way of saying every Turner in Nuckton was related thrice over.

Well Rachel, she took her leisure with that glue. By the time she locked up shop I was a good way through the plug she'd given me. Her daddy's land lay two or three miles north up Lazy Boy Hollow, hollows being what we call those little dells that go back deep into a mountain. So the Lawsons' place was a big place at the end of the hollow, and we walked it fairly fast so there would be light enough for me to see by and dowse a good well, or so my thinking went. But as I stated, I knew of Rachel. Good old Rachel Lawson. Even before I'd left Nuckton or so much as chipped my chin on a razor her name was known to me. She's what we boys used to call 'deciduous' in her habits, shedding garments like leaves for anyone who would give her a good shake.

More than once Rachel Lawson suggested we depart from the road and step down to the creek for a peek how high the rain might of brought it. By and by, I agreed. The creek wasn't much higher than I remember, though quick as gypsies, and the cottonwoods were beginning to turn. Yellow leaves were collecting all along the bank and you could smell the mulch of it. More than anything it was this smell that made me realize I was back. I was home. The horrors I had left behind were left behind.

I pointed out the lights. White and blue. I saw them swinging about, just under the water but Rachel Lawson professed not to see. I figured she saw all right, and knew what it meant too, only she didn't care much for the meaning.

Besides, she was taken up with a powerful notion about then. Deciduous as ever, she made to get plenty friendly down there in the shady seclusions of the creek. This time she lifted that dress with a purpose.

Now some'll say a womanfolk's beauty, her everlasting charm, is inversely proportional to her scruples. I'm of a different camp. I'm no saint, mind you, and will gladly thump the man that slanders me so. But my heart just doesn't work like that. Old Rachel Lawson, I wasn't mean to her, but I told her how it is.

"I love another," I says, plain and simple, and to this statement her little forehead wrinkled up, incredulous-like. She barked a quick laugh, cut it off sharp with a look of seriousness, eyebrows drawn, lips all pouty, then burst into laughter again. "Dannon Lereaux, I ain't asking for your love! Just a quick tumble down here by the creek!" She laughed, not with me, as the saying goes, and you might of thought I was a fool by the way she kept smirking at me sideways as she shimmied out those skirts. "Now come on and get them overalls back off you. We don't got a world of time."

Thing is, I did love another. Only the time wasn't yet right for us to be together. There would come a day, howsoever, of this I bore no doubt. There would come a time when I would lay with my love and leave her heavy with kisses and shelter in the bonds between us.

Except I wasn't thinking about that right then, for Rachel Lawson, what with that pale little face, was making good headway in the transposition of her garb and it took most all my strength to keep that girl clad. So I picked her skirts back up from the leaves and pressed them into her arms. "My apologies," I says. "I just don't work like that."

It took powerful encouragement, but we made our way back to the road. The sun was just dipping behind Henry's Backbone, but there was light yet, mountain light, which is different from the stuff you see elsewhere. The west slope stayed bright with the last rays of the sun while the east slope came alive with crickets. And I listened. I walked and I listened till I faded away, just disappeared, with nothing left but a bunch of crickets all singing this mind.

That time of year, the Blue Honeys are a dream. A misty, luscious, horse-drawn land as colorful as any paint-smeared palette. The old country roads are all hemmed with long grass and meander as aimlessly as the cow that first made them. And follow any road far enough, any road at all, and you'll find yourself winding up and up into hazy blue mountains, finally vanishing into the shade of dark woods.

The road up Lazy Boy Hollow was no exception. Almost immediately, it tapered down to no bigger than a trail, a muddy path rutted with hooves. We stayed mostly to the grassy shoulder, except where the cockleburs grew wild and pushed us back in. As we climbed, we passed many a sight that was like pure ache to my memories. Back in a copse of dogwood there was that old pine barn, empty and leaning, just like I remembered, where I used to pull nails by the pound and sell them for books. Then there was the old Nuckton silo, peppered with rust, where Mama said the skull of a dragon had been dug up in her youth, packaged in plaster and sent on to Washington Museum. Then the Hamptons' bottomfield, pumpkins coming on. A dead snake on their fence to draw rain.

I saw a nanny goat peeking through a split-rail fence, and she saw me. And there ain't nothing in this world like the Holy Spirit seeing the Holy Spirit in another.

Now these woods were nut-bearing woods, which are best in summer, but you can pretty well gather nuts off the ground all through autumn. Old Rachel, she stopped to collect herself a lapful of walnuts. The grass beneath the trees was littered with them. I'm not much for autumn nuts myself as they have a way of sneaking worms into your mouth without your noticing till it matters. But Rachel, she appeared not to mind and commenced to cracking them up between two stones, when I says, "Be getting dark soon."

She scowled out the corner of her eye and kept cracking at those nuts.

"If I'm to be dowsing this day, perhaps we best keep on."

"Don't take but two minutes to crack a wad a nuts!"

That Rachel was in a huff. Shorn of her ardor, she was in quite a huff. So I squatted down there beside the path and let her crack up those nuts while I listened to the bonk of geese overhead. I watched a woodpecker berate himself. I smelled the sweet rot of autumn and saw a manbug itch a ladybug's back.

It has long been a failing of mine to get caught up in the sound of a thing, even a word, at the exclusion of its meaning. Don't ask me why, just something that happens in my head. When Mama first taught me to write, I filled whole notebooks with, "Chaos is a pretty haos by the C." When she would ask what it means, I'd ask what she meant.

So as Rachel stood up to leave, with all the accompanying boot-scuffing and rustlings of departure, I failed to make the connection till she shouted, "All right! I'm done! We can go now!" Then she stamped up the path with an apron full of wormy nuts. Half of them, at least, she ended up pitching away upon closer inspection. She'd chuck them hard as she could, and I asked her how come girls always throw with their wrong arm, and she says how come men don't bother to wipe the tobacco juice from their beard and let it dry there like they was god-damned mammals, and I says, I don't know, do I got tobacco juice in my beard, and she chucked another wormy nut with the wrong arm.

Before long the Lawsons' gates were clacking shut behind us. Rachel let out a long sigh and took me kindly by the arm and says sorry about all that, all that silliness back there. She says, don't mind her, it was just the glue talking, and I was left to marvel at the labyrinth of her world and the twisting paths of her emotions as they had traveled between our first meeting and the present, realizing it is no wonder women complain of exhaustion. Surprise, suspicion, intrigue, passion, frustration, regret, kindness. She had just walked a hundred miles to my two.

She perked up when her daddy Lawson came out on to the veranda, and she introduced us cordially. Theirs was a big old place with stone chimneys either side, Lawsons being some of the only slaveholders in all of Nuckton, with a host of magnolia trees out front and plenty of bean rows climbing up the mountain, corn rows where the hollow was flattest. The slaves were thick as kindling running about the place fetching this and that. How the Lawsons afforded them, nobody knew, so the talk goes it was them that found the treasure of the Barbary pirates. Only now that I've traveled some and seen the distance to the sea I have some doubts about landlocked buccaneers in the Blue Honeys. Still, it is a mystery. The Lawsons are just mountainfolk like the rest of us, always have been, talk like us, church like us, only sometimes they pretend a difference, folks say, and take on airs what with their fancy manor and all those slaves.

But I never pay much mind to talk. Old man Gideon, who was Rachel's daddy, he was plenty kind in my book. Before they sent me away I knew him good, as everyone did, him keeping up the only general store in Nuckton. He was one of those opal-haired old fellas with stubble goes gold in the sun and says shick-shick real satisfying-like when he brushes his knuckles up his cheek.

Mr. Lawson, he pumped my hand real good out there on the veranda and says, "I know this boy! A Mr. Dannon Lereaux needs no introduction here! Welcome home son. How is it, how long you get back?"

But I was momentarily distracted by a moth on the sill, this side of the window—once beautiful, maybe, but now quite dead.

Little legs pointing to the sun.

"Dannon?"

"Sorry, what? Oh just now, sir. Yeah, I am just getting back now."

"Just now, just now. Well that's fine. With the war over, I suspect you boys will be trickling in by and by. Well it's an honor to have you. I'm sure your folks, God bless, would have been proud to have you back safe and sound too. But you'll have to come in and tell me all about it. Mexico! By God! You'll have to tell me all about it."

"Actually, sir, I come by to help with—"

"Laurel!" he called back into the house. "Laurel, the first of them's coming back from Mexico! The heroes is here! We got a guest needs something thirsty!"

With my new hat wadded up, I pointed back over my shoulder. "Like I was saying," I says when his eyes came back to me, small and watery and blinking all over the place like his glasses were mislaid. I says, "It'll be getting dark fairly quick now, and Rachel here tells me you need a well found. I thought if I could just—"

"Now who is it?"

Rachel's mama. She flew out onto the veranda in a vapor of excitement, all homecooking smiles and smoothing her dress. She wasn't near as old as old Gideon, being the second of his wives, but old enough to have those marionette-lines running down from her cheeks to her chin. And she had puffy cheeks too, which only added to the look. Another girl, just coming on to womanhood herself, she came out with Laurel but hung back some, staying near the door. This one looked electric-shocked or scared, I don't know which, her eyes all big and bug-like. Only she always wore that look, no matter what she was staring at.

"Well don't just leave him standing there, Gideon, introduce the man," says Laurel, who I sort of remember from way back, but not really.

"It's Dannon, hun! The Lereaux boy, from up Blackwater Hollow! You remember Dannon, what used to hang about as a littlun out front the store, scaring folks with his queer talk. Oh you did boy! I'll reckon you don't remember that!"

"Well he ain't a boy no more. Look at him Gideon! He's grown giant!" She took a step closer, hands on her hips, apprais-ing me like a slave on a trading block. "Well Dannon, it's a pleasure, and more so getting you all back in a piece. We get mighty bad reports of the fighting went on. Was it bad?"

A little fighting's bad. A big fighting's worse. A good kind of fighting is mighty hard to come by. "Some maam. Not much."

All fairness to her, these were still the antebellum days. We hadn't yet fought our Civil War and this little foray into Mexico constituted one of our country's first marches against a foreign nation.

Laurel gave me a nice doting smile, maternal and naive. The other girl, the hanging back one, I saw now she was ready to pure litter. She had a woolen shawl around her shoulders, which covered her belly too, but it wasn't hard to tell. Her arms and legs poked out spindly as a spider but her goddamn belly looked complete to bust. "You go on hun," Laurel tells the littering one, whose name is Ducie. Ducie Lou. "Ducie, you help the nigras get something together for our guest now. He looks like he could eat a load." She smiles. "What brings you out this way, Dannon?"

"He's trying to tell you all," says Rachel, puffing the hair from her eyes. "He's here to dowse your well, Daddy. Just give him a pair of willow switches and he's good as done."

I was promptly fitted out, and by the time the fireflies came blinking out, as they like to do upon an autumn eve, I had located three spots for well-digging. None of them satisfactory. The first water was too deep, near a hundred foot, and would've needed the negroes' quarters get torn down. The second came straight out the mountain at the edge of their property, but the water was no good, reading like sludge. I mean real slow. Less than a gallon a minute. The last site was my hope. It was dead center of their corn, which was still standing brown and unturned, south side. Plenty of good water, maybe twenty feet down. My switches were going wild there, crossing and flipping to where I commenced to feel that feeling I get, as if the water in my body and that in the earth is all skipping up my spine in a fountain of purest nectar. It is a delicious sensation unlike anything in this world, except maybe the shiver you get after a good piss in the cold.

Problem was, old Gideon already had a well-digging company come out there and they found the same site, only the stone getting down to the watertable was too thick to bust with a drill. Old man Gideon, he was pleased all the same, feeling satisfied my switches had found what the company had, claiming it was something of a peaked experience watching me work. He seemed especially fond of me after that.

Naturally there was a supper. I was plenty hungry, what with walking all the way from Fort Brown on the Rio Grande, twelve weeks in coming with scant rations at best. But old man Gideon, he had fought the war in 1812 and so kept pressing me for campaign stories, features of the battles in Mexico, shot and slash type stuff, wanting to know if General Taylor actually led his charges like they say or just commanded from the rear. I didn't have much to tell on that account. Fact is, I'm not much proud of it, or anything else I did south of the border. We were the invaders so far as I am concerned, and the only bullets fired in the right were aimed at us.

The women kept on about this and that, mainly just jabbering to keep the rhythm of noise at a certain pitch. Even Ducie Lou, the hanging back one, was bailing words out of her mouth like too much water. "He did what?" she whispers across the table when she thinks me and old Gideon were too caught up to hear. "What did he do?"

And that Rachel, she leans forward with an elbow on the table, her hand at her cheek to shield her words. "He came strutting right in, like nothing was amiss, and asks me for a pair a denims as though he wasn't wearing nothing but his party suit on."

Her ma. "You mean his birthday suit, dear. His birthday suit you mean."

Rachel. "That's right. Nothing at all. But you should have seen him. It was like—"

Her ma. "Now Ray hun, let's not poke fun. We don't know nothing about him except he's had a hard life, and we ain't got no right passing judgment on another's tribulations."

Gideon. "Now it is one thing to shoot a man at a distance, but the charge... bayonets lowered, bugles trumpeting. Now that is glory. Something you take with you. Was you boys fighting hand to hand, sabers and all, or was it all musketwork down there?"

Rachel. "Ma! I ain't passing judgment. I'm just trying to say he carried himself better as a naked man than most ten others in their Sunday best. More dignity-like, I mean. What if Daddy were to help him out some? Give him some work?"

Gideon. "Oh ho yes! I remember a time, back when they had us down in Norleens and the British was coming down on us, a company of us, and we set up behind a stack a cotton bales and I seen a man get blown straight—"

Her ma. "Now Ray, we don't know nothing about him. For all we know he—"

And so it went. On the whole I was itching to leave. I was damn near to just coming out with it about the devil at the crossroads that stole my clothes and bidding everyone fare thee well. Let them sort it out on their own, I figured.

Nevertheless, I stuck around, my skin crawling in a juxtaposition to such unnatural talk and manners. Do I just take a bite from my plug of tobacco, or do I offer it around? And when I blow my nose, does the napkin go back like a hankie, or do I leave it setting in my lap just so? I never did know how to conduct my own with such folks, me the only one at the table without shoes.

The fare, however, was pure fine. Corn pone and fresh corned beef. Turnip greens and butter. As it was Ducie with the negroes that engineered the meal I offered her my thanks. She nodded, not at all warm-like. Figuring she expected more from me in the way of conversing I says, "So how far along are you?" And upon that remark, my mistake bucked up in my chest, me taking notice of the looks all about me. Only I never was much a wizard with words.

"How far along what?" says Ducie.

Not at all warm-like.

The big clock in the parlor must have tocked five or six times. I cleared my throat. "Well maam," I says, letting go the towrope. "Either I am mistaken, or you are with child."

Someone dropped a fork. Someone else coughed. All credit to Ducie who kept a calm face, but whose voice was tight with emotion. "You are mistaken."

Never did a silence roar louder in your ears. Sometimes, when the artillery stopped thundering and the musket-smoke hazed the field, the ringing hush that followed seemed to creep right up from the depths of death itself. Yet it was nothing compared to this. I could hear the blood pulsing through my ears, and the ears of everyone present, as though we pulsed together as one, in harmonious horror at my wayward tongue, until old man Gideon got up the nerve to clear his throat.

"Reckon you'll be looking for work, now you're back," he says to me, and everyone appeared plenty grateful for the break in tension.

"Work? Oh I reckon, sir. I reckon. Only not much."

There was another pause. So many looks crossed that table they would have made a cat's cradle with thread.

"Sure. Sure, I understand," says old Gideon with good-natured approval. "A fellow likes to take it easy after three years in the fray. Lay up and enjoy life some."

"I reckon, sir," I says. "Only I don't know about work."

"Oh there's a plenty, when you're ready of course. You looking to get back into your pa's line? Millwork? Not a bad way to go for a man like yourself. Put them long arms of yours to use."

My old man Phinny, he may have been a drunkard and an ass, but every soul in Nuckton knew he could work like a Clydesdale. After he died it took four men to replace him at the mill.

"No sir," I says. "I mean I don't know I'm up to it."

"Up to what?"

"Work."

Old man Gideon, his face got kind of queer. His lips sort of sawed back and forth like he was tonguing a sore inside his cheek. "I understand. I understand. I myself, as a young man subsequent to 1812, I vowed not to work upon any day had either a P or Y in it. Ha ha! P or a Y! Get it? But things have changed, as you can see. Things have changed. You grow up some."

There was an uncompanionable silence.

Thing is, that P or Y bit, I cannot stand a poor joke. It gets me down, thinking about the person saying it and how they thought themselves pure comical at the time when, point in fact, they are just another ordinary soul trying so hard to be special.

And that got me down. Real low like.

"Welp," says I, untucking my napkin. "Reckon I best be on. I thank you." I scritched back the chair and walked out the door.

<hr />

When I came to the road it was plenty dark, and none too inviting without a place to go. I looked down that path all funneled with trees. Just dark. Nothing but dark, and somewhere out there a place, maybe, where I could rest this threadbare soul. For it wasn't until that very moment I came to understand, with a most abrupt and heart-sinking lucidity, returning home to Nuckton just wasn't what I hoped for. Not where I was supposed to be.

The porch lantern flickered as something passed before it, and I turned back to the house. Above the creaking of treefrogs I heard the gates clap shut and understood, more than saw, she was coming back out again.

"You know she's got a bellyworm," says Rachel, halting in the dark before me. "She's got a bellyworm that does it. Makes her belly like that."

"Yeah, well," I says, looking around for my escape. "You really can't hardly tell."

Rachel glanced back over her shoulder. She looked up at me. "Sure I can't interest you in nothing? Last chance." Her face was so pale. I could smell the corned beef when she breathed.

"Nope. I best be on."

"You're sure now. We can do it right quick."

"Nope. I best be on."

"Fine then," she says, only she didn't go away. She just stood there, so small in the dark, and I saw by her silhouette she was holding something in her hand, about big as a satchel. Finally she comes out with it. "I won't begrudge you your love. What I came for was to give you these."

It was a pair of boots. Fine made too. Truth is, I'd never worn anything on my feet till the day I volunteered, but I got used to it marching about in Mexico. Shod was now my preferred mode of travel.

"I thank you."

"Belonged to my brother," she says. "You ever recall a Will? A Will Lawson?"

"Nope."

"Well you pray you don't. He is a world of trouble. No matter now, as he ain't home, gone to town with his nigra, and I'm plenty glad to help you along at his cost."

I returned the boots. "These boots ain't mine then, if they're belonging to him."

"Oh that's all right," she says, pushing them back into my arms. "He's got two pair. Besides, it's me what's stealing them, which makes them my own. And now I'm giving them to you."

I pondered on that one, weighing all sides till my head got so scrambled it hurt to think. Just to be done with it, to be done with this place and the ache in my chest and all these feelings that wouldn't stop jabbing me, I says, "Well in that case, I thank you." I took the boots and turned to go.

"But if you do meet him, just don't tell him it was me."

"It was you what?" I says, turning back.

"What gave you them boots. William had them special made. They were his Sunday boots, only wore them on Sunday, but as he ain't much a churchgoer these days I don't see the point. Still, I reckon he'd know them right off. Just don't tell him it was me what gave them to you."

"I'll do," I says. "I thank you." And I strapped on those boots and started down the road, fireflies blinking. Treefrogs singing. I was just itching to be shut of that place. But here I was with new plumage, so to speak, right down to the boots and with the soft thud of them upon the earth of the road I commenced to swell up right grateful. I stopped, turned around. There was Rachel, still standing in the dark. Her face so small, just looking at me.

Now up till this point, my schooling in chivalry added up to Pa telling me to wipe the outhouse seat before a woman set down. I was sort of winging it here. I walked back to Rachel and before I really knew what I was doing, I'm giving her a kiss, a nice one, right there upon the softest lips you ever imagined.

"You know I ain't like that no more," she says in the dark. "The way I used to be. I ain't like that no more."

"I know it," I says, because I did. I knew it was true.

"I just didn't want you to go away," she tells me. "And my old habits come upon me like a fever. I know it's foolish, you coming into Daddy's store without a stitch, and me falling for you like that. But it is the way it is. Something about you, Dannon Lereaux. Even Daddy knows it's so. Still, I don't begrudge you for going. I thank you for the kiss though. It was a fine kiss."

A fine girl too, that Rachel Lawson. Maybe she really didn't know what those lights meant.

"So long," I says.

"So long."

I headed back down the road.

———◆———

Because the thing is, I spent much of my youth trying to get out from under the boot heels of this world, what with having a pa like mine, then none at all, then discovering my own way of seeing things just doesn't balance with the rest.

Mama, who had taken to sucking on lozenges since The Loss, she used to say to Pa, "He ain't crazy, Phineas, and not another word of it. The boy just ain't got no guiles is all, and no fist of yours is gonna bring it on. Now leave him be." A hundred lozenges a day she sucked. All for loss.

Nevertheless, I've been called crazy in one form or another most all my life. And it may be. The way I figure, if I am crazy then it's the truth, and there's no use in denying it. And if I'm not crazy, then it's not the truth, and therefore ain't worth getting worked up over.

It was the parson in particular who first spited me and told Pa my skull was good for nothing but driving piles and such. I never did understand why.

"Hi there! Hi, Mr. Parson?"

"Yes, what is...oh no. No. Please, boy. Not you again. Not today."

"Well, sir, I was just a'wondering."

"Can't you see I'm walking, son? I can't be always—"

"Yeah, well I was just a'wondering. If all the bad folks go to Hell, and only Pentecostals go to heaven, then where do all the good folks go when they die?"

"Son," says the parson, pausing to sigh at the sky. "You are a chancre in the heart of the Lord."

Far as I could tell, most folks shared this opinion and liked it best of all when I did not speak. Others, my pa among them, took special delight in making sure I knew I was dumb.

"What you talking about, Dannon, not going to meeting this Christmas. Are you stupit? Huh? You want to go to Hell, is that it?"

"Naw sir."

"You think the parson's stupit?"

"Naw sir."

"What then? Tell me what."

"Well, sir, if Jesus was *born* on Christmas, and even he never went to no meeting, what are we all fussing to do there?"

"Hide idgits like yourself from the devil, is what. Now get your damn coat on. And not a word to the parson."

So it may be I'm a little slow in some respects; maybe even missing a few buttons, but given the chance I can cough up words nearabout half a foot long, and I reckon I've read more books than most five men together. I read Cervantes. I read Dante. I read Virgil and Homer. I even read that new fella, what's his name. Dostoyevsky. For a while there I read history, and then politicking and government. I tried to read William Shakespeare once but had to put that man down, figuring I was better off waiting for the English translation.

I even read the King James, cover to cover, not once, not twice, but seven times for it was the only book in our cabin till the age of nine, but never could I understand our Lord being three things at once, because frankly speaking I've seen the Holy Ghost in most every object a person could imagine, from axle grease to musket-wadding, to cows on the road and their dung, not to mention the shine of a person alive which burns so bright in some as to make your eyes tear up. Anyhow, lacking any means to square up my seeing of the world with that of most holy scripture I more or less set the whole thing down.

"Touched," they would say. "That boy is patent bizarre."

But I figure sometimes a whole thing can come about by mistake. Take the word 'solemn'. The way I figure, it was just somebody mispronouncing the word 'calm' and then another body figuring it was word enough on its own and thereby worthy of a second spelling. Like that. That's my take on dogma and said trappings. Somebody mistaking one thing for another, nonsense for fact, and giving it a new name to suit. Had nobody ever devised a pew or a hymnal, I reckon the Holy Ghost would be here all the same.

I used to walk to the edge of Nuckton where the road broke off leading to the Presbyterian. And I'd look down that road, 'Church Road' we called it, green with the growth of six days neglect because Sunday tread just ain't enough to keep a path clear. And that means something. Even if no one else cares to see it, the meaning's there plain as day.

So people call me crazy. Maybe I am. But I'd rather be crazy than fool.

<hr>

A good mile out from the Lawsons' place I paused for a set beside the path. The woods were thick here. Mountains run up like a cliff of shadow to either side, and in the slot between them I saw the sky was soft and smooth as velvet. The moon, corn-colored, was just hanging its chin over the V of Coalstoke Ridge and Little Partridge and the insects were pulsing like blood. I had nowhere to go.

Nowhere that meant anything, anyhow. After we, the Union element, overran Mexico and sacked her capital, held president Santa Anna hostage and enticed him under duress to sign that pretty little treaty that doubled Union landmass overnight, president Polk told all us boys, "Now come on home. You all made your country proud in the eyes of God."

Problem was, home ain't always a place on earth, and pride is but a gnat in God's eye. So the army booked steamers, take us anywhere could be reached by sea. Lots of men heard of gold out west and decided to try their luck. But that was a long, long trip by way of Magellan's straights, and busting into the earth for gold just didn't interest me. Besides, I felt sorrowful enough about having just stolen the whole territory of California from thy neighbor. To get dripping rich off her now would just be rubbing Mexico's face in it.

But truth be known, I wasn't about to get on a steamer of any kind. No thank you. 'Seasickness' is too tame a word to describe the inglorious tempest that sweeps through my bowels the moment I step foot upon deck. I swear to you, seeing the waves upon a bowl of whipped cream is enough to put a sweat on my skin. It's the reason why you won't hear me making all those nice authoring metaphors about 'sterns' and 'bowsprits' and 'navigating the seas of life' and such, for frankly speaking I hate all things kin to a ship.

"But it is a straight shot across the gulf to old Norleens," they try to tell me. "And from there you can book passage up the Mississippi." And I said I would gladly walk to Beijing before I booked passage upon anything floats, so it was only natural I would find my way home by footing it. Except I didn't give much thought beforehand as to where I should go. Thusly I strode twelve weeks over hill and dale to get back to Nuckton and the Blue Honeys only to discover 'Nuckton' was just another way saying 'default.'

Our family's cabin, if it wasn't cannibalized for cordwood, would have gone straight to the bank after Mama died. The rest of my relations would be holed up down in the bayou of Louisiana somewhere, producing unholy spawn and eating banjos and gators for all Pa told me of the place, though I never met a one of them. I did once hear of a Lereaux out of Dorinville, a hemophiliac glasscutter they say, man of impeccable faith, but Pa said we weren't kin but in name. All down in Baton Rouge, he said. Still, old Phinny hated everything about that place and vowed we were to be Blue Honey folk from here on out, and if the south ever seceded from the Union, as the talk often went, well then Pa would choose his allegiance according to whichever way Louisiana went for he was sure to go exactly opposite.

Anyhow, standing out there beside the path I could smell the smoke of a woodfire off somewhere. The woods were plenty thick, as I stated, and it is no small thing tracing out smoke on a breeze but I got myself a sniffer. Quite a sniffer, in fact. I dipped into those trees and picked my way through the brush until I came upon the steaming coals of a hunter's camp. Not long abandoned. The skins and inners of two or three squirrel lay heaped on the rocks ringing the fire, all oozy and dried and sticking to the stone like worms trapped overlong in the sun. The coals were fresh, however, so I stirred them up till I had a decent blaze. As good a place as any for the night, I reckoned. Someone had swung the skinny end of a long deadfall into camp, lining it up beside the fire like a bouncy bench, so I tucked in, keeping close to the fire for warmth. Overalls were fine for daylight but without a shirt of any kind the night would be pure bitter.

A whippoorwill started up in the big limb over my head and then the lights commenced their bouncing through the trees. I watched them for a while, feeling all the melancholy and the joy come together in my heart.

And that's typically when I start pining most for my love, the girl I once saw and vowed to care for. It was three years ago, and happened in a nameless little town, twenty mile south of Carter, just before I enlisted with the volunteer regiment and got on a coach headed south and west. Where she was from I did not know, but when I first saw her there in that old country store I knew she was from somewhere else. Somewhere farthest away. Another world, it seemed to me.

I myself was out front on the porch, chewing a plug, minding my own so to speak when in comes this girl, the hues dancing about her head so bright I nearly choked and swallowed my chaw.

She wore a bonnet, tied low at the ears, with just a sprig of black curl coming out underneath. Her eyes were dark, but real dark, so they lit like candles. She was little Bo-Peep all full grown and blooming in a nice clean dress, and so far out of my league I was a fool to consider.

Thing is, I knew she was for me. It sounds odd, I know, what with me barefoot and mountain-wild, fresh from the asylum. Next to her I wasn't better than a tag on a pretty dress, but I knew the heart of that girl like I know my own, and they were not two things but one.

She went straight up to the counter, me following behind with about as much choice in the matter as her shadow. She asked if her paints were in. That was all. She asked if her paints were in yet, and the young man at the counter, he says, "No maam. Afraid not. Everything coming in from Bethel this week is stalled. But I can have them sent up to Valhalla for you when they arrive."

Valhalla. The girl from Valhalla.

I hadn't the first idea where that was, or if they'd let me in when I got there, only that all things shiny on earth and above had convened in this golden person. And should my poor station in life ever take a turn for the better, should I ever unsnarl all those tangles in my head, become presentable, upright, wiped clean of perdition, well that's where I would go. Valhalla. To find my girl and love her.

She wrote something down on a piece of paper, an address I figured, and I took notice how she used her own ink, a bottle produced from the deep well of her handbag. As she wrote I stepped closer, and I saw the little wingbone in her back wriggle beneath the white of her dress as she maneuvered her quill upon the counter. The hues leaping from her skin were like sparks from the sun, and I could smell her, that musky skin-scent that comes natural off a woman though she bears no awareness of it. It was too much for me.

So lost was I in fever and flood, that when she turned to leave I didn't think to move and she near slammed into my chest. But she didn't, and we stood like that, her looking up without blinking, and me deafened by a clock-stop glory. For we were two sides of a window, one soul split in two, and her bearing showed she knew it too.

She took one breath, long and slow, smiled the smile that has become the signature of my salvation and then stepped past me and out the door. That was it. I never saw her again, that girl from Valhalla. She walked out that door, never speaking a word and my world's been five feet smaller ever since.

But sometimes I suspected she left me something. She'd tucked it deep in my skin like a secret missive I might one day read. And if I could just decipher that moment and everything she said without speaking, I reckoned that ache in my chest would uncoil and sigh and I could rest easy for the remainder of my days.

The moment I lost sight of her my head commenced to spin. It took a good minute to catch my balance. I went directly to the clerk at the counter, who didn't look up. He had mislaid something and was busy shuffling around the counter, yanking out drawers, then noticed his quill setting right there in the inkwell and plucked it out to write two words atop that paper, the paper she gave him. Two words.

"I need to see that a minute," I says, breathless.

He straightened and set the quill down, blinking at me in confusion. "Wait, who are you?"

"Dannon Lereaux. I need see that there receipt," I says, pointing, for I saw then that it was a bill of sale she had written upon. Problem was, the bills from that store were green. Green paper, they got.

"And... wait a minute, were you—"

"Don't you mind. I'll give it right back." I slapped my hand down on the bill of sale before he could fuss and turned to the door for better light. Only problem was, I saw then the bill wasn't just green, but my girl, my love, the right pinecone of my heart, she had written whatever she had written in red. Red ink.

I believe I cried out. I must have yelled, "Red!" like it poked me with a stick, for next thing I heard was the clerk saying, "It's like her trademark. Some reason she always writes in red."

I couldn't read a fleck of it, what with the red from the green, especially with the fuzzy fibers of that cheap receipt-paper breaking the script all up. My eyes went all screwy just from trying, but it was no use. The only thing I could read were the words at the top, the two words the clerk had printed in black after she left.

Madder Carmine.

Her name was Madder Carmine.

Something you should probably know. By medical standards I am, in point of fact, a little touched in the head. Mentally ill, they say. But I don't buy it. *Acute Onset Mania with Episodic Hallucinations and Secondary Daltonism (Color Blindness)*; a diagnosis tailored special for me, I am told, when all other Latin failed to wrap proper about the haywire in my head. First they said 'Epilepsy', but without the fits. Then they thought 'Phrenitis' but without the fever. 'Melancholik' without the sorrow. Neurosis. Dementia. Idiocy. They didn't know what to make of me. Did I drink paint as a child?

Had I suckled from a slave? I told them about the breath that night, the night my siblings all died, and my mama's demon lover on the mountain, and they summarily plunked me with a title too fancy for a duke: *Acute Onset Mania with Episodic Hallucinations and Secondary Daltonism (Color Blindness)*.

But I don't buy it.

It all came of pure spite, if you ask me. After Pa died, when I was twelve years of age or so, I learned to thrum the washboard fierce as a Hittite. Supernatural rhythm, I was told. Even the negroes were in agreement. So I started up a jugband which I aimed to call 'Parson Farted' only the man himself took up and had me sent to Carter once and for all, on account of they have an asylum there for the mentally downtrodden. The Pain of All Saints. Established 1804. But to us residents it was simply known as the shriekhouse.

Mama was heartbroken and took to sucking lozenges day and night, never less than two in the pouch of her cheek. But the truth is, I didn't mind being there. The shriekhouse is where I got to read all those books I mentioned. I don't think a day went by I wasn't reading *Don Quixote* or the *Inferno,* particularly the *Inferno,* so all-in-all it was a decent show. Sure I had to do the icebaths and the swinging chairs. And they shackled us more than I generally like. But it gave me plenty of time to sit and think, to try and build some sense around the goings-on in my life which had hitherto been chiefly calamitous. Besides, it was during my sojourn at the old Pain of All Saints that I began to fathom the meaning of the lights, all those hues I've always seen dancing about every living thing. I am grateful for that, the time I spent there. The hues have come in mighty useful since, but never more so than my first night back in Nuckton, tucked in there by the fire, just off from the Lazy Boy road, for it was the hues that set me off to the trouble brewing.

I had tossed a moist log onto the fire and now the sparks were popping up a storm. I jumped back with a whoop and swatted the sparks from my face. I stopped, looking out into the trees. Something about the way my whoop carried, it got me thinking.

Whoop. I did it again. It occurred to me with the force of thunder that it is a pure miracle we can speak at all. I figured the earth, given this grave task some many years ago, would've had to muster some real know-how to up and fashion its mud and rocks into animals like myself with lips and tongues and voice-strings.

I whooped again. Quite a miracle. Whoo-oop. Whoop whoop. Only with all the ruckus I was making I managed to draw some attention from the woods. I heard something big coming, horse probably, then one man's voice to another in low tones.

There wasn't much to do now but set and wait and see what I'd brought on. I'd banked the fire pretty good so I was fireblind as all hell, and couldn't see much beyond the yellow dome of it.

I heard a faint bray through the trees, then a mule snort. Then a man bowed his head through the brush and stepped into camp, hard as winter, barely glancing my way as if we were already acquainted. With his back to me, he snapped a middling branch off a nearby birch, about head high, and hooked the loop of his mule's reins over the snag. He untied the end of a lead rope from the mule's saddlebag and gave it a good tug, and into the light stumbled a negro, bound at the wrists.

Now I could tell you this negro was a hefty-looking negro, going a little bald up top with a skein of white fuzz scattered round his chin and jaw. I could tell you his face was wide and shiny, handsome, baby-smooth, with nostrils like a bull and a gray ascot about his throat and the sort of trousers and coat as a tramp might use for bedding. But such words tell you nothing but the weather of a man, as likely to change as mean nothing at all. For there are souls out there who jump free of all words and trying to describe them is like corralling a fog.

The white fella, he tugged again at that rope and then turned toward the fire. "You keep quiet," he says over his shoulder to the negro as he resets his floppy hat and comes toward me with rope still in hand. He was a big man, this man, and about as affable as broken glass, and everything nose-up stayed put in the shadow of his hat.

That negro, he stayed put too, eyes on his toes while the big one set himself down across the fire from me, slow and easy, hands on his thighs as he let himself down, and goddammit if he didn't remind me of a thunderhead lounging. He rubbed the back of his neck, which was stump-thick, and studied the coals some. Lastly he picked up a stick and poked about.

"Now you get out from behind me," he says to the fire, and the slack in his rope drew taut as his negro stepped around to the side and into his view.

"Little closer now," he says, still stabbing at the coals. "That's right. Little closer. And you stay." He tossed the stick into the fire and went quiet, sucking his teeth.

And I may as well tell you the hues coming off those boys were bright and dark, just like their skin. Only their hues were in reverse, with the negro all haloed up so bright his face was just a blur a light.

"You found my camp," says the sitting one to the fire.

I tossed my chin at the negro. "He a runaway?"

To the fire, the sitting one, he says after a good suck on his teeth, "Reckon a man with a drink might share it around."

I didn't say anything, for the plain fact I didn't have any drink.

The sitting one, he hawked up something thick. "A fella, he might take offence," he spat into the fire, "if another stumbles into his camp and then holds on his liquor."

This time I made a sound, only it wasn't on purpose. It was like my belly set to squawking, but way up in my throat so it came out like the vowels of a baby. And the sitting one says to me, "Did you, did you just *coo* at me?"

"No," I replied. "Or not much."

He threw me a look somewhere between disbelief and disgust, and I says to him, "Got me some chaw though. And you're welcome to it."

He spat in reply, but through his teeth and without moving them. It was like a click of his tongue, and I have since tried but failed to duplicate it. I tossed him my plug through the flames. He caught it, turned it over once and then took hold with his teeth before sawing off a powerful big chunk with his knife. His teeth were bad. Real bad. Only he didn't give that plug right back. He just kept turning it over in his hand, testing its weight, waiting for a challenge-like.

"Keep it," I says.

"Nah." But he didn't give it back.

Next thing he reaches into his belt and tugs free his pepper-box, a rotten old pistol he must have dug direct from the earth by the look of it. The hammer looked bad as his teeth. But he commenced to play with that hammer, setting it and releasing it, setting it and releasing it, sighting the barrel by firelight and checking for burrs, all the while talking, talking, but never meeting my eye.

"We was tarring and feathering a thief back in town," he says, glancing at my boots. "Should have been there."

My eyes kept drifting back to that negro. Standing there, staring at his toes.

"Tarring and feathering. Which is pretty kind handling in my book. I'd rather see a thief lynched." Still toying his pepperbox, then pumping in some wadding and a ball. "Or barring that, make him too leaky for mischief. Six holes'll do if one will. But I'm sure you got ideas on how a thief is best treated." He snapped the hammer back, sniffed, and looked up at last, staring me dead in the eye.

"You are mighty close to my folks land, I noticed."

The hues floating about him, they were black. Black as hate. I tried to brighten them but those hues just wrestled me back like a catamount.

"If my nigra here hadn't slowed us up so, we'd be home about now. As it is, we had to stop for a bite, but I figures the delay, it come about because he is lacking in boots."

That negro, he didn't move a muscle.

"What I mean to say is, my nigra, this one standing here, he ain't got no boots. But you there who is setting got a whole pair to yourself. Not much sense in that, is there."

I didn't say nothing. Nothing to say when a man's hues are black.

"Mind if I take look? Cause them boots look mighty familiar."

"You saying you want my boots?"

"Ho now! And so we come to the knuckle of it! It is only the knuckle of a thing that matters, am I right? Because, you see, you asking me if I want your boots. Which is a funny thing. Because I already know they're mine."

"I ain't a thief."

He pointed that damn pepperbox at me. "Why don't you tell me how you came by them boots, then. If you ain't a thief."

And I wondered to myself, but aloud, which will sometimes happen, "I wonder what a measure of honesty do for me about now."

And he says, "Perhaps earn you one last demerit in Hell, for I am about to send you there." So I stood right up and upon the clack of his misfire I threw a few fists in his face and he fell right over. For I much preferred not to lie about those boots.

———◆◆———

I don't know why it is we're in such a hurry to get back up when we fall. You might think we would just lie there for a spell and rest awhile. Leastways, that Will Lawson had it right.

Once I climbed back onto the Lazy Boy trail, I commenced to walking. I'd reclaimed my plug, which was only right, and tore myself off a goodly chaw. I had that rhythmic heel-slap gait you get when you're going downhill fast, and all the sudden I came around a bend and got slammed with a view so dramatic it stopped me dead in my tracks. It was the Nuckton river valley all spread out below, the Shallewapre gliding its course. The trees on the hills were dense as black but the river, lit by the moon, was total clear. It made a dull, sad, distant sound like the haaaaa of a bottomless exhale.

From up here, looking so far down, the town proper looked small. It was just a handful of flickers like stars dropped from the night, but the sight of those lanterns got me thinking about Mexico again, and how I had once imagined this homecoming scene exact, for home was never finer than when remembered from afar.

There was a time, just after I'd arrived at Camp Camargo down on the San Juan River in northeastern Mexico, when I would have traded anything to be back here in Nuckton. I hadn't so much as been issued a rifle and taught to shoot when I heard the *beddy-beat beddy-beat* of First Lieutenant Beighman come galloping up through the mud on that gray mare of his. It was a stormy night and we were camped up on the bluffs of the San Juan, but you couldn't barely hear it over the sound of the rain. Yet I heard that mare of his whinny, for she was just outside my tent, and then the fwapping of canvas as the doorflaps were thrown back. Lieutenant Beighman stood hunched in my entry. I saw the puddles around his boots go bright with lightning.

"Son, get you hat on." Swiping the rain from his shoulders.

"Yes sir. How come sir?"

"I said get you hat on. You going to see the chaplain."

"Yes sir. I got it right here, sir. But how come?"

"Because she is dead, son. You mama's gone to glory."

A sorrier bulletin I never did hear. Seems the roads all through the Blue Honeys had slumped out, some of them swept away completely by the rains that year, and there wasn't another shipment of remedies due into Nuckton for at least two months. Even the traveling wagons that sold snake-oil weren't venturing that deep into the mountains, and Mama was clean out of lozenges and most likely hankering like the devil. So she set out.

That's right. Mama, who had never in all her life ambled more than twelve miles from our front porch, set out to find her some lozenges. But in the haste of delirium she started east instead of west, crossed the Blue Honeys entire and keeled over dead of exposure and exhaustion just across the Carolina border.

Thing is, I had to come all the way back here, twelve weeks walking, before I understood more than Mama had died in these misty blue mountains. Home, too, had passed from a place on Earth to a dim corner of my mind and now there was nothing left for me in this world but the Holy Ghost, a ripe ache in my chest, and the promise of a girl in Valhalla.

The Lazy Boy path widened here, becoming a road proper, falling straight and steady the rest of the way to Nuckton. Mist was already fingering about the lower slopes of the mountains but I could still see the odd haystack of light over on Little Partridge. I thought to keep on, maybe find something in town, maybe crawl under a wagon or find an old springhouse to sleep in, when I heard a ruckus behind me and spun in the road. Out into the moonlight steps that negro again, with a great big straw hat on this time, and behind him was the mule going buckwild at the end of his rope. He was a regular squall, that mule, like he's seeing nightmares and nothing else.

I ran back to proffer a hand. But that mule just wouldn't quit. He near to kicked my head off and the negro's too until I thought to blindfold him. That's a trick I learned, way back in my gold-eating days.

"Give me your hankie," I says. Then I tied the negro's hankie to my own and made a blindfold for the mule. He went immediate calm the moment I covered his eyes.

"I know how it is," I says, stroking his muzzle. "Sometimes I don't like to see neither."

"Mighty grateful for you cutting off them bindings like that," says the negro. "That Mista Lawson, he cold-blooded in his heart, but you done him up good. You done him real good. And now we got us a mule."

"He's ain't mine, that mule. And I've no use for a slave."

"Nor do I wish to be one, suh," says the negro to myself. "Fact is, I run off tonight once already. But that Mista Lawson, he caught me and bumped me up good. So I says to myself, I just try again later. I says, I just take this here spade he keep a'tied to his mule and slap that Mista Lawson up the head."

"So you're the ruthless type then, are you?"

And he replies, "Nawsuh. I got plenty ruth in me yet."

Which was plain already, for this negro, he wore the sun on his brow and ain't no man with such hues going do me harm.

"Welp," says I. "This mule ain't mine. And I don't want no slave. I don't know what you're gonna do, but there ain't much use tailing with me. For the sole reason I don't know where I'm headed for."

"Oh that's all right, suh. I already know where I'm a'headed," he says. "Right back to my Miss Odessa. She was my masta previous, you see, and kind as the baby Jesus. Before she sold me to that Mista Lawson she says to me, I don't like it, but you got to go. And when the time is right, I spect you be coming right back to me Virgil vol Krie. That's what she says to me. You be coming right back when the time is right, and I figures the times ain't getting no better. So that's where I'm a'headed. Back to my Miss Odessa." He gave the mule a friendly slap on the haunch and looked me direct, and I saw his eyes were deep-water blue. "Reckon you can come along if you like."

Imagine that. Never did I hear a suggestion more queer, and never was I more willing to oblige.

"But that mule," I says. "That mule'll have to go back. He ain't ourn."

"Oh I hear you, suh. I hear you," says Virgil vol Krie, who's king of the slaves so far as I'm concerned. "But I think I'll keep him around some. He'll be belonging to me now."

"Can you even ride a pack mule?"

"I don't see why not," he says with a smile. "But then again I don't know a first thing about mules myself. Do you?"

I didn't, not beyond what Pa told me the day he died. "Welp," I says. "That chattel then. Them saddlebags got to go. Leave the saddlebags and we'll make do with your mule."

"You sure, suh? Oh but this a powerful good musket Mista Lawson got here. Might come in handy down the road."

"Nah," I says. "I'd be beholden to him, and that won't do. Return the chattel and we'll be on our way."

So Virgil, he slung those saddlebags over his shoulder like an ox, musket spade and all, and humped it back to the very man who would probably kill him if he could.

Not ten minutes later Virgil popped back into the road. I kind of smiled to myself when I saw Will's other pair boots on his feet. "That Mista Lawson," he says to me, "You sure done him good. He still cold out. Still a'lying right where you set him. Where you learn to brawl like that?"

Me on one side of the mule, Virgil leading him on the other, us walking down the road to Nuckton.

"I ain't never seen a fella brawl like that before," he says. "Where you learn to brawl like that?"

"Just learned."

"Learned where? I ain't seen nothing like it."

"Just learned, is where. Learned myself, as I had to."

"What you mean, had to?"

"Well I'm coming back from a'warring, is what I mean. Just give two fellas hell, then tie them at the wrist and they'll learn to fight all right." The blindfold was starting to slip, and that mule was building up. I retied it and says, "Reckon that's the thing about warring. You either figure it out, or you don't. No three ways about it."

"So you figure it out then."

"Yeah," I says. "I figured it out."

Then Virgil vol Krie, who's not like any negro you ever hear of, he says, "Then tell me what you figure."

And so I looked at him and I looked away, and I says, "Ain't nobody wins a war."

⟫⟫◆⟨⟨

Now slaving's one of those things makes about as much sense to me as feeding bacon to the hogs. It strikes me odd that there we were in the year 1849, at the very peak of modernity so to speak, where a fella could hop on a train and fling himself across the country at the breakneck speed of eighteen miles per one hour and yet fail to see slavery goes both ways round. Which is to say, no man's so free as to escape a good whipping from his own conscience.

"I never hear of a negro with a last name," I says. "Virgil vol Krie. Where you get a name of vol Krie?"

"Oh yessuh. A Miss Odessa, she gave it to me. On account of that's her name too, and she say I could use it long as I stay true to her service."

"You're loyal then."

"Oh yessuh. Mighty loyal when folks done me good. And that Miss Odessa, she kind as the baby Jesus."

"And the Lawsons?" I says. "They weren't good to you?"

"Some was. Some wasn't. But that Will Lawson, he extra bad."

Me and Virgil, we were about a half mile straight shot down the road from our little treaty with the Lawson boy. Which is the approximate distance, you should know, that a musketball can travel when fired in a line. Half mile.

"Welp," says I. "Whichever way you put it, you are a runaway Virgil vol Krie. At least in the eyes of another. That puts you and me both in a position, until you catch up with your Miss Odessa anyhow."

"So happens I been thinking on that, suh," says Virgil. "Thinking perhaps it is best if I says I belong to you. Should anyone ask."

About that time I heard something click behind me. I spun about and by light of the moon I saw something tiny, just a blur of movement, as it skipped off the packed clay of the road. And coming right for me. It skipped again, slower this time, then once more, and as it rolled to a halt at my toes I picked it up. It was about the size of a cherrystone and near hot as a coal. I held it up.

And may I burn in hellfire if I wasn't holding a musketball right there in my hand, and at the very moment I heard it too. Crack, it says, right there between my thumb and forefinger, for it took that long for the sound of Will's rifle to reach me.

Now I don't know if other fellas, holding the bullet aimed to kill him and hearing it same, experience what I did, but my mind turned something like this:

I am told it is a rare man that realizes his potential. But I say rarer still is the man that realizes his potential ain't very much but does best he can with what's been granted. An honest man, so to speak.

"Perhaps we should keep on, suh," says Virgil. "That Will Lawson is most like reloadin' about now."

"I am eighteen years old," I says, staring at that musketball. I suppose every bullet has to drop somewhere.

"That right, suh? Well then, you plenty young still. Plenty reason to keep on and not fool about here on the road."

"I am eighteen years old, and younger today than I will ever be again. I believe that means something." That musketball, it was longer in the middle. Not perfect round any more. "You understand what that means?"

"Nawsuh. What's it mean?"

"I don't know," I says. "Something." I slipped that ball into the chest pocket of my overalls. "Something, though."

Thing is, that something hit me right then and there. The moment that musketball slipped in next to my heart, it hit me all at once, like I was a man shot true. I realized, with the brassy-hued-cymbal-splash of revelation in my soul, there simply isn't any time for atonement. No time to wait about. The haywire in my head isn't likely to fold itself neat. And while no man can say for certain what lies ahead, he can be certain hanging onto the past ensures a miserable future.

"I reckon," says I, "it means I don't need to lay about any more, feeling sorry and tainted, like I ain't good enough for what's right. I reckon," says I, "it means it's time I take myself to Valhalla."

———◆———

Upon those words, that Virgil vol Krie, he grabbed me hold at the shoulder and pulled me off the road and into the woods. Except they weren't woods any more, but a trail through them I ain't never seen.

"The hell are we?" I asks him, and he just smiles. Him with that old straw hat and that great big negro stride, and he just smiles and says, "Why, we on the road to Valhalla, just like you says."

"Then I suspect I should be leading us."

"Fine by me, suh. You lead, and I just tell you where to go."

That damn smile of his. I'd never seen a thing like it. Then I saw the sun on his brow and I says, "Are you a king, Virgil vol Krie?"

The paper-white of his teeth. "Nawsuh. I just a messenger. My Miss Odessa, she said I might be bringing a body along. And here we are both headed the same place. Val-halla!"

"You know where it is?"

"I do, suh. Yes I do. It's where me and my Miss Odessa is originatin'."

Now this news near took my top off, for I had yet to meet a person in all these mountains that could find the place. I asked around plenty, but there wasn't a soul that could give me directions without tying their tongue or drawing me up a sail-or's knot on paper.

"Is it close?" I asked. Somehow I always imagined my Madder lay a world away, beyond the veils of my Herculean sorrow.

"Oh I reckon," says Virgil. "But it's a ways too. Folks don't know it. That's why you need old Virgil vol Krie to take you there. Not quite Kentucky, but not quite Tennessee neither."

"Virginia then?"

"Oh you'll see. You'll see."

And I suspected I would, too. And something about the notion of a colorblind dowser and a runaway king leading a blindfolded mule to a land not entirely of this world appealed directly to my curious sensibilities.

Which is what the whitecoats called them back at the shriekhouse. My curious sensibilities. I had a friend there by name of Erasmus, next cell over, who used to say he could read a fella's future in the graffiti of our walls. So each day he had me write down whatever was written upon the bricks beside my bed and shoot it over to him through a tiny hole in the wall. Then late that night, after a good think in the dark, he would stuff his lips into that hole and translate for me, in the hellfire voice of a preacher, what was to be the makings of my days to come.

So anyhow, along came a day when I wrote to Erasmus, I wrote to him, "Root knows water. In every blossom lies the distance to the sun." Only I didn't tell that old fella it was me who etched those words into the wall with the burred edge of my own shackle. Still, just like ever before, I woke up in the middle of the night to old Erasmus hollering at me through the wall, "The message is clear, young fella! In his glory and grace, the good Lord has deigned to speak to me, his humble servant once again! Though I am a God-fearing man and a sinner too, I have unciphered the text which he has laid before us, this message which near to smote my soul. That the Lord says 'Root knows water' means in the source is your salvation. Only in the source will you step free from captivity. And when he says 'blossom', he is here a'speaking of your soul, my young friend, which is mightier than most, but he lets on to say how your mortal lot is to be constant mistook in this world. Ever will man swap your genius for dust. Dust, I say! But alas, there are some among us who shall comprehend the glory of your torment. And I am one. And I say unto you, nigh is the day of your judgment, my friend. A choice like no other shall be placed in your care, and the grooves of your life shall be determined. On the one road is your blood, for it shall be a'wrenched from your veins, and on the other road is the blood of many another."

Then I heard the sound that old man makes when the invisible lizards come to get him, for he had taken off his slipper and begun to splash it about the cell.

I wasn't sure what to make of it all, but very next morn, who should enter my cell but a solitary whitecoat with a document and a quill. Seems a new treatment was being made available to folks like myself, folks who failed to respond to all others. It was called 'Moral Management' and meant our cells were to be made more homey-like, believing a domestic feel might eradicate our troubles. Only this doctor didn't believe a word of it, he says, apart from "the environment playing a vital role in a patient's recovery." His job was to move us stragglers along, and that was all. This doctor, he says what I need is something drastic, something to put the lead in my soul and drag my skyward mind back to earth. Something like, say, *a war* he says, which happened to be brewing south of the border just as we speak.

The harsh realities of combat were sure to put a fix to my delusions, and if I was willing, I could just sign away right here.

And why not, I thought to myself. Armies had ever relied upon the able-bodied and warped to conduct to earnest business of slaughter. And volunteers, the doc says, were in such heightened demand that boys like myself were being welcomed like royalty.

Option number two was not a new treatment, he went on, but about the oldest around, saved special for folks without a hope. But I needn't worry. That old doc assured me the survival rate for bloodlettings here in the Pain of All Saints had gone up considerable in recent years. Five, at times six in ten lived to tell of it later, and an encouraging percentage of them had shown improvement.

So there were my roads, just as old Erasmus predicted: Bloodletting, or the letting of blood. Such are the ways in which we choose our destruction. Even as I signed I knew the true nature of that covenant, for a man does not enlist with the devil unknowingly. And for all my days after I regretted that choice, and denied myself others in retribution.

Like my Madder. The pinecone of my heart.

Who at long last I was set to find.

⟫⟨

For all the haywire in my head, you might be thinking I raised pure bedlam as youngin. Truth is, I stayed in line pretty good. My mama, what with nine children tugging at her skirts, she had a right preternatural sense of mischief and wasn't afraid to skip a plate off your skull if the occasion called for it. Generally speaking though, it wasn't us little ones but mostly Pa she laid into the when the Lord's wrath took hold of her throwing arm, especially after he got some drink in him. That's when he'd get to 'feeling downright religious' and take up with his 'poetree,' which Mama spited like a backtalking devil.

You see, down there at the mill it became plain that old Phineas Lereaux had a middling mind, and if they could just keep him off the drink long enough to learn him his letters, well they could promote him, on account of they were in need of someone crafty enough to look after the books. So that's what they did. And Pa learned his letters all right, and like a child with a shotgun, wasted neither time nor discretion in exploring the limits of the damage he could wreak. He'd come home from work, go straight to his desk and stay up all night with that quill scribbling away. Thus dawned a new chapter in the evolution of smut.

Between coon hunting and beating on me, Pa's choice of a nice summer evening would be to get ripping drunk right there in his old chestnut rocker and recite his verse out loud to Mama and us little ones in his boomenest voice; lines so crude and depraved as to put color on a sailor's ears. And Mama would flip benches and chuck pans about the cabin like grain at a Roman wedding.

So anyhow, I kept my nose pretty clean back then. Besides, apart from the small issue of my eating gold, my queerness wasn't ever more than half-awake in those days. It wasn't till after The Loss that things started swapping about in my head.

Even the whole Daltonism thing, nobody knew till I was instructed to pick apples one day and came back with a sack all mixed up with reds and sour greenies. But it's not like you think. It's not like I mistake red for green, or even the other way round. It's like I can't tell them apart. They both look the same in my book, the way it does for you, I'm told, when the reds and the greens get all blended up into gray when you're seeing them in a calotype photograph.

Welp, me and Virgil and that mule on a rope, we were deep in the mountains that night, and getting deeper still, when Virgil says, "I believe I call him Jimmy Brown On A Rope," he says. "Yessuh, Jimmy Brown. A fine name for a mule like this."

And when the wind blew you could hear the whole forest go fluttering, and the moonlit leaves just raining down like gold flakes.

Old Virgil with his straw hat and new boots, he stayed just ahead of me on the trail, leading a blindfolded Jimmy Brown between us. I could hear him whistling in the moonlight, a nice negro tune, and when he turned about on the trail I saw his big white teeth in the night.

"Hows about we set on down, have us a little lazy awhile. Could use me a decent set on the ground."

So we sat down with our backs against a pair of oaks, facing each other across a whole scatter of leaves. "Nice night, ain't it?" he says, looking up at a patch of sky. Enough light was coming down through the canopy that the earth between us appeared all glowed up.

By and by, Virgil slipped a hand into his coat, into the pocket of his vest and pulled out a beat-up square of sandpaper, unfolded it carefully, the creases white, fuzzy, torn through in places, and then from another pocket hauled out what looked like a ball of mottled gray marble, about half the size of a lettuce head. He hummed quietly to himself, shaving away at it with the sandpaper, so satisfied with the pastime as to make my own mind fall still.

"Chaw?" I says, holding out my plug.

"Oh nawsuh. I don't mess round with that stuff. Nawsuh, I'm a snuff kind a man myself."

From a third pocket, this one in the breast of that tattered old coat he withdrew a little cloth sack. He opened the drawstring and dipped out just enough tobacco snuff to make a nice acorn-cap on his thumbnail. "Try some?"

"Might as well."

I gave it a good snort, straight from his thumb, and goddammit if it didn't put a circus up my nose. My eyes went pure fire and I kept coughing up slime, ropes of drool stretching to the ground, and all the while that Virgil vol Krie slapped at his thighs and cried "Who-boy!" when he wasn't choking himself blue on the laughter.

I sniffed one last time and spit up a clump of something awful.

"I thank you," I says, struggling to stay ahead of the coughing. My voice was all parched up and morning-raw. I palmed the tears from my cheek.

"Can I have another?"

And that Virgil vol Krie, I couldn't hear a thing in the dark, but the way his straw hat was shaking up and down I knew he was just gone with laughter.

"Oh yessuh. That you can. That you can."

⊷◈⊶

And the door to the woodstove would creak as Mama slammed it shut, locking it with a twist of the handle, and she'd say to me, clanking down a skillet, she'd say, "Dannon, if any single day don't find you a better person at the end, you failed to live that one." The lively crackle of pork-fat. Cracking eggs with one hand. "So how about it, little Dan? You live today?"

By that reckoning I suspect I'd lived two, maybe three years total. Just enough to eat without a bib and throw a quality tantrum. So it didn't make sense that I should be all on my own, walking this world without a guide. Who, if not Virgil, could tell me why a leaf might throb with such splendor, or come alive as it fell; why my heart should keep busting open and open. Here I was with the devil on my heels and all I could think to say was, "Hell sure is mighty nice," and old Virgil would say back, "Oh yessuh. Folks don't know it."

Sometimes the ridgelines in the east would spit up stars slow as honey and I'd imagine my darling belle in bed. Sleeping, her breath soft as silk, bright-cheeked and downy, lips parted in insatiable innocence. I could watch her sleep in my head forever.

And then not one moment longer—for I would be compelled to lean in, smell the perfume of her skin, my senses taut, tuned, induced by her scent, I am intoxicated by the play of light in her hair, and then ever so gently, because I have not the power to stop, I lean a bit closer, feeling the sweet brush of her breath, mad with longing and the tyranny of love, I drink in her sigh and let it roll through my soul as I place my trembling lips upon hers.

Back at the shriekhouse I used to have the same dream night after night. Mama would be tossing me in the air, just tossing me and catching me, with everyone all around shouting, "He can talk! He can talk!"

Then one day, one of those whitecoats took a look in my records and said it was so. Said such a thing happened when I was a youngin. He told me there was a good year or so, right after The Loss, when I refused to talk at all. But what alarmed me most wasn't that such a thing took place. It was that I could forget it. My past was all slipping away, trackless as boats a'row. Of my eight sisters departed I could only name six, and the only one of them I could still see in my mind was little Maggie, who we used to call "Little Magus" and was but a biddy baby when she died. Memory of my youth had become a pathless wasteland with the solitary exception of The Loss, for I will recall The Loss unto my dying day.

At the approximate age of seven I was not yet an only child. Four sisters older. Four of them younger. Me right smack in the middle. Then one night the heat-lighting took up. It was all over Little Partridge, flashing so close the whole mountain lit up, and yet silent as a breath of wind. We children all went to sleep, stacked like trout in the bed, but Mama stayed up praying as she knew something wasn't right. The way she told it, a queer wind raced down from the mountain. It swept all through the cabin, unnatural as could be, and next morning not one child woke up but me.

From that night on I couldn't see red any longer, for my colorblindness set in with the wind. But Mama said not to tell anybody on account of she was ashamed. Said she knew that wind was the breath of her demon lover, come back to haunt her with sorrows galore. True or nay, nothing went right for a Lereaux ever since.

———◆———

Me and Virgil and Jimmy Brown On A Rope, we were treading through a thick stand of pine, the smell of it sharp in my nose when a mourning dove let loose with a couple sad cries.

Mourning doves are one of the few birds you'll hear at night. "Best we stop here, suh, till we figure what he saying." Virgil searched the trees for the dove. "Or least see if he's got more to say."

Our trail was wide, near enough to be called a road, and cut sidelong into the slope. You could see the exposed roots of trees in the cut of it, some of them gripping stones in their fists and the fiddle-neck ferns looked blue in the moonlight. The dove cried again, and Virgil says, "There you go, suh. I knew it. We got company. I just knew we should have kept that rifle along."

We both turned to squint back down the trail. I listened, but couldn't hear a thing. I stood so still I could see the moon shake, ever so slightly, each time my heart pumped blood through my eyes. Then someone stumbled and cursed, not twenty paces down trail. My back went straight. Next thing I knew a silhouette detached from the main, about the size of a person, and crashed sidewise into the brush alongside the path.

"The hell?"

"Good Lord."

Virgil tugged on the lead rope and we went back down the trail for a look. We could hear whoever it was struggling to get themselves vertical again, cursing and clawing at the soil as if there was no more menacing a force on earth than gravity. I saw someone, a form, crawl slowly out onto the trail on their hands and knees and then push themselves up, one tottering leg at a time, until they stood before me, but in the way a broomstick stands when you balance it on end and know the miracle cannot last.

"You there!" a man cried with finger upraised, and the heat of liquor hit me so hard I blinked back tears. "I got a message for you!"

The man took a step forward, then lunged back two just to square his balance. The whole world appeared to be wheeling beneath his feet.

"Your salvation is near at hand!" he cried, and I knew right then I was in the presence of a saint. Not for the words he spoke, but because he should have been dead of poison. This was no common-type drunkenness before me on the road. No, this was a whole new level achieved, a feat of mystical immoderation. The man held out his hand and I took it with reluctance. He had a handshake made you think of a horse's lips. When I let go, he fell back a step and then cried, "Ho!" like he'd seen something there in the road. With a crack of the knees he stooped down to fetch it, swayed there a moment, put one hand on the ground to steady himself, then came back up, and goddammit if he wasn't holding a hoe.

Not a bad one, either. At the spade-end of it was tied his bundle, containing Lord knew what, and he slung the length of that hoe over his narrow shoulder. "Name's Levi," he says. Though actually he said about four-five names after that. Levi Such-and-Such-and-Such-and-Such, except I didn't catch any of it but just the Levi.

Reason was, my mind began to foray, thinking about how I'd always been rather partial to the name of Levi. If Madder would have it, I even reckoned we'd name our first son as such. He would be little Levi Lereaux and she'd teach him to paint and mix colors in a palette and how to stretch a canvas across a frame and I'd say, "Levi, my son, Levi how about you and me doing some of them things boys and their fathers are meant to like doing?"

But now that I'd met this drunken old coot, the name of Levi was suddenly tarnished in my head. Whereas most folks are named after hotshots from scripture and revolutionary generals and great-grandpappies dead in the grave, I was named after three days of drunken revelry by a father who once knew a sot by the same name, and I did not wish to carry this tradition.

So this Levi fella says, he sways there on the road and says to me, "Name's Levi Such-and-Such." And he says this while staring, tranced-like, at a point precisely between me and Virgil, patting Jimmy Brown with a wooden motion. "And I tell you what," he says. "I am in sorry company. Ain't none of you going to drive me away?"

"Not that I planned on."

He slumped down onto a log with a whoop and began to unlace his boots. "I got no trust for a man that trusts the likes of me," he says. "Not that I am iniquitous, mind you. Lord no, I am a God-fearing man. There ain't a wicked bone in this body, but to look upon it in a mirror is a fright to my heart and ain't no man in his right mind gonna shake my hand in the dark."

He slipped off one boot and started in on the other. For the first time the moonlight caught him good, as he leaned down for that boot, and I saw this fella was small and wiry as hell, like scrambling mountains was something he did for a salary. This Levi had a billygoat's beard and long oily hair which in color was either green or red. I could see through to the shine of his scalp. His cheeks were hollow and weather-bitten as a sailor's with a nose swollen purple with veins. In all the time I was to know this man, I never saw him eat a bite. Got all his corn from the jug, as the saying goes.

"Well, I got good news and bad news," he said as he peeled off a threadbare sock and went about flossing his toes with it. "Which one you want first?"

And I says, "Don't matter, so long as you speak true."

"All right then. The bad news is you fellas ain't the first I encountered on this long and lonely road. No sir. There is another not far behind, says he's fixed entire in a murdering way. Says he's on the path of the man stole his mule, and the nigra what run away."

"That would be us," I says, and saw Virgil throw me a look like I was a million dollars on fire. "Only not quite like he tells it," I quickly added.

"Well he is a'telling it to many. I passed him up whilst he was near to preaching your shame to a pair a fur trappers right there in the road. They was offering him up supplies that very moment."

And Virgil says, "So he a ways back then."

"Oh yeah. A ways. Several mile maybe. But the manner he is going about it, he'll be upon you before long, and most like have something of a posse."

I wasn't overly concerned. For one thing, I had old Virgil along, my guide through the night. I doubted Will Lawson would ever find Valhalla alone. I said as much aloud.

"Well, that's all fine and goodly," says Levi. "But insofar as this Valhalla is concerned, I been just about every part of these mountains and unless Valhalla got another name to go by, it is doubtful to exist."

It occurred to me that for all the juice in his veins and the spinning compass in his eyes, this Levi spoke clear as a bell. As if he could no longer recall the last sober notion invaded his skull, and so like a blind man walking home without a falter to his step, had long ago learned to operate smoothly at a deficit.

"The good news," says Levi, slowly, carefully untying the knot of his bundle, "is I meant what I said."

"About being in sorry company?"

"Chuu! Come on now, don't you know wit when you hear it? No sir. I mean about your salvation being near at hand."

<hr />

I figure there are three kinds of hisses come to mind when a person says, 'hiss'. The first is the hiss of a log when you throw it on the fire and the steam spits out, high and sudden and makes you jerk in your seat. The second kind I actually forget, but I had it a minute ago, and it was a perfect example, a really good one, and the last kind, the third kind of hiss is the sort nobody likes to hear, not underfoot anyhow, or without good warning and a stick.

"Can you keep a secret?" says old Levi, untwisting the neck of his sack.

"That would depend on a number a things," I told him, for a promise is not something I take lightly.

"Won't do," says Levi, "as I need something of a collateral before I show you my hand. There's those who'll prosecute me and my kind."

"Fair enough," says I, "I can pledge secrecy to you, allowing for the terms is within practical reason."

I had to say that, to add the "within reason" bit, otherwise I'd be obliged to keep mum under all manner of torture, and I hadn't known this man but a minute.

Old Levi, he grunted and scratched at his jaw, and then opened the sack wide and I leaned in for a peek, and that is when I heard the third kind of hiss. You've never seen so many serpents knotted up in a pile. Copperheads and water moccasins and no lack of fat rattlers. I jerked back just as one lunged at my face and that Levi, he just gave the sack a quick twist, tied a rude knot and giggled like a shriekhouse regular.

"What exactly are you and your kind?"

"Revivalists!" says he, lifting the sack like a trophy-fish. "Folks who ain't afraid to put their faith on the line. For the good Lord sayeth, Mark sixteen verse seventeen, 'they shall take up serpents and drink any deadly thing and they shall not know harm!' And you, my young friend, are cordially invited to a tent meeting."

A tent meeting. Imagine that. I quickly explained I was no stranger to Christianity. Beyond the velvet-pistoned elegance of the word itself, I had next to no use for the thing, and I told the man so. Well, he came back and says his meetings were different, of a different sort entire, and salvation was all him and his lot were fixed upon. And I told him my salvation was in Valhalla. It was my Madder Carmine. And the color red.

And he says, he says to me then, that is three things I am speaking of.

Three things, whilst in salvation there is but just the one.

<hr />

So that's how I came to join up with old Levi Such-and-Such, and me and Virgil and blindfolded Jimmy Brown On A Rope, we followed that coot up hill and dale with his sack of snakes swinging side-to-side from the end of a hoe. He said we were headed for Stilton, which the Cherokee call Adayahi Tsilihu Digugodisgi, or something along those lines, being the more lyrical way of saying, 'Grove of Sleeping Judgment'.

So we walked. Sometimes the moon was so bright it burned my eyes like the sun. At intervals in our passage, old Levi would sally from the road to flip rotten logs with his hoe, poking round for serpents. I saw him catch two myself. Just as often however, it wasn't serpents he was after but those little liquor-stills tucked back in the hollows. Without warning old Levi would peel away from the path, cutting into the woods, declaring it was time to, "say how-do to a friend." He had quite a knack for hunting out the rogue element in those hills, seeming to find them by some imperceptible change in the sound of a creek, for creek water was always preferable for the setting of a good still.

General speaking, they were little camps we came across. Little one-horse operations, for any bigger was likely to draw the taxman's eye. You could pretty much count on finding yourself a bit of dried possum and a tater or two, and of course a cauldron of sour mash going over an ashwood fire, for ashwood was near to smokeless, copper run-off coils bursting every which way and one or two fellas passing a jug. Old Levi seemed to know them all.

"That good?" they would say, pouring from their jug to his tin cup.

"Very," says Levi, angling the jug on his own. "And more is ever the better."

Virgil was only a little less shy, never asking for more, but never covering his cup to seconds. Me, I'm more a connoisseur of cheap wine myself, but I'll allow for a taste of good whiskey. Except I never could get over to the custom in those parts, which was to let raw meat ferment in their brew to give it "that mellow spice."

We never stopped long for these sojourns. Exactly how long is difficult to say, given the nature of our visits, but you had to hand it to old Levi Such-and-Such. He had it down to a method. He could locate his next liquor-still like a point on a map, tanker himself up, offer a few slaps on the back and we would be on the road again before you could say fare thee well.

And old Virgil. Good old Virgil striding alongside me, never saying more than enough. Usually it was just wink and a smile, and then back to whistling those warbly little tunes like he wasn't really among us but on a whim. Sometimes I'd look over, and he'd catch me looking, but he'd stare straight ahead, trying to whistle through a smile like he was stuffed so tight with mirth he was set to bust. "Just you wait," he seemed to be saying in the space between notes. "Just you wait, Dannon Lereaux, for all things broke gets fixed in the end."

So we followed that Levi up and up in the mountains, him staggering about in his infallible zigzag, chattering on like a tree full of jays. There seemed no end to the topics he could speak upon without the least response from myself. I reckon he was the sort of person would see nothing amiss in conducting a lengthy conversation about people who talk too much. Clever though, in a witless sort of way, a phenomenon best related to you by means of his unsavory dialogue:

Him. "You got littluns?"

Me. "Littluns? Not yet I don't, but I aim to have about as—"

"You're lucky!" he says. "With littluns it's the same thing, every damn day. Never let up. Tugging at your coat. Pawing your leg. Whining and whining. *Can we have some food? How come we ain't got no food? All our friends is got food.* Wah wah wah, till you get so fed up, you finally find them some food, and then you know what? You know what happens? Starts all over. Very next day. I say the human race is better off without them, thank you very much. Now this here hoe, howsoever, you see this here hoe? Am I right in saying this is a fine-made hoe?"

Our path was burnished with moonlit leaves, the air was autumn sharp. We were coming upon a stream that played across the trail and sang songs like tinkling glass. In regards to the hoe, I wasn't quite in agreement, for the spade-end had been refashioned all queer, rendering the tool useless for all but hooking serpents.

"Guess how much," says Levi, not slowing one jot before picking his way over the creek stones.

"Go on. Guess. Now don't, now don't touch it! Christ Almighty, you want a get bit through the sack? Sweet Lord, now just step on back and guess before I crack you one."

"Don't know," says I. "Never bought a hoe. A dollar?"

"Chuu! A dollar! Listen to you! What if I was to tell you this here hoe, this fine-made hoe didn't cost me a red cent."

"I'd say you was a gambler, and luckier than odds."

"You'd say I was—now listen here. You ever hear a place called Indya? Well now in Indya they got them a phosophy what's called karma. No, I says kar-ma. Like karma. That's right. And don't forget it, for it works mighty smooth-like, about as useful as any apparatus you're like to find. So let's say you done something right and good, for a sample. Well then life pays you back, and with interest to boot. And when you done something low-down, say, well life finds a way to bring you up square. So I sees this here hoe, just sitting lonesome in a shed, and I says to myself, Hell, Levi, you sure could use you a hoe, and the bank won't give you no credit. But with this here karma business, you can take what you need now and circumstances will bill you later-like."

"You sure you worked that one right?"

The unspoken lesson here seemed to be that, according to Levi, for the small toll of self-loathing a man could have just about anything he wanted from life.

"Darn straight I got it right!" he replied with heat. "I have it on high, for my late brother-in-law, God bless, was a English spice-trader what used to play poker with the sultan."

The brother-in-law got himself a hand-chopping for thievery, finally dying of privations in a dungeon, but that was beside the point, as Levi so ardently assured us. The real point was that there was system in place, a divine coordination. And if you were astute with the Lord you could work it like any other.

We dropped down into the dry riverbed of a shallow canyon and the trail quickly scattered itself among the stones. We had to scramble to find it, following the cairns people stack on boulders to show wayfarers the trail. Jimmy Brown stumbled all over, his hoofs making scraping noises as he swatted for purchase. Yet still that mule would not let Virgil remove the blindfold. He'd snort and bray like a squeaky-rust-door the moment you even touched it, preferring blindness altogether to sight. Suddenly that mule froze, right there in the canyon.

A howl geysered up from the woods, way up on the bluffs above us and Levi, he gripped his hoe a little tighter and says, "Just wolf. They'll be following our scent, see what we're up to."

And I says, "Rascal," for that was the name of my Pa's favorite hound, the one that got killed the night Phineas threw himself in the Shallewapre. That was Rascal all right, howling away. I'll grant you a wolf and a hound will sound alike on a wind, but I reckon I was nigh weaned onto the yowling of hounds, and I'd know that Rascal about anywhere.

Old Rascal, he howled again and Levi grimaced, saying, "Haste now, come on. Let's get on up that gap and be done with it."

I glanced up and saw him, that Rascal. Just a flash in the dark, eyes bright as huffed coals, but I saw six of them. That is to say, I saw three pair of eyes for each his three heads because in these mountains he wasn't Rascal but Cerberus.

"Who-eee," whispered Virgil, nudging Jimmy Brown along. "He don't like the sound a that one. Let's go, Jimmy. Nah, this way. Let's go." And I could tell Virgil knew the difference same as me.

Some time ago, can't say precisely when, but back when Mama and Pa were still around, I used to hanker for gold the way other youngins did sugar. Whenever gold came into the cabin, I felt it all through me. It didn't happen frequent, mind you, but when there was gold in the cabin, I knew it true, just as I know water when it's flowing deep in the earth.

And every time it was the same. Late that night I would get up and hunt around in my sleep till I could find that gold and eat it. Whether bauble or coin, I would swallow it down and wake up next morning with a bellyache. Then I would stumble around, shaky as colt, moaning and slobbering till I stuck a finger down my throat and chucked it up again.

Welp, this went on for a number of years till one morning I woke up with a bellyache like no other, having dreamt I swallowed Mama's own wedding ring. I lay there curled up like a prawn and hollering till I could cough it up proper. Then I cleaned it off real good and gave it back to Mama, saying, "Here you are, and I am sorry, Mama, for I didn't mean to go and swaller your ring."

And she put a hand to her heart, and then real quick to her mouth and her chin commenced to get all quivery, and she says through her fingers, "Bless your little soul, Dannon Lereaux, if it's not the very ring I dreamt of last night, and on so many another. For your Pa never found need to give me such a thing."

I never ate gold again after that. But when Pa found out about that gold band, he went and took it from Mama and sold it in town for the money to buy Rascal with. Needless to say, I never was too fond of that hound, and had little doubt he was now the herald of pure trouble.

We climbed up and out of that canyon, steep going, filed through a rocky gap and came down the other side a little ways. We paused along a broad outcrop that was near to bald on top, except for a stack a flat boulders. Those boulders jutted out from the slope like a row of felled dominoes with one of them, the biggest, hanging over the edge of the mountain like a perfect platform put their for your private viewing of the valley below.

"There you are," says Levi, stabbing a knobby finger at the distance. "That's your Stilton. Just cross the River Caroline, down there in among them oaks."

But I had my qualms, you see, on account I couldn't see anything but the river and the woods, and suspected this Stilton lay beyond the gates of earthly vision. To Virgil vol Krie I says, "You reckon I'll make it?"

And he says to me back, "I reckon you got to. Unless you want to turn around, there ain't no other way to where we is a'headed." But the look in his eye said I was in for a ride.

Then old Levi pointed out the steeples of several tents, some of them huge, rising out of that oak grove down below. When the wind blew, I even saw the flicker of firelight through the trees. But there was something queer about those oaks. For the life of me I couldn't say what. Just gave me a feeling, is what it was, a feeling that defeats all narration, and I noticed Virgil was watching old Levi like a hawk.

The River Caroline was all brighted up like a silver thread below, working its way down through the valley. You could hear it too, faint and rippling, like the applause of a thousand unseen hands. We scaled our way down the knoll till we came into a patch of willows and the sounds of the Caroline grew louder. Soon it was a roar in our ears and we popped out from the trees and bumped right up against its reedy banks. Levi had us hunting all through them, swatting around, until we found the raft his folks kept moored there. He ferried us across, me clenching my teeth and holding my guts until we could clamber the far bank and come right up on the verge of those oaks.

Instantly, I saw what was wrong. Those oak trees, the whole forest of them, they were all lined up in perfect rows the way fir trees are when a man plants timber. They fashioned avenues all side-by-side with great hoary arms going every which way, eerie as all hell and sent my nerves into turmoil just to enter.

"I ain't never heard such a hush," says I, listening to the hollow whispers of our footfalls on grass. And Levi, he says we were in the Grove of Sleeping Judgment, as the Cherokee so named it, for the Cherokee were nigh the only ones who still attended these woods.

Levi said these oaks were all that's left of the village called Stilton, for the whole habitation of them died of smallpox more than a hundred years prior. They had lain, bloating, without a solitary survivor until along came a young Cherokee trapper who was collecting ginseng one summer and found the complete village all rotted asunder. The Cherokee boy's name was Big Water, they say, and he razed the place to the ground. Then he dug a thousand-and-one graves with his dark lonesome hands and the hickory paddle he carried to prize up roots. And as he laid each body to rest, just before he backfilled the pit, that boy placed an acorn in the mouth of the deceased. Now it was those acorns, said Levi, that took root and drank bones till these oaks were all that remained of old Stilton.

I asked Virgil if this was the way he had come, and he reckoned it was close enough, and we were arriving none too soon what with old Will Lawson making headway behind.

Before long the keen of a fiddle, somewhere ahead of us in the grove, came haunting through the trees and I swear it was the voice of desperation itself. It whined and it cried and made leaves shiver and float. They were playing a downright wicked fiddle whoever it was, and as we closed in, the ting-tang-tang of a banjo picked up and began to roll about the wood, a sound that always reminds me of a pair of dice tumbling down hill.

And it was upon the sound of that banjo, plucked by the devil's own hand, that I felt the slipknot of destiny yank tight upon my throat. I would have stopped right there and run back the way I'd come if I didn't know reining up would've choked the life clean out of me.

⟡

But that fire, that great pagan blaze! It was through a break in the trees I first saw them dancing around it, demons shrieking and leaping about. Satyrs and maidens, diabolical grins, bodies writhing in a gloss of animal sweat.

I had to blink twice, three times, then give my head a good shake before the caprice of my vision retreated. Then it was just regular folks dancing, just a bunch Christians stomping their feet, clapping to a dosey-doe.

"*Shew!*" I hissed to myself as we entered the light of their fire, trying my damdest to recover from the apparition, when without warning old Levi hollered out: "Behold, I give you the power to tread upon serpents, and nothing by any means shall harm you!"

The fiddle screeched to a halt. The grove filled to bursting with the echoes of whoops as folks spilled every which way to greet us. "Always does it," says Levi, shifting his hoe from one shoulder to the other. "Nothing'll rile them up like Luke ten-nineteen. But just wait till they see the mixed load we're bringing them. It's been a tolerable stretch since we've had fresh rattlers to play with."

The fiddle burst back in with "Fox in the Holler" and a whole bushel of folks commenced stomping about the fire, their shadows swinging round on the tents. There was a whole camp of them, like they'd been here for weeks, living off nothing but acorns and Jesus-meetings and music to taste.

Suddenly old Levi thrust the hoe at me. "Here, take it. Take it!" Overcome by zeal, he did something that looked like a jig but near laid him to the earth, his knees unequal to his fervor. It is a well known fact that holiness folks is disallowed from liquor so Virgil, in his intransigent kindness, took Levi by the back of the shirt and held the old man up so he could dance right into camp under the auspices of his own steam. With that sack of serpents over my shoulder I followed behind, leading old Jimmy Brown On A Rope.

"Brother Levi!"

"Hows about it!"

"Ho, what you got now! Let's have a look!"

Half-naked children chased a dog through the crowd. Women twirled and yodeled and clapped hands above their heads. Levi slapped me firm on the back. "Now you're about to see the Lord's true hand at work. This here's a Jesus jamboree!"

Virgil slipped back into the shadows, just watching and smiling, scratching old Jimmy about the neck. He got right in under that straw hat of his so there wasn't any way to tell his thinking.

That fiddler, he was a pear-shaped fella with a beard down to his belt, and he played that fiddle from the hip, sawing away at it while calling out dance steps through his nose. Folks clomped, clapped, swung little girls around. Levi's sack got passed around with all the fanfare of applecakes, and folks peeked and poked and exclaimed such approbations as to make me wonder what precisely I'd missed.

Someone shouted a particular murky verse from scripture, and all those revelers piled back into the main tent with whoops and barking dogs and a whole heap of excitement. I helped Virgil water Jimmy Brown. Then we hitched him up among the teams of horses and mules already corralled beneath the oaks.

When I turned around, Virgil was gone, and a wave of panic overtook me. But he'd only let himself down in the grass, his back against a tree. Without a word to me, he'd taken to shucking away at that ball marble of his, scuffing it round with the sandpaper.

"What do you say, Virgil vol Krie?"

"Oh, I say they strange folk, these folk you got here. Strange folk. But you got to do what you got to do."

Good old Virgil. I says to him, "So you coming in?"

"Oh, nawsuh. Ain't nothing in that tent for old Virgil vol Krie," he says. "Nawsuh, I stay right here, mind my own. You go on ahead though, for you got to do what you got to do."

I took that as a sign. Virgil would never tell you a thing straight out, but he let you know. He let you know what had to be done all right.

But that tent. It was pure humming with menace. I could feel the shadow of it, like a thing alive, and knew a trial lay just within. "You reckon there is another way?" I glanced down at Virgil, shuck shucking away at his orb, then I saw him face down in the dirt. Dead. The blood flowed out back of his head and mixed in a puddle of my own. Our blood, all mixed up in the dirt. Then it was just him again with that ball marble.

Shuck. Shuck. Shucking away.

"Ain't no other way I know about."

⋙◈⋘

You could tell the water moccasins from the rest because when they opened up to hiss the insides of their mouth were all white as cotton. The copperheads, they were actually kind of pretty with their burnt gold banding and yellow caterpillar-looking tails which they used to lure in small victuals. And the rattlers, well anyone can tell a rattler. They were all three kinds dumped together in a wooden crate, hissing and writhing with nothing but drunken Levi and his hoe to keep them from climbing back out and spreading about the tent.

From amidst the pile I saw something spring-like, which was a mouth, thowing itself forward and then recoil into squirming anonymity. "Oh don't mind it. They's more afraid a you."

Old Levi assured me they were the serenest class of serpent, and I pointed out there were three, and every one of them showed colicky, and asked how a man makes his choice between them.

"It's the good Lord does that. Ain't no choice a man makes but the wrong one."

Apart from those serpents, the tent was empty save for a couple coal-oil lanterns, a few rows of stump-seating and a rude cross nailed together from fallen oak limbs. The folks were already hallelujah'n left and right and throwing their hands in the air and shammying their heads like a dog coming out the water. Their eyes were either pinched shut with passion or else open and bewitched, while one of those folks, the most feverish of the lot, thumped a leather-bound bible and shook his fist in the air.

"So the good Lord spoke unto Jesus!"

"Amen!"

"Who was received unto heaven!"

"Hallelujah!"

"Jesus, who sat at the right hand of God!"

"Praise be!"

"And went forth and preached ever where he could!"

"Go Lord!"

"From Nazareth to Galilee!"

"To Galilee!"

"From Gethsemane to Jerusalem!"

"Take me home!"

"And then the good Lord a'sayeth!"

"Glory be!"

"In thy name ye shall cast out the devils!"

"Ain't no Satan here!"

"And ye shall speak with new tongues!"

"Tell it like it is!"

"And ye shall take up the serpents!"

"Hallelujah!"

"And drink any deadly thing without harm!"

And upon that last one, about the swallowing of deadly items, that last one appeared to be the cue for everybody in the tent to go pure buckwild, frothing at the mouth and scooping up serpents like sideshow bushmen. They weren't gentle either, like you'd think folks would be with five or six copperheads in their fist. No, they hopped about like they were barefoot on a griddle, shivering and shaking till they went cold-out and flopped around on the earth spouting gibberish.

It was getting downright feral in there, to say the least, and when the music took up again I saw a spare banjo lying about with no one to play it. I felt the spirit move on me, instant-like.

Now if I had known then, as I rightly do now, this was the very banjo Satan had played I have no doubt I would've kept my distance. But as I've stated, I've got something of a natural rhythm in me, and it drew me in thick, and even though I never played any banjo I could pluck out a mean tempo on just about anything. All around me folks were shouting me on, hopping around in a sweat and trying to press me with those quart jars of strychnine they were drinking from.

"Who-boy! Look at him go!" they would holler and then jerk back like something punched them in the chest and start jabbering away in tongues. I swear there was smoke coming clean off my fingertips. I was pure whipping it. Then one of those folks, a man total heaped in serpents all round his neck and arms, he asks me if I wished to testify to our Lord. And I said that sounded about right. And so he asks if I might like to tote a deadly serpent. And I said I believed I did. So he up and placed a rattler about my neck like a diamondback-scarf and goddammit if the Holy Ghost didn't go sprinting through my inners.

I set down that banjo and took hold of that rattler and next thing I know I'm up and dancing with the rest of them. I was voltaic with joy, just zipping with vigor. I was Dannon Quixote, primed to take on the world, and so I holler, "Open your doors, Avernus, for I am a'ready!" and that bearded fella with the fiddle, he looked up at me queer, halting his bow midstroke with the kind of sound makes your toes curl up in your boots. On the instant, everybody fell hushed and a howl pierced the veil of night.

Rascal.

It was that Rascal again. I heard him clear, only this time he was howling in harmony, what with those three heads of his, and that rattler bit hold of my arm.

———◆———

If I learned one thing from it all, it is don't ever play the devil's banjo. Any man doesn't take my advice is setting himself up for a whole succession of woes. I suspect it is even written somewhere.

"I believe I been bit," says I.

You might think a fella would know right off, but when a rattler takes hold of your arm you don't feel the pinch of teeth first thing. Nope. Feels more like a blacksmith just cracked you with his hammer. It'll jolt you up pretty good, but unless you saw the actual bite, you don't know what happened right off.

I looked down and saw the twin beads of indeterminate color pooling upon my forearm, and I says, "Yessir, I believe this here serpent just took a taste."

It was Levi himself who yanked that rattler from my neck. Only he just passed it to the woman beside me, her all barefoot and jolting with a suckling child in one arm and my rattler in the other, for the music had picked back up again. I looked around and saw folks laying-on-hands and fish-flopping on the ground like the doors to bedlam clean busted.

"Levi," I says. "Levi, I am a might bit befuddled here."

Still dancing, his whole face opened into a grin and he slapped me on the back. "Bible says take them up! Never says they won't bite you!"

Granted, I wasn't feeling particular organized in the head about then, but I seemed to recall a bit about "ye shall know no harm" and wondered if the good Lord wasn't splitting hairs when he drew the lines between hurting and harming.

And it was about this time I began to feel mighty poor. An unspecified number of mallets commenced to thumping at my skull and I had to blink hard to keep the black away. Only the black kept getting heavier, and filled up in my chest and then spilled down my limbs. I looked down and saw a bruise, about the size of a potato, already purpling my arm and the room began to spin with considerable vigor, though no one else appeared the worse for it. The odd one of those folks stopped jolting and babbling long enough to shake my hand, saying the Holy Ghost had done taking a liking to me, having chosen me out select at my very first meeting.

And I says, "I wonder if perhaps you got some place a fella can lay up and die proper."

And those folks, they were regular bastions of solicitude. They hooted it up and elbowed my ribs. "You hear that? Listen to the man speak!" They pressed me with those jars of strychnine, wanting to know right then if I'd join up with their outfit. I said I'd consider it, should I survive the ordeal. But happy as those folks were, I reckoned I couldn't do this sort of thing every week. My liver would put up a fuss, or just plain abscond, and I reasoned I couldn't rightly commit to anything in this world when I was just setting up to leave.

Without warning, something up and cracked me in the head and I says, "Umph." Then I opened my eyes and saw the beautiful face of old Virgil vol Krie crouched over me, for it was only right he'd be coming along. He hefted me up from the ground and says, "Lord damn you heavy. I can't be carrying you all the way now. Come on now, can't you stand?"

"We still friends?"

"We got to get you on that mule, is what. Get us outa here before old Will Lawson come in. That be him just outside the tent now. You here that? That be him a' pushing and hollering to get in here. Now stand you up and walk like a man."

"You coming with me?"

"Course I coming with you. Oh no you don't, git back up. Come on now, stand on up."

"We in Hell now?"

"We in a fix, is what we is. Can't you stand none?"

"We're in Hell proper, right?"

Old Virgil, I felt him come around behind me and lace his arms about my chest, dragging me out back of the tent. And as the blackness came over me, pushing the last vestiges of this fine world from mine eyes, I heard old Virgil vol Krie mutter between breaths, "Hell. Oh yessuh, I spect it for real now."

PART II

CIRCLES IN THE DARK

MAMA, SHE LIKED TO DECLARE WE WERE ALL BORN with mansions in our heart. Mansions stuffed with golden treasure and knickknacks galore, all of it our own, and our only God-given task being to treat it precious and honor it for the gift it was. So what we do is, as folks full grown and gluttonous, we get all dressed up in bandit's black from head to toe, smash through the window on the lowest floor and make off with all the silverware.

Mama used to say pilfering such a treasure is like the right hand stealing from the left, and there wasn't any more sensibility in it than sweeping a dirt floor. She said we settle for the cheapest of gifts, and every man does it, even though we know there is better.

And Mama, she wasn't any sweaty-faced preacher spitting fire and brimstone, but she and those preachers were in agreement on one point in particular: Before that treasure could be regot, every man had a stout justice to pay.

So it goes. I was cold-out by the time Virgil dragged me clear of the tent and tossed me, face down, like a pair of saddlebags over the bony ridge of Jimmy Brown's back. For purposes unknown, old Levi caught up with us, having come at a run, and

I reckon Virgil allowed it for the simple reason he lacked a third arm to beat the man back.

Before we knew it, Levi was directing us to a place, safe place he said, and knew a man there that could fix me up proper.

Meanwhile my head had become the ill-fated location where distant worlds collide. I was battered by visions of pure fever doom. Virgil said I cried out in my delirium. He did his best to quiet me, for there was no telling just how long before Will Lawson caught our trail.

So while they were trudging it direct into the black of mountains, I was total busy in my head, communing with Madder who had come to me in my hour of darkness, her lips moving, speaking, without saying a word. She pointed to my chest and I found a secret pocket there. I reached within and found the missive I'd always known she'd hidden inside me, only it was written in blood, just like the receipt, and I couldn't read a jot of it. And as I watched, those words began scampering about the page, rearranging themselves until the letters were plain before my eyes.

Dannon,
Thanks.
Love,
Madder

That was it. That was her message entire, the one I'd been pining to read. Considering how long I'd been waiting, you might think it wasn't near enough, four words. But they were four words more than none, which is all I had up till that point, and what more could Madder really say?

Between herself and me, there was only thanks and love.

I reached out to touch her but she stepped back, receding through a stone archway until only the archway remained.

Inscribed in the black granite of its lintel, I read the words, "Abandon all hope, ye who enters here." And above it, a sky filled with stars. I pondered their brightness and their number. So many... so many.

"So many!"

"Shhh."

But compared to what other sky? What other universe? Maybe the universe ain't big at all.

"Maybe it's normal size," I says.

"Shhh. You got to whisper."

"And we are just... very small," I says. "Like a speck. Or even smaller."

"Yessuh. Now you be quiet."

"Like a... like a speck."

"Yessuh."

"Are we specks?"

I heard Jimmy Brown bray, for he had stumped on a root. I experienced the odd weightlessness in my limbs that one feels at the peak of a fever, and also when tossed through the air, and then I hit the ground.

I lay there, considerable stunned by the rock beneath my head, and resumed my contemplation of the cosmos.

"Waste of hide." That was Levi, spanking Jimmy Brown with the rope till he brayed again. "This mule is whole useless, ain't worth his weight in sand. What you all doing with a mule like this anyhow? Can't see nothing, can't walk straight. May as well—"

"Mule can see fine," I says, rubbing the fresh lump on my head. "It's what he sees is the problem."

I sat up and blinked into the darkness. We were in a ravine of some sort. The slopes to either side were just tall enough to hide our passage. Virgil crouched beside me, inspecting the lump on the one side of my head, and then the lump on the other, and finally my arm. "Like you got a collection going."

"Let's get him up," says Levi. "Think you can stand?"

There were approximately three or four livestock tromping around in my belly, churning it up pretty good, and my whole arm was swollen black to the shoulder. My forearm particular looked set to burst, the creases in my wrist deep as a milkfed baby's.

"I could stand," I told him, so Levi came around the other side to help, crouching down beside my arm. My hurting arm. "Some fancy work you got there, " he says to me. "Reckon you paid off a big one with a wallop like that."

"What?" says I, near to retching with the spins.

"Paid off the karma, boy. Like them Indyans I told you." Levi indicated my arm with a brusque nudge of his own elbow and the blackness nigh swooped me up. He says, "Don't take more than a few travails of this caliber to settle up a man's account in full."

Then old Levi, he slipped an arm under my shoulder and gritted up like he was going to lift me, and if I haven't said so already, you should know the man had pure spectacular body odor. It was like skunk and turned onions, and it hit me with a force. My guts turned near inside out.

Bad is it was, there is in fact one smell that does me worse, and that is the smell of burning cloves, for that's what they used to hide the sickly-sweet reek of gangrene in the infirmary when I took injured down in Monterrey. Surgeons said I was the first fella they ever heard of went onto the battlefield with his own set of teeth and came back with another man's. And the stench of rot in the infirmary got so ripe under a Mexican sun, they burned those cloves day and night, to the point I now got the two smells mixed together in my head and will retch myself empty over a whiff of either.

Anyhow Virgil, he cleaned me up pretty good and the two of them tried to stand me again. But it was pure useless. I was a ruin. They had to hoist me back onto Jimmy Brown, only this time I sat him proper, my boots near scraping the ground and my head folded forward in his withers while they roped me tight to his back.

"He don't look good. Uh uh," says Virgil. "I never seen a man's arm do that before."

Levi said we were close now, close to the miner's cabin where we were headed, and for Virgil to shut his goddamn perseverating for it was clouding his mind. Virgil kindly feared he didn't know the meaning of that word 'perseverating' and so Levi, he came back and says it meant Virgil was bothering him with all the wrong facts at once. And so old Virgil vol Krie, who always knows more than you'd think, he says, that really what the word mean, suh? And Levi mumbled curses and took the lead.

Far as I could tell, the two of them had been going head-to-head like that since Stilton. Virgil staying mostly quiet, his straw hat like the sun, never rising to the bait, Levi growing more livid by the minute. He told me direct he would never again stoop so low as to work shoulder-to-shoulder with a runaway nigra and I would have asked him, right then, why he had come along at all but I knew it required them both together to keep me saddled. So they walked either side the mule, holding me up like a pair of bookends. My arm swelled up so tight I could have blubbered like a baby. But there's little sense in crying all night when the crickets can do that for you.

It was the yowling of twenty-one coyotes set me up straight on that mule. Twenty-one of them will make quite a commotion. They started up just as we broke free of a thicket of mountain laurel and came into a clearing where the moon shone so bright I could hear it humming in the sky. I could see the shadows of individual grass blades. The clearing ran up against a lake on one side, molasses-black, which hung in the saddle of two mountains. They were part of a rocky range that lined up like a row of horse's teeth, getting bigger and bigger from east to west.

The coyotes themselves were all gathered outside the leanenest old miner's cabin you ever saw. Cabin lay at the far side of the clearing, almost at the edge of the woods, with a sagging shake roof and a porch running its length, but near overgrown with honeysuckle and brambles. There was smoke coming out the chimney.

"That'll be Chief's place," says Levi. "He'll set you up with that arm of yours."

My head was ringing like a bell, and I could feel my arm throb with every beat of my heart but I was raccoon-suspicious. It wasn't till Virgil nodded to me that I knew it was all right. Because that meant I was about to meet the sibyl.

A few of those coyotes were tied to the porch railing, and they were now whining and panting at the end of their tethers, choking themselves up onto two legs. Old Jimmy Brown On A Rope, he didn't like it, and Virgil vol Krie said so while resetting his hat.

"What, you want to carry him in then?" says Levi, referring to me.

"Nawsuh. Just speaking for ol' Jimmy here."

"Then quit your nigra mouth and lets git this boy inside. Hey! Chief! You in there? Just look at this place, sweet Jesus."

Several coyotes jumped up on Levi and he wrestled them down or threw them off, affectionately cursing and shaking their muzzles. "Them's just coy-dogs. Half-breeds. Won't hurt you none. Coyotes'll come down and make a bitch of your she-dog, and now old Chief here's got a right kennel of them." He clomped up onto the porch. "Eh! Chief! You in—oh hey, didn't even see you there."

The man Levi called Chief was sitting right there on the porch, watching us with eyes so steady and black you might have thought they were of pair of puddles reflecting the moon. An old Cherokee man, with long silver plaits and a buckskin shirt, woolen pants and moccasins. Looking at the creases in his face, you couldn't help feeling he didn't quite belong here, like something spilled off the top of another era, another world.

"Oh yeah," he says in that deep slow voice of his. "I am here." His voice came up from the center of the earth, only he's got a churgle, way back of his throat like he's got to swallow but just can't bear the taste.

Without another word of greeting, Chief bowed his head, moonlight bright on his hair, and resumed his carving symbols into the carapace of a living turtle. The turtle pawed at his lap, but the old man kept at him with the tip of his big knife. Near every scale on that turtle's shell was ornamented with some mark or another. Chief blew the shavings out of a deep groove and says, "Can put your mule in the corncrib out back. It'll be empty. Dogs won't bother'm. Can put your snakebit friend on the cot beside the fire." He blew the shavings again, and went about scratching out a last symbol before descending the porch with a cane in one hand and setting the turtle on the ground. He mumbled something to the turtle, I couldn't hear what, for that churgle in his throat was powerful distracting and gave me the constant urge to clear my own throat. Then that old Cherokee gave the turtle a friendly nudge and turned him loose toward the lake. He stood up and says to me direct, "Snake said ye be on your way." He clack-stepped back up the porch, cane in hand, and ducked into the cabin, dragging his right leg after him like it was a stump of driftwood.

※

Chief says, "Turtle knows water. Can take your words to the deep."

Virgil had pulled me off Jimmy Brown and helped me inside. Levi led Jimmy around back to the corncrib.

Chief says, "Ye can count on Turtle. He wears your words in his shell. He'll be letting folks know ye coming through."

Virgil laid me out on the cot, which was slung with deerskin webbing and made soft with layers of pine boughs.

Chief says, "Turtle tells them below: This boy is a'coming. Best ye all make way for his passage."

With that big Cherokee knife he made two long cuts in my arm, near flayed it to the bone. His voice was a chant in my ear.

"Snake's eyes cloud over before he sloughs his old skin. He goes blind and fasts from his food."

I could hear the slow rhythm of pounding. Someone pounding up roots. I could hear burl-knots pop in the fire.

"Snake welcomes the dark, for he knows what comes after."

And a restlessness came over me. A heat slithered under my skin.

"Snake burrows down into the earth. To the world he is dead."

And I writhed on that cot, my eyes slitted with fever.

"But he is not dead."

I wished to God I knew why.

"He is on a dark journey."

Words like firebrands in my head.

"And when Snake comes to the surface he is new."

———◦•◦———

I woke up, my mind total looted, on a pine-bough cot in an empty cabin. The fire was low and danced in step with the shadows, and my skin felt hot as embers. I watched the moonlight slowly glide down the log wall, the chinks of mud in between, then down to the floor and up over the foot of my cot. Only it confused me some, for I used to watch the moon do the same thing back at the shriekhouse, and I began to think I was there again.

There was a time back when the whitecoats would come into my cell fairly regular, usually first thing in the morn, and set themselves down for a cozy little chat on a stool that would leave when they did. And they would say, so Dannon, I need you to be honest with me. I'd say, all right. They would say, Dannon, I need to know if you ever imagine God has given you certain instructions, or powers other folks simply don't have, and I would say no sir, but if you'll allow me to stay here forever and ever I'd be willing to change my answer to yes, and they'd frown a bit and scribble it up in my chart and tap their chin to show they were thinking in earnest, and then they'd say, Dannon, I'd like to know what *you* think is wrong with you. They loved that one. What do I think. Welp, I would tell them, I believe the problem with me is that I am here, and don't particular want to be. Which is to say, I ain't elsewhere, and would swap the two if I could. And they would say, of course Dannon, of course, but do you know *why* you are here, and I would say, yessir I do, I am here because I ain't miserable like most folks is, though I tried my best, and no matter what I do I just pure fail to see things like I'm supposed to. And they would say, do you mean your Daltonism, and I would say, no sir, I mean I got me a different set of eyes to see with, and they would say, uh huh, and scribble it up in my chart.

Now about your eyes, they would say, Dannon if we could just come back to your eyes for a moment, what is it that makes you believe your eyes are special, and I would say, go to hell, and they would scribble some and say, this is important, Dannon, as we want to understand you, but to do that we have to understand what you believe. So if you could just tell us why your eyes are special, and I'd say, I don't mean my eyes you fool, if you would just stop listening to my words and hear what I'm saying you might—and they would interrupt, reminding me that porters were just outside the door should I get too uppity, and they would say, Dannon, it sounds to me like it's you who is miserable, and I'd say, I reckon I am, and they would say, but you just said it's everyone else who is miserable, and I'd say, I reckon they are too.

Scribble, scribble. So Dannon, are you saying I'm miserable? And I'd say, you and your old lady both, and they'd make their eyes jump back in their skull and try to the hide the strain in their voice when they says, that's quite a presumption, and I'd say, it's presumption that pays your bills, doc, give it up now and you'll have to find a new line a work, and their chin would get all flexy and white while we listened to the distant rumble of the plumbing. Then I'd ask how they felt about me skipping my ice bath today for they were chapping me up pretty good, and the guy in the cell next to me, not Erasmus but the other guy, he'd yell 'I got new legs!' two or three times, like he did every morning and the whitecoats would say they had to continue their rounds and we could discuss these features again next time.

I reckon you can see why war, and my probable demise, might have struck them as a suitable therapy. Thing is, I managed to come through it all with my madness intact. Nothing but another man's teeth in my head to show for it.

At some point in the night I got clear on my locale. Chief's cabin. I looked down at my arm and saw the two knife strokes he made, both stuffed with a poultice of root pulp. Probably Klamathweed, as I saw a bowl of the wilted yellow flowers on the table. My arm didn't hurt near like it did, either. It had gone from black to purple, which I reasoned a good thing, and the swelling had gone down enough for me to wiggle my fingers. Still laid out on my back, I shimmied my way over to the edge of the cot and sat up, but the room began to twirl and broke apart in my eyes till there was nothing but pirouetting snowflakes.

A long while I sat there, feeling the pins poking my lips and the sweat breaking cold on my brow, just waiting for Chief's cabin to quit unraveling. I rubbed my eyes so hard they made squishy sounds. When I could finally stare at a solitary nailhead in the floorboard without my stomach going dark, I reckoned I was at my best. I took a deep breath, feeling equalibrious at that moment, and shoved up from the cot in a single movement. Only that feeling vanished the instant I stood, and the wall and the floor, in that precise order, came swinging up at me, clapping me up like a regular one-two punch. When I came to again, I was crumpled sideways like a toe-kicked can with my legs spraddled on the floor and my cheek pressed to the wall and my arm pinched tight in between.

I rolled onto my back. I laid there flat on the floor. I had I fairly nice view out the window. Through the tears in my eyes I could see the stars stretch blurry and the mountains panting like a row of dogs. The yellow moon, it hummed aloud in perfect G. As I lay there, wrinkling my forehead to feel the stickiness of dried sweat, I reckoned one or two more lumps like these and my skull would start to feel like an ear of corn.

I heard voices out on the porch. I refused to crawl across the floor. But when I finally made it to my feet again I saw my problems were manifold. I had a powerful dose of the spins, true, and an arm that looked like salt-pork, but the cabin was so damn decrepit it shifted under your feet like the whole thing was pontooned on water. Starting at the far end of the cabin, opposite the door, I made my way around the edge of the room, leaving the sweat prints of my good hand on three of the cabin's four walls as I went. When I came to the door and opened it, the voices stopped.

There was Virgil vol Krie sitting right beside Chief, just sitting there on that pineslab bench, peering out at the night through a screen of honeysuckle. Virgil was shucking away at that ball marble of his, and he tipped back his straw hat and smiled up at me. "Who-eee! Now don't you look like a bar of golden sunshine!"

Chief says to me, "Snake talks loud, when ye don't want to listen." And it occurred to me the man had yet to speak of anything but critters. What's more, I saw only half his mouth worked when he spoke. The other half collected white foam in the corner, and that entire side of his face, his whole body actually, may as well been frostbit for all it moved. Even that one eye wouldn't blink so he had to do it manual-like, and a steady stream of tears trickled from it like the man had seen something once, and half of him would remain ever steeped in sorrow.

"I hear him, though," says Chief, gazing out at the lake. "Snake said ye be coming. Says to me, look out, for there is a strong spirit a'coming, and he be riding a blindfolded mule to git to ye."

I says, lifting my arm a little, "I thank you for the fixing. It's a lot better now." I wondered how long I'd been asleep.

And Chief, still watching the lake, he says, "It is Snake what fixed ye. And ye'll observe your mule is near to fixed too. By the time ye meet up with the mayor, he won't be blind to ye no more."

I couldn't confirm the fact of that right yet, as I hadn't the first clue what the man was speaking about. I asked if that snake of his had said any more to my providence. And Chief says, "Yee," real low and slow-like till I wondered if he was finally clearing his throat. But then he says, "Yee, Snake spoke some. But I hear it through Deer." And from there old Chief went on to describe the peculiar menagerie of his world, and how gossip makes its way circuitous to his cabin. He says, "I seen Deer come tromping stiff-legged out the woods like he just hear warning from Crow." He coughed once and the churgle popped in his throat. A tear dropped from one side of his jaw. "Old Crow, he'll do that, he'll tell Deer what he knows, particular when he gets word from Mockingbird. For they rely equal upon Mockingbird's announcements. Now Mockingbird, he says he hear Bullfrog go quiet, which Bullfrog will do when Snake come down to the lake for a drink."

In this way I learned it was Bullfrog that first heard tell of my debacle, passing it on in like manner till old Chief, last in the line of communiqué, says to me, "Snake says next time ye and he meet, it will be different. Ye'll meet eye to eye, and know each other for brethren, and Snake'll pull ye out of a scrape."

Even over the smell of twenty-one coyotes, which bear the eccentric tang of ripe socks, I could smell old Levi come stumbling out from around the cabin—for I've got quite a sniffer, as I believe I've stated—him staring up at us from the bottom step of the porch. He had a look in his eye, restless and wild, a look that says there ain't a drop in this place and he could feel the threat of sobriety creeping on.

"Well I see you're up," he says to me. He kind of sneered about, looking distasteful at all three of us. I don't know what went on while I slept but I suspect it wasn't friendly, for it had sent old Levi out and about, scouting parts unknown and brought him back all wretched and wroth-like.

"So what you been up to there, Levi? Where you been at?" says Virgil, cordially enough, and Levi replied with spite, "That there's none your business, is the fact of it." He gave an exploratory sniff of the air. "Come and go as I please." He sniffed again, looking about, finally crinkling his nose like a rabbit and scowling hard at Virgil. "The hell nigra, you go and step in something again?"

And Virgil, shucking away at his ball, calm as can be he says, "Nawsuh. I reckon that just your own moustache you smelling there, suh."

Levi barked something between a laugh and a yell, but he sort of choked on it and had to swallow real hard to keep from coughing, his eyes gone misty and bloodshot. "You let your nigra talk like that?"

"You know he ain't mine."

Levi raised a finger, palsied with emotion. "I tell you he needs a whipping. A whipping, I tell you! I'd do it myself if I weren't parting ways this moment."

"And I'd help you too," I says. "Only I believe Virgil vol Krie here would whoop us both." And so help me Lord if Chief didn't cackle out loud, a sound so sharp and unexpected it folded me double with laughter and sent old Virgil into silent convulsions. "Besides," I says to Levi, clutching the stitch in my side, "you got to go. Like you said."

Old Levi shook his head, ugly with hate. "So that's your thanks, is it? After saving your life? Bringing you here? Well then, you all can sit round and rot. Our ways is parted, far as I'm concerned. And these here is just cough-tears, don't mean nothing. There's others out there who know how to return a favor."

Which is, of course, what it all came down to for old Levi. The trafficking of favors. The currency of good turns. Needless to say, I had not one misgiving about seeing the man go. I watched him zigzag out onto the clearing, back the way we'd come, and heard the coy-dogs bark when he stumbled midway, and you could hear him yelling break-voice curses back at them till the rim of the treeline swallowed him up.

"He'll be back," says Chief, pushing himself upright with his cane. "Bad spirit got ahold of that one. He'll be back."

Chief tottered across the porch, one hip clicking with each step, then cane-clacked down the four stairs and out into the night.

I threw myself down onto the bench beside Virgil. He slapped my thigh with natural exuberance and says to me, "Glad to see you looking better, suh. Up and about as you is." He caught sight of my arm. "Who-eee, look at that, though. He cut you *deep*. You got pain enough?"

I had a goodly supply.

"Damn!" whispered Virgil, bending closer and squinting as I wiggled my fingers. "Is that… is that bones moving? That is, isn't it! Oh damn, that's…" he turned away. "That there is a nasty looking wound, suh. Powerful nasty."

I took a peek myself. You couldn't hardly see the bone at all, actually, for the poultice covered it mostly.

"It's all right," I says.

Virgil looked at me. "Oh yessuh, ain't nothing atall wrong with that. Just a scratch is all. Fact I's surprised you noticed even. Tell me though, seriously. Can you feel 'em, them bones? What is bones feel like when you touch it?"

"Nothing," I says. "Don't feel like nothing. Listen, can we talk about something else? Anything, I don't care. Hey, is that water there?"

I saw a water dipper balanced on the railing.

"Nawsuh, empty. But there a whole barrel of rain-catch round the side of the cabin." Virgil folded up his sandpaper, the creases fuzzy and white. Tucking it back into the pocket of his vest he says, "Anyhow. I sure is pleased to see you up, suh. Mighty pleased. And it'll be nice finally talking to somebody about matters beside beasts and bugs."

I took up the empty water dipper and walked round side of the cabin, Virgil talking louder so I could hear him while I had a sip.

"Not that I am complaining, suh!" he called out from the porch. "But be nice to final leave this place too, you know? Find some real food? I reckon that injun's too old for a'farming and trapping and such, for he appears to live off nothing but dogs' milk and ginseng. He tells me he been hiding out up here over ten years now."

I sat back down beside Virgil, supporting my bad arm with my good. "That right?"

Virgil gave a slow nod. "What he says."

"Welp," I replied, wiggling my fingers again. "That old Chief did me up fine. Could use a bandage to hide the gore, but there ain't no doubt I am on the mend."

And Virgil says, "Something you ought to know, suh."

And I says, "What is that, Virgil?"

And he says, "Just cause that Levi call him Chief, that don't mean it's his name."

And so I says, "What is it then?"

And Virgil says, "Didn't say I know, suh. But it ain't Chief, I tell you that." Still holding my gaze, he dug his snuff-sack out his pocket, loosening the drawstring by feel. "And another thing, suh. That old Will Lawson."

"What about him?"

"He is coming. I can feel it."

"You think he'll find us?"

"Ain't no think about it, suh. I know."

"You can feel it?"

"I can feel it. And there be a whole *mess* of bitchfire when he does."

I took that in.

Then Virgil, he says to me, "That old Will Lawson, suh, he a different sort of man. He find us. Whatever it take. Don't you forget, me and him knows one another personal."

I turned to my guide. "What then? What do we do?"

And he says, "Ain't no place safe for you and me both. No place but old Valhalla, and I am itching to git there."

I was all for that notion. Madder had become nothing less than my Dulcinea, my Beatrice, my pole star in the night. Every step I took was to get to her. It wasn't entirely true, but I says, "I am ready. I'm ready right now. Just put me back on Jimmy Brown and I can hold my own."

Virgil gave me a dubious look, then smiled to himself and snorted. "Don't mean no disrespect, suh, but you ain't anywhere near ready."

"I can. Nah, serious, I can! I can and I will, better than waiting around here for that bitchfire you're promising."

"And how you gonna do that, huh? How you gonna hold on to old Jimmy? You in no shape for nothing, and that injun about the best thing you got going right now, so you may as well just—"

"I can ride."

Virgil fell silent, just looking me over and shaking his head.

I worked my hand into a fist. My fingers were slow and thick, but I reckoned I could hold on. Problem was my fever, and the way spots kept slamming round in my vision. But then there were ways to take care that, ways I knew. I had a trick, is what it was.

Way back, some time after that wind came down and stole the breath from my sisters and The Loss stole the heart of my Pa, I myself, as a boy of seven, commenced to feel like my spirit deserted and had taken solace in the stars. Like it quit this earth and marooned me in my body.

It was to rectify this feeling, and not to dig wells, that I first took up the habit of dowsing. I don't know how I first conceived of the notion, young as I was, but seeking out the blood of this earth with a pair of willow switches was about the only way I could think of to remedy this gloom. Because the moment I felt water stirring below, deep down in the rock, I felt it rushing through my body and knew my body and the earth were combined-like. I knew I belonged here, and my spirit would come snapping back into my breast, and walking barefoot on the soil was like a love affair.

"Give me an hour," I says to Virgil. "See if you can have Jimmy Brown ready, as I aim to have this thing licked in an hour."

But first Virgil bound my arm. He quickly made a sling from one of Chief's old shirts and then went out to get Jimmy watered. I started off across the clearing, my head throbbing with the moon, stumbling over my own feet till I reached the lake. I wandered along the grassy shore in hopes of finding a willow. Willows love water, and you'll general find them nearby. To watch them grow, you'd think they could smell it the way a hound smells coons. I reckon that is why willow switches work so good for dowsing.

Story. And this one's true, though you may not believe it at first. If Mama was alive she'd confirm it. One time, long time ago, I asked Mama how come we have willows out back of the henhouse if there isn't any creek. She says it's cause your Pa's got willow-piss in him and can grow them up from the dirt with his very own water. It is true that after a good night on the jug, which was most every night, Pa was in the habit of relieving himself out behind the chicken coop because it was a shorter route than the outhouse by an approximate twelve paces. So night after night, year after year, Pa watered that ground until one day a willow sprouted. Jumped right from the earth.

Pa was total spooked. He took to relieving himself else-where, but still nearby, until a second willow popped up its little green head. This went on until we had five or six willows strug-gling up from the earth with nothing but Pa's liquor-piss to go on. Pa scratched his head over it for a good while, and finally resolved to undress the miracle. He got out his spade, and then later in his excavations, an adz, a chopping ax, a rusty old stonepick and a wheelbarrow to help him quarry out the root systems of those mysterious saplings.

Turns out a quarter mile up Blackwater Hollow stood a solitary willow, an old granddaddy willow that grew on the banks of Wiles Creek. Except Wiles Creek had dried up years ago, and that old willow sent out a single root, straight as an arrow, down to the place Pa laid his water. All five-six trees out back were actually the same tree, and the same as the one up on Wiles Creek. If you don't believe me you can go see for yourself, for I doubt anyone has ever backfilled Pa's trenches.

Down on Chief's lake I found myself a willow and bent off two switches of equal size. Just holding them and I felt better, like both my feet were firm on the ground. I commenced to wander back across the clearing in search of water. Right off, my head began to clear. It's nearabout magic what a dose of dowsing will do for my body, like my inners just crave it, like I'm drinking it up, and there was plenty water in Chief's clearing. I'm not talking about the lake water. I'm talking about something deep and big, practically reeling me in, and I began to walk faster to get to the spot. It took me direct to the cabin, which confused me at first, but then I realized the cabin was just in the way. I went around it, continuing on, the pull of water nigh yanking me along. I'd never felt such a draw that I could recall, it was like being swept along in a current. It led me toward the tree line, where the laurels stood thick as a wall. But it happens I saw Chief standing there, just standing there in the clearing, looking out into the trees. He wore pants but no shirt, long silver braids, and he kept his back to me.

As I made towards him, I realized the willow switches were in agreement, only halting me when I came up against his back. It appeared he was standing directly on the spot they were leading me to. Excepting the way those switches were crossing and dipping, it was like they were pointing to Chief. Like he was the water. And lots of it.

Without turning, he says to me, "Ye'll be wanting to head straight up this mountain, this one with the burn-patch up the middle. When ye get to the top, don't go back down direct the other side, but follow the ridge northwards a good mile. When it cuts east, then ye drop down. Ye'll come to a road eventual what runs the side of the slope, and ye'll follow it east-northeast a good ways till you come to the crossroads. From there ye'll take the fork what goes to Union Fog. Ye can rest there. They'll hide ye good. Just ask for the mayor."

I looked down at my arm. "You think I'm full better now? You think I'm ready to go?"

And he says, "Ye hear them treefrogs?"

I didn't. I listened, but I didn't hear anything. "What treefrogs?" I says. "It's total quiet out there."

"Yee," says Chief, nodding real slow. "And by this time tomorrow, there'll be one day between us." He turned around then and I saw the tears streaking one cheek. He put something in his mouth. It was an acorn.

Then I heard the crack of a rifle and that old Cherokee fell forward, and Will Lawson leapt out from the woods.

<hr />

It'll take the average man nigh two minutes to reload a musket, and considerably longer to fire a pepperbox that's never going to fire. I ran back to the cabin, dipped inside, saw it was empty, and jumped back out just in time to see Virgil vol Krie come round from the corncrib with Jimmy Brown On A Rope. Virgil's eyes were wide. I could see the whites all around.

"Who's firing?"

"It's old Will," I says. "Other side of this clearing. I think I seen Levi skulking around back there too."

"You seen 'em?"

"Seen them both, and reckon they're right behind."

Virgil grabbed Jimmy by the withers and yanked him up alongside me. "Get on up," he says. "I'm gonna go get that old—"

"Dead," I says. "Will got him."

I saw Virgil's chest heave up and down, two or three times. Then he says, "Come on. Get on."

"I can walk now. I just ran even."

"I says get on!"

I threw a leg over Jimmy and grabbed hold of his reins, and I learned something then. Something most folks have little need to discover. A mule can gallop. Virgil had to sprint the difference of the clearing to keep up, and then took hold of the rope again when we reached the trees.

"This way," he says, panting.

"Uh uh. It's up this mountain. We got to go up."

"Nawsuh. Valhalla's this way."

"May be, but this here's a rout. We been routed, Virgil."

He seemed to gather my meaning without further account. We crashed through the underbrush, Virgil leading the way. Next thing we were headed straight up that mountain without a trail to speak of, the backslap a branches thrashing us up pretty good. Old Jimmy Brown nickered in protest. Virgil would shush him, shove him a handful of weeds, then tug on the rope with a few kind words and Jimmy Brown would follow along sort of tractable-like.

"You think we lost him?"

"Nope," says Virgil, breathing hard through his nose.

"Can you hear him?"

"Ain't no time to talk about it. Yaw! Come on, Jimmy." Breathing hard. "Come on now. Keep it up!"

Over the course of our journey I was coming to learn a few things about mules. For one, they aren't stubborn. Just too smart to follow commands that'll clearly bring them no profit. Where a horse will run till he drops or his heart explodes, a mule will stop when it's time for stopping. He'll face a whip before a rickety bridge and he won't ever ride into battle. He's dignified, it what it comes down to. Only misunderstood is all, thereby endearing the beast direct to my heart.

"You arm's bleeding."

So it was. You could see it come through the sling, a patch of black on moonlit cloth.

"Yup."

"You want me to stop and wrap it tighter?"

"Too tight already. That's why it's bleeding."

"Nawsuh. It's bleeding cause we riding hard up a mountain, and you arm is scored to the bone."

Jimmy Brown had been fitted out with a saddle at Chief's place. Virgil had found it, an old heap of a rat-chewed thing rotting on a shelf in the corncrib. It was a little big too, made for a horse, and shifted side to side on a mule's swollen belly. The squeak of its leather beat out a little rhythm as we climbed, and I strained beyond it, listening for the sounds of Will Lawson.

I says, "You know Union Fog? Other side of this ridge?"

Between the huff of breaths, "Oh, yessuh."

And I says, "How about hiding there for a time, and making for Valhalla when it's clear?"

He says, "You arm that bad?"

I says, "I don't know. Maybe. But it was Chief's last words that we go there, and I suspect a sibyl knows something of these matters."

Me and Virgil and Jimmy Brown On A Rope, we came up hard and quick on the ridge Chief spoke of and stopped there for a breath. Virgil was breathing it for real now. "Here, you ride," I says.

"Nawsuh. Mostly downhill from here."

The valley below was lost in fog. Only the ridgeline circling above was visible. We followed north about a mile, just like Chief said, then dropped down into that misty dale when the ridge cut east.

Without warning, we popped out onto a road of hard-packed clay. It was like it materialized out of nowhere from the fog. It was wide enough for two wagons to pass.

We followed the road east-northeast, as per Chief's dying directive until the road widened out. I could feel the space around us, though couldn't see the edges. I fathomed we had reached the crossroads. The fog was so thick it muffled our voices and dampened our clothes.

We parked there in the middle of the crossroads, turning slow circles. All told, there were now four possible roads to choose from. I says, "So which way now?"

Chief had said to take the road leading to Union Fog, but gave no hint as to which that would be. Nor could Virgil vol Krie recall one from the other, or having ever encountered such relentless ill fortune. I pointed out the omega-tracks of shod horses in the mud, but they numbered equal in every direction.

Virgil sat right down, right there in the road, and set himself up with a pinch a snuff. He sniffed hard, arched his eyebrows and gave a little waggle of his head and says to me, "Just don't know, suh. Fact is, I don't recall no crossroads atall." He said he was of a mind to consult the spirits, for he carried a charm that allowed it. Said his own daddy had purchased the charm direct from a genuine Carolina mountain witch that could spit sparks from her tongue when she incanted. And I said absolutely not, no way in hell, and nor was I going to sit round here and think about it a moment longer for I had made that mistake once before. As you may recall, it was upon the juncture of a crossroads that the devil last caught me. The very event that cost me my clothes.

It all happened just past Hickamaw, as I was walking the homestretch so to speak, having followed the Shallewapre River for nigh three days running. Mexico was far behind and I wasn't barely fifty miles from Nuckton, practically close enough to smell the pine of its hollows, when the road suddenly cut east from the river and I came upon the lonesomest old crossroads to ever converge upon a wood.

It confounded me some, as I had never heard of any Hickamaw crossroads. It certainly wasn't there when I left. Furthermore, I had once traveled six days in the exact wrong direction as the result of one tiny, impetuous moment at the fork of two paths. That's when I learned there's no such thing as a small decision.

So... there I was, standing at the Hickamaw crossroads. Totally fed up, hungry, tired, and possessed of a sudden inflexibility, I resolved not to take another step until I knew precisely which road to take. I would not budge, I decided. Only the shining path of certainty could upend my vow, that or a person generous enough to point me on my way.

A long while I waited. I began to look for symbols of portent in the blowing of leaves, signs in a bug-tangled web. But nobody came along to help me that day, and the following morning I woke up stiff with the cold. That next night was colder still. By the third morning I was feeling put out.

I woke before sunrise that day, just sitting there on the X of the crossroads. Arms wrapped about my shins, chin resting upon my knees as I gazed out at the forest with eyes half-open, closing, half-open, closing. There was still mist on the road, as the sun was just coming up. The air was dark blue with dawn.

Then I saw a woman in a long white gown go gliding through the trees. Her skin was pale and lovely. Her movements effortless. Her head was on fire, however, so I did some quick thinking and concluded I should run for my life. I crashed through the woods, sprinting fast as I could, my breath steaming out my nose like a stag. But sure enough she found me, stepping directly onto my path. I cleared my throat and kindly asked her to step aside.

In response, her hands combusted, and that's when I knew for certain she intended to hassle me. I tell her, "Look here, I got no debt this side or the other. If you coming to collect, then you best pass me by."

What she did to me, however, was simply too weird to describe and I've yet to sort it out in my head. Just know the sum of the affair left me without a stitch of cloth. I believe you know the rest.

The point of that story is that a crossroads is no place to bide your time. I believe I told Virgil something to that effect. And when it came to devils and haunts and ghosts and such, Virgil was more than rational. We left the crossroads immediately, taking the road leading north.

We hurried along maybe an hour more, north as I said, my arm in a wicked turmoil and soaking the sling clean through, when we came to a washout. Recent rains had yanked a wall of mud across the road. It piled fifteen feet high, obliterating the road. Virgil led Jimmy Brown right up to it, then backed away, retracing their steps the way a fox does, back to a point where our tracks had neared the edge of the road. From there we dipped into the woods, subterfuge-like, leaving no sign of said departure except the false ones that would lead Will Lawson right up to the mudslide.

Cutting through the woods this time, we backtracked all the way to the crossroad, knowing Will Lawson was likely to presume the mudslide had sluiced our tracks. He would probably fight his way over the pile up and continue on in hopes of catching us.

Having returned to the crossroads, we didn't so much as pause this time. We took the road due east, for no better reason than it was nearest, except we stayed to the woods just beside it so's to keep our tracks hidden and prolong the ruse.

Before long our bellies were rumbling. Virgil suggested we call it a night. Following no path that I could see, Virgil led us away from the roadside, deep into the woods and far from the road, then up a rocky little gulch till we came to a beaver pond. The little critters had gnawed all the stumps and dammed up the creek so the water spread out in a big puddle. All the trees standing in the middle of the pond were skeleton-dead, for they were five foot submerged, and the shore was tangled with cattails and deadfalls. It offered just enough cover for a little camp.

It was getting cold, and Virgil judged it safe enough for a fire. But he kept it small and burned nothing but the driest wood.

By and by, old Virgil stood up. He put on his straw hat like he was taking his leave. "Where you off to?" I says.

"Well suh," he says, "I believe I'll go strangle me a goose." And so help me Lord if that's not exactly what he did. As you may have suspected, Virgil had some real woodsman in his blood. He had spent most his youth working Alabama cotton, his kin slaving the plantations down there for nigh three generations. But there were rumors always, talk of a movement in the north, a mystical force some called 'abolition.' But the deal was, you had to be there to make it work.

What little information he gathered was sparse and contradictory, but over time he managed to sketch out a map in his head. Somewhere beyond the mountains to the north lay a negro paradise of milk and honey. A land of abolitionists with open arms.

He was the age of ten when he packed his pockets full grits and said farewell to his Mama and his Papa. And it was some fourteen siblings he left behind in tears, spending most all the next year alone. Trekking. Hunting up grub, hiding by day, eating frog legs kicking. When he finally crossed the Blue Honey Mountains and came down into the hills below, he saw a sight like something from dreams. Instead of cotton plantations far as the eye could see, there was nothing but fields of tobacco. He was north. North at last.

So noble of heart and certain of freedom earned, he practically strutted right into Roanoke, no doubt flashing that beatific smile.

"I'm here for the abolition," says Virgil to the first man he found, a big man who smiled right back. "Nigra, you reined yourself up about two states shy. For there ain't no abolition in Virginia."

"No? How much farther I got to go?"

"Oh, long way. Long way yet. Fact, farther than you're like to go."

Laying claim to his windfall like a coin in the dust, that fella had Virgil scrubbed and naked and chained to a block and ready for sales by sundown.

Except fortune was on Virgil's side, for the person that purchased him was a traveling man by the name of Jeremiah vol Krie, from a little village deep in the mountains. A little place known to some as Valhalla.

So it was back to the mountains for Virgil, which turned out to be the next best thing to abolition true. In the mountains, white folks scratched out such a hard, isolated, toilsome life they were obliged to live side-by-side with their slavefolk. Negroes might well be treated like kin, taught to run a family business, or in some cases paid wages fair.

Jeremiah vol Krie raised Virgil up alongside his three sons, teaching him the ways of the world. He was taught how to grow corn and beans on a slope, how to make fine whiskey from mash, and though I cannot be certain, I believe Virgil even learned how to read.

For all these things Virgil was a grateful man, and loyal, as you already know. So when old Jeremiah died, Virgil stayed on with the family. He became the property of a Miss Odessa vol Krie, the benevolent granddaughter of his kindly old master.

But back to the goose. Virgil caught us a big old gander and he dragged it squawking into camp. Then he gripped the neck in one hand and the head in the other and spun it off like a bolt.

"You know how to cook?" he says.

"Let me put it this way... Nope."

He tossed the carcass direct into the fire and we watched it with watering mouths for all of three minutes, and then the belly began to hiss and we leaned forward in anticipation until the whole thing exploded, spattering us with boiling gizzard juice.

"That mean it's done," says Virgil. The feathers were still sending up black smoke like a chimney but he waved it away, choking and coughing as he hauled it from the flames.

"I don't know, Virgil. Still looks like a bird to me."

"Oh, this be a good one," he says, appraising the carcass in his hand. "This here what a done goose look like!" He took a webbed foot in each hand and began tugging until the whole thing ripped in two. "Now hows that!" he says, handing half to me.

"That looks just fine," I says. In fact, it looked more like something rescued from the fire than cooked in it—just a cold, dripping, feathery mess, but if I closed my eyes and kept away from the feathers, it wasn't half bad.

After a deep sleep by the coals, we hiked it back to the road. We had to walk upon it now, for it filed between hills so tight there was no way to stay beside the path. Furthermore, the hills were dense with woods and still smothered with fog and twice we jumped at the echoing report of a rifle.

"They's hunting in there," says Virgil to my unspoken query. "Can't be too far from a town now, suh. Look at that. See there's a cabin already."

The cabin was decrepit and abandoned, practically reclaimed by the woods, sitting just off one side of the road. Grass was growing tall on the roof and through a wagon's skeleton in the yard, bits of rusty iron poked up through the weeds. From here on, a split-rail fence hedged one side of the road, and we followed it till it stopped sudden at the mouth of the next hollow. You could hear the sound of a creek back in there somewhere, not far away, but the mist was so thick you couldn't see a thing.

And there was a glow in there, a lantern or something, just off back in the wood.

"What you doing climbing that fence," says Virgil. "Nahsuh, get on back. You know better'n go following lights through the woods. That there glow is unnatural."

Which was plain as can be, and yet somehow I'd nearly fallen for it, one of oldest tricks in the book.

"Should call this place 'Tuley Fog'," he says to me then, our footsteps hollow and dull-sounding. "Not no Union Fog. Should call this place Tuley, if you know what I mean." For that is what we call a mist in the mountains when it's so thick you can cut it like pie. And it was true, what Virgil said, for even as the hills grew bigger, becoming mountains proper, and our little road came straggling into town, that Tuley fog hung so tight it was like the whole settlement was hidden. I'd doubt there was any way you could see it from the peaks above.

<hr>

You know how Nuckton splits up like a turkey's foot, with the three main hollows branching off the Shallewapre and the main road? That's Union Fog too. Does the same thing. Hardly a house in town, with every one living off back in the mountains, but that little lane going through Union Fog was crammed dense with rickety old shops, usually stacked, sharing sidewalls without an inch between them. If you were to look just beyond town into the surrounding dell and those rolling foothills topped with oaks, you could see the rumpled quilt of fields, turned and fallow, an earthen patchwork of yellow and brown. But any further on and your eyes came up hard against mountains. They ran up steep, hemming this place in, and you could only guess at their height for that fog hung solid as a creamcap on a bottle of milk.

The streets were dark without one lit lantern, but there were plenty folks about, strolling and haggling and selling their wares as vigorous as Saturday noon. So far, Jimmy Brown hadn't eaten anything but grass and we needed to find him some feed. Virgil, too, was eager for warm victuals, but what I desired most was sleep. I had no idea whatsoever how to find this mayor we were after.

"Now don't you go worrying about money, suh," says Virgil vol Krie as we tied Jimmy to a hitching post outside a tavern. "Let's get all what we need. Provisions is mighty hard to come by in these mountains, and I myself is in the mood for some bacon. I can eat me a whole lot a bacon."

I says, "Where did you get money, Virgil?"

And Virgil sniffed, pausing to set one boot on the edge of a water-trough, brushing off the dust all meticulous-like. "Well suh," he says, "so happens when I come across these here boots, these boots good fortune was kind enough to lay before me in a time of superlative need, well these boots was hiding a fair bit more'n a whiteman's toes in the tips of them."

And I says, "How much exactly is a fair bit?"

And Virgil, he patted his trouser pocket, twice, hard, and I heard them. Not the jangle of a few loose coppers or a couple gold pieces butting heads. What I heard was the dull, unyielding grind of too many coins rubbing up against each other when they were stuffed tight inside a purse.

"You like bacon?" he says, making his way up the steps to the tavern. "I reckon I eat me a whole side a bacon right now."

Even from outside, the tavern was soiled and mournful, the clapboards dark with the grease of time. Countless inscriptions were graffitied into their grain. In truth, this place was no more than the bottom room of a teetering tri-level shanty, unfit for swine where I come from.

Hanging about the plank-benches out front were a couple fellas with the scurvied look of rapscallions. One of them was hollow-cheeked with a matted beard, lazily plucking at his banjo with a purple thumbnail. The other had sideburns long enough to comb back over his ears, which sported little tufts of hair, white as dandelion fuzz. He whittled at a stick, throwing splinters about his bare feet but otherwise producing nothing definitive from his efforts.

"Howdy," I says, tipping my hat.

Neither man replied. Their eyes were dull and cowlike, wholly unafflicted by intelligence. One look at those fellas and you knew they were prepared to sit right there, forever, without a single complaint if that is what the job took.

"This here a boarding house?" I asked.

The banjo-plucking one stopped plucking his banjo. The other cut a splinter, long and slow. The silence carried. Then their eyes narrowed with a mixture of dimness and suspicion as me and Virgil climbed the porch and brushed past them to the door.

I peeked inside, smelling the rancid smoke of tallow. There were two tables in there, empty kegs for sitting, a solitary shelf of unmarked bottles. Against the back wall I saw a ladder going up through a hatch to the second floor.

Only two folks were in the tavern. The one was nicely dressed, drinking a snifter of something in the corner, a puddling candle and an open book before him on the table. The other was the proud proprietor of this establishment, splashed out in a hammock slung between rafters.

I called to him. "You got rooms for sleeping in?"

"Hyup," comes the proprietor's voice, only I couldn't see him, for his head was buried in the hammock folds. All you could see of the man was the one leg hanging out, giving a little kick to the floor every few swings.

"And beds?" I says.

"Not unless you brought one."

Kick. Kick. Kick. He said there was a bale of hay probably moldering out back, which I was welcome to, and a horse blanket round somewhere, though he couldn't be sure of that, for the horse last used it was dead. And he didn't cook meals or supply washing for clothes. Latrine was three doors down.

I says, that'll do fine.

Proprietor says, should I take offence to the vermin, I could purchase turpentine across the road and paint myself with it prior to sleep. Just make a point of smoking outdoors should I do so.

I asked how much for the room.

He showed me the grime in the creases of his chubby vertical palm.

Five dollars, I says, that's quite a lot.

And he says, cheaper'n a pound of grief.

And I says, are we talking with or without water?

He tells me there's a tub out back. Baths were ten cents for clean water, five for used. And don't expect him to be carrying no buckets. Nor messages for that matter. Nor wake up calls prior to noon. Soap was a quarter.

I says that all sounds pretty good, so long as he allowed us our privacy, and he sat up in his hammock and looked at me and Virgil for the first time.

"Nope. No nigras."

"He is a free man," I says, Virgil vol Krie at my side.

"He got papers? Papers says he's free?"

I didn't say anything, and the man flopped back into his hammock. "No nigras."

It was at this point the fella in the corner, the special dressed one, he quietly hailed me with an open hand. "Something to drink?" he says to me, shutting his book and loosening the ascot round his neck.

"You may as well, suh," Virgil says to me. "Ain't no bacon in here nohow. You'll keep an eye on old Jimmy Brown for me?"

I says, "Where you gonna go?"

"Just be across the road. See there? Nah, the other one, see with the grain sacks out front? That'll be me."

"What you getting, just buying stuff?" I wasn't too easy about letting Virgil go it alone here.

"Just a few things, suh, things we'll be needing."

He smiled again, then turned to go. I watched Virgil cross the road, watched his broad shoulders and back till they disappeared into the general store's gloom.

"Brandy?" the man says to me when I turned back around. He stood up in greeting. Then to the proprietor, "Can we get another glass here? Great, that's fine, thank you. Sure, no, just set the bottle right there."

This fella, he wore one of those English waistcoats, pocketwatch on a chain, sideburns, spectacles. Total dapper. His hair was a little long for his type, perfumed, but he's got a good handshake, like he's sawed a few logs, and when he tells me he's a professor I didn't hold it against him for I could tell he was smart nonetheless. Says he's an ologist of some sort from the university of such-and-such, down here studying the fog patterns in this town for they were peculiar as all hell. Says it took him nigh six weeks just to find the place.

I heard a snort, derisive-like, and saw those fellas from out front had taken up at the second table. "Only thing you need to know about Union Fog," says the whittling one, who's now rolling something suspicious between thumb and forefinger, "is that the nunnery is at the one side of town, and the whorehouse is at the other, and I'll be goddamned if there is a soul in this place knows which is which." He wiped his fingers on the table's edge and asked the proprietor how his credit was looking today.

The proprietor leaned sideways from the hammock, put a finger to one nostril and emptied the contents from the other onto the floor. He stared at it for a while.

"This is a great place," I says, and my friend at the table here, who tells me his name is Throckmorton, well old Throckmorton says, "People round here are pretty close-lipped on the whole. I've had an awful time of it just trying to learn anything about the place. All I know for certain is they like their privacy. And are good at keeping it. Speaking of, you have any trouble with bandits? This town's on fire with talk of bandits right now. "

I took a sip of my brandy and then held it up for a closer look, pondering what the big deal was, why city folks want to forfeit a ransom for poor whiskey. I figured it was the bottle. Bottles were classier than jars, I suspect.

"Nah," I says. "I never seen a bandit in my life. So what you reading?"

He reached forward with both hands, a nervous movement, and adjusted the book so it ran exact even with the table's edge. "Oh, this? This is just... You read?"

"Some."

"Oh," he nods, a little more relaxed-like. He took a breath. "Well, this is Sturluson. On Norse Mythology. It's a little tedious, I suppose. And definitely archaic, but it's all here, all the good stuff. There's certainly better out there so far as storytelling goes, but he makes a point of—"

"Can I see?"

"Sure," he says with a jolt of enthusiasm, standing up and handing it across the table. I cracked it open, took a peek.

"So it's worth reading, this book?" I flipped through the pages.

"Go ahead, try it," he says with a wave of his hand, sitting back down. "Keep it, actually. I shouldn't be reading it anyhow, just an excuse for me to avoid working on my—Jesus! What happened to your arm?"

"What, this? Nothing."

"What do you mean nothing?"

"Just what you get for broaching hell, is all."

"My god," says Throckmorton, leaning forward for a better look and crinkling his nose in disgust. He sucked air through his teeth. "I mean Jesus, look at it. Don't you think you should see a surgeon or something?"

"Why? Does it look bad?"

He blinked at me. "Are you serious? You're dripping blood on the table for godsake."

"Sorry." I tried to wipe it up with the sling, but as it was pure soaked I just spread little swirls on the table.

"No, I'm just saying you should take care of that," he says. "Looks bad. If the green rot gets in there, they'll just take the whole thing off."

"Yeah," I says. "Yeah. Only I'm here to see the mayor."

He looked at me some.

Just then, the whittling fella came over and clacked a filthy glass down on the table. "Compliments," he says, still standing there, looking down at me. He filled the glass, pouring from a dented tin bucket. The moment I caught a whiff of the stuff I knew what I was in for. He lifted the glass without ceremony and drank it down in a single helping, his throat-lump jerking like a trapped toad with each swallow. He says, ah, and poured another, pushing the glass in front of me. He says, "You're looking for the mayor, just look right out front the door."

I leaned back and looked around him. "There?" I says.

"That statue," he says. "This town's only monument."

It was across the road, a wood carving, set out front the store Virgil had gone into. It was hard to tell, but it looked like somebody with a shotgun on a horse. Only the dimensions were all queer, which I attributed to the fumes coming off the bucket.

"Joke is," says the whittling fella, "so many nuns and whores is migrating back and forth from one side of town to the other, ever ten years or so they just switch billboards out front." He pointed over his shoulder with a thumb. "Anyhow, mayor's in with both. It's why we got ourselves a monument right here, middle of town, to mark which side is which."

I tell him how my friend's mule has been a bit high-strung of late, pretty emotional, isolating, definitely worrying us, but anyhow my main fear being he was internalizing a whole lifetime of subjugation, you know, just letting it fester in there without really dealing with any of it and not having the skills to communicate. Which was none of my business really, I ain't one to interfere, except now you could see it all coming out in this weird, malingering somatoform kind of thing, with a fetish-like fixation on blindfolds, or blindness, or maybe even just the loss of vision in a metaphorical sense but all of it stemming from a perceived lack of power and deep-seated belief that life on the whole would be more consequential and gratifying and universally meaningful if he could just, you know, sing. Like sing his heart out, no matter how big the crowd.

"Drink," says the whittling fella, and he tapped the rim of my glass with his yellow-calloused fingertip. Click, click.

Beyond a showdown, I saw little choice in the matter. I swilled the glass around, sniffed it once more by accident, and threw it back in a gulp. I turned my head to the side and pinched my eyes till the shiver ran through me.

"May joy hunt you!" I says, clacking the glass down. "Hunt you to a man!" For I can do bravado in a pinch.

It was the stomaching of garlic-wine I could never handle. The whittling fella, he gave a mirthless laugh, then took up his dented tin bucket and filthy little glass and sat back down with the purple-thumbed fella at their own board.

"You handled that all right," says Throckmorton. "I've probably drunk a bucket of that poison by now, and the taste only gets worse."

I was still fighting back a grimace, for it kept climbing up my face every time I swallowed and tasted the stuff again.

"So what brings you here, anyhow?" says Throckmorton, who was watching my face real close, like he's waiting for me to hack.

"Oh, just trying to get to Valhalla really."

"Yeah," he says. "Aren't we all."

"You know of it? You know how to get there?"

"Valhalla? Yeah, well…" He blew out his cheeks and sat back against the wall with his hands on his head. "Can't help you there, friend. I'm afraid that one's between you and your maker."

I knew it. Every time. Doesn't matter who I ask, mention Valhalla and folks are all the sudden gypsy mystics giving me all manner of nonsense. Everyone but Virgil, that is. Good old Virgil would get me there.

"Well, tell me this," says Throckmorton, cracking a sly smile. "What about your girl?"

"What do you—what? What do you mean?"

"Your girl. Your love. Whoever it is you left behind. It's plain as ever you're pining for someone."

"Oh," I says. "You can tell?"

He gave a little chuckle like we were in the same boat. We were peas in a pod. He says, leaning forward all conspiratorial-like, he says, "Not with a barrel of paint could you hide the love in your eye! So. Where is she? What happened?"

I says, "She's in Valhalla."

"Ah," he says, making a face like he's pulling a sliver. "Sorry. I understand now."

I actually understood less. This conversation was dumbing me. "I think I better go now."

Once outside, first thing I noticed was Virgil wasn't there. I became apprehensive. I looked around. He should have come back by now.

The second thing I noticed was two fellas crouched down beside Jimmy Brown. One of them pulled a pipe from his mouth, pinched a loose flake of tobacco from his tongue and pointed to old Jimmy's crotch. "This mule yours?" he says.

"Sort of."

He squinted at me like I was hard to see. "What, are you like stupid with liquor?"

"No. I mean…no."

"Your mule's intact," he says, pointing to old Jimmy's balls again. "You can't be walking around town with a stud mule on your hands. It's dangerous, for christsake. Lucky he hasn't killed somebody."

"That right?" I says, dropping down to take a look myself. "Yeah, I suppose he does have something of a set on him."

"You suppose so, do you?" the fella snorted. "Well you got to get this animal off the street. A stud like this'll snap on a dime, go crazy on you. He'll just—"

"How come?"

"How come? Well because his chemicals is all mixed up! On account of the sterility! Sure, a mule can kick out in any direction too, he ain't like a horse. You mean to tell me you didn't know this?"

"Huh," I says. "Ain't that something." Digging an itch out of my ear. "Well I guess you're always learning something new, huh?"

He just looked at me. Hard.

"So. What you reckon I should do?"

"You got to geld the sonavabitch. And right away. And what is—Christ, is that a blindfold? Boy, do you have any clue whatsoever what you're doing here?"

"Not really, no. So how do I geld him?"

"You don't!" he says, exasperated-like. "You take him to someone else who can! Boy, I don't even know where to begin with you. Listen, you take this animal up to the convent, up at the end of this road here, and you ask for Sister Dinah."

"Sister Dinah?"

"That's what I said, isn't it? She knows horses, all right? They got a whole stable up there, and if she don't break your neck first, she'll take care of your mule here. Castrate him proper."

"So just take him up to Sister Dinah."

A pained look came over his face, like he's so puzzled it stings. "You are a hard man not to shoot, do you know that?"

"Yes sir, I do."

"Christ," he says, shaking his head at the mule. "Just try not to let him murder nobody, all right? And keep him away from the children."

"I'll do," I says, tipping my hat. "I thank you."

I heard one of those two fellas murmur 'hillbilly' as they crossed the road together and watched me from the other side, conversing between themselves. Probably waiting to make sure I did what they told me, I figured, but I wasn't going anywhere till I found Virgil.

I sat down on the bench outside the tavern and had myself a chaw, keeping an eye out for my guide. Problem with me is, I get so caught up in a person's hues I'm inclined to miss what they're saying to me. It's like trying to track two conversations at once, for my mind will take off trailing the one, then jump back to the other, then jump again to the first until the talking's all finished and I'm left standing there, befuddled and panicky, with the broken halves of two different dialogues and trying to piece it all together.

Shortly following, I saw old Virgil vol Krie come strolling up the road with a new towsack over his shoulder. His hues never gave me trouble. Always the same, simple and bright, and always matching up with his words. He tipped his straw hat, and I saw he wore a smile of pure triumph. "Twenty pounds," he says with those big white teeth of his, slinging the sack down on the bench beside me.

I says, that is a sight a bacon.

He says, oh yessuh, I eat me a whole lot a bacon.

Welp, old Jimmy Brown going in for the works was a grievous blow to our hearts, whichever way you look at it. It was the first time I ever saw Virgil pure sad. All the way up to the convent he kept patting Jimmy, telling him everything's fine, everything's good, but Jimmy was too clever for that. He became downright mulish, tugging against me as I led him along by the rope.

Up top of the road, the Daughters of Providence abbey marked off the extreme north end of the town. Coming upon it, I was expecting twenty-foot battlements of unassailable granite, gorgons out front wagging their midnight tongues and arrows of fire raining down from above. But the convent was common timber, total unmenacing, with an apple orchard set in neat little rows and a lazy little fountain out front the gate.

"Who-eee," whispered Virgil, looking up at the place and shrinking back with feeling. "I don't know, suh. Don't know about this. Just ain't right, nuns stealing you jewels. Whenever did they get into the emasculating business?"

"Actually, I think there's something about that in the bible," I says, then pounded on the gate with the meat of my fist. While we waited for an answer Virgil tells me he hears nunning just doesn't pay like it used to. He hears they were hard-up these days, and reckons we best be on our guard for those sisters were likely to be cunning. Bloodthirsty even. And not to look them in the eye or drink water from their well or else we were certain bewitched and disaster-prone.

As my guide I was obliged to heed Virgil's warning. I had my reservations however, owing mostly to a longstanding notion that all women were innately virtuous, the whole rib-pilfering issue aside.

I felt a chill wind, then the hackles back of my neck. Virgil grabbed his straw hat to keep it from blowing away, and then just as suddenly, everything fell deathly still. I heard a hawk cry somewhere high above.

Without anybody needing to tell me, I fathomed something wicked in the air and knew my soul was laid before the doors of perdition. I heard footsteps beyond. A single clink in the lock. There was the muffled scrape of wood against wood as someone lifted the plank-bar and then a girl, tall, too young to be full-nunning, opened the gate.

Whereas some females are easy on the eyes, and others easier, some are so damn easy they go full way around till looking at them makes you downright troubled. This girl, this young apprentice at the gate, she had the habit and the headdress, all of it white. Her face was porcelain with moist little lips and a pale air about her that said, *stay the hell back*. My belly clenched up for she frightened me considerable, so young and severe, and my imagination set about wrapping her with fantastic powers.

This girl bade us step into the portico and asked our business. I tell her our mule here needed to be clipped, and I wasn't too sure how to proceed for these matters were both novel and mind-jarring. Furthermore, I had been envenomated by a deadly serpent and wondered what they had in the way of shelter, as we happened to be seeking asylum from a most heinous pursuant. She tells us we could wait in the chapel, next room over. The abbess would see us shortly.

We left Jimmy Brown hobbled out front where he could sniff out apples from the grass. I was careful not to let my arm drip on the tiles when I came in. The chapel was vaulted and cold, with rows of straight-back pews and a remarkably blood-bespattered, gaping-mouth-twisted-in-anguish Jesus mannequin nailed to a cross above the rostrum. Apart from these thoughtful little touches the place was desolate of all welcome. Its success lay wholly in the yearning it inspired to beg God for his mercy and grace.

Virgil, refusing to sit down in a pew or take one step further inside, stood rigid as lumber at the chapel's threshold. In his one hand was the sack of raw bacon, hanging greasy and limp. In the other was the charm his daddy gave him long ago. It was the ear of a stillborn lamb soaked in a witch's dreamsweat, and he rubbed it to a shine while mumbling protective prayers and incantations.

I myself kicked up my heels and laid down for a spell, as I had to, and might have slept right there in the pews but for the chill of the place. The cold went deeper than skin and clouded your breath, and when you lay still, the silence came down like an anvil.

I still had the book old Throckmorton had given me, only I was tired of carrying it and had no place to put it. I resolved to choose one page at random, tear it out and let it speak for the volume in full. So it was that page one hundred and eleven went folded to the chest pocket of my overalls while the remainder I stacked with the hymnals and whatnot they store beneath the pews.

By and by, I heard the hollow ring of footsteps on tile, and then that icy breeze came whipping through the chapel, which told me that girl was approaching, that girl in white with the venom-wet lips. I threw myself upright in the pew, my whole body tense, my breath parking in my throat like a wad of dough. She came in through a side corridor, halted, specters caressing the white of her habit, her china-doll face shining and dreadful. She says Sister Dinah would see us now, only the abbess was busy out back in the stable. We were to kindly gather our mule and follow.

"Inside?" I says. "You want us to bring the mule inside?"

Her young voice was so smooth it sent my skin all prickling. "There are many exits, but only one door into our Lord's house."

Me and Virgil shared a look. "I thought we were going to the stable."

The girl's robes snapped when she turned, and I saw Virgil give a jump. She started off down the corridor without us. I'd never heard of a mule allowed in chapel before but figured regulations were probably slacker within this particular circle of Hell.

"I get him," says Virgil, rushing out to fetch Jimmy, all the while rubbing that lamb's ear so fast I expected it to burst into flame. Jimmy brayed when he came in, like he knew something was up, and I prayed ardently he wouldn't drop anything. We hurried down the corridor trying to catch up with that girl, those white robes swishing and sweeping the tiles. But even after we reached her side I had to practically jog to keep up, like she's got herself a set of wheels going under that gown.

She led us directly through the back of the chapel, behind the pews, into the corridor leading to the abbey, requesting only that we avert our eyes from the left where a single stairwell led up to the cloister. I did so, not knowing what manner of consequence—*face peels back, flickering tongue, kiss of death*—that snowy little lass was capable of and felt no inclination to test her clout. Old Jimmy's hooves clomped on the tiles, past the rectory, past the courtyard, past several other corridors that seemed to branch deep into the gloom. We finally came out onto the hoof-torn dirt of the stableyard, nice little stable with two lines of stalls and bales of hay stacked against the back wall. You could smell the dankwet of leather and of mildew in the hay, and of course the horses.

I suddenly felt a warm breeze, notably warm, not at all like the chapel, and realized we were not alone. For right there in the middle of it all was Sister Dinah, abbess of the Daughters of Providence, mucking out a horse stall by the shafts of moonlight that glowed upon the floorboards of the stable. Sister Dinah's habit was rolled up to the knees. Her boots were crusty black. Sweat gathered like dewdrops above her lip and I had to physically shake away the sudden impulse to lick it. It came out of nowhere, that urge, and left me blinking in surprise. She showed no sign of having noticed.

Sister Dinah was a robust little lady with extravagant hues, looking about strong as miniature ox. She took one look at me and says, "Chee-zus." Then tossed her shovel into the corner and brushed her hands down her habit as she stamped through the muck of the stall. "Now aren't you nice and gory!"

Which was true enough, just not your commonest greeting. With my hand slung to my breast as it was, the blood trickled steady from my elbow. Sister Dinah clucked her tongue a few times and shook her head in dismay, then brushed past me to have a look at old Jimmy.

"Thank you, Daughter," she says to the girl in white while inspecting Jimmy's balls. "I'll take it from here. And there they are, yup. So this mule's giving you grief, is he? No wonder. Look at the size of them plums." She spat a black stream of tobacco juice, wiped her chin with her palm, climbed up onto a stool and then went about poking round in Jimmy's mouth, counting years in the wear of his teeth while the girl in white glided away. "So what are you boys doing leaving this mule intact like that?" she says, talking into Jimmy's gullet. "He should have been clipped years ago. Right away even."

"We only came by him recent," I says.

"Huh. And did he do that to your arm?"

"No maam. This here was the devil's doing."

"Don't doubt it. Well, you're right screwed whoever is the villain. Make your donation in the nave and I'll see your mule gets fixed. But your arm there." She climbed down from the stool. "That's another affair. Gruesome. Does it hurt bad as it looks?"

Little wisps of hair were escaping her headdress.

"Some."

They were the color of fresh-minted pennies.

"But not much."

She was real short, Sister Dinah. Real short lady. Fact she was the shortest lady I ever seen by half, and I've always had a thing for small women. In total, there wasn't more to her than was necessary to leave tracks in the dust, but she was old as my mother. And looked a little like my Pa. But still…

Damn was she short.

Sister Dinah rinsed her hands in the trough, then at her request I crouched down so she could untie the sling. I saw her chubby little fingers working the knot. The moment it came undone my arm swung free at the elbow, slapping the wall beside me with the sickening sound of wet steak. My knees buckled in reflex and the ground began to pivot just as the black sponge of oblivion commenced to sucking me under.

⟫◆⟪

Clearly I was being tested, for I'd never before borne any desire for a nun. Nevertheless, knowledge of my own fickleness came like a hammer slap. Literally, for my head spanked the earth at the precise moment of revelation like it was truth itself that was knocking me wise.

What of my Madder? The right pinecone of my heart? Could the winds of lust so easily rumple my fidelity? I thought hard on the topic while I lay there in the stable, the stench of horsemuck curling my nose hairs. When I cracked my eyes open I saw Sister Dinah fanning me with the hem of her habit. I pinched my eyes shut, praying she'd go away, would just leave me alone to love my Madder in peace.

I lifted my head, just a little, and says, "You should know, maam, that I am not easily inveigled," then dropped it back with a squelch.

"Shush now. Just you lay calm."

There was a revolution rumbling all round in my heart. Images of nuns warred against those of my Madder.

She kneeled beside me, and I hollered, "Back woman! You've misjudged my temper! My soul will not abide here in lechery!"

And she says, "Shush now. Just lay still."

I sighed, my head pulsing like a star, my arm pounding in rhythmic lagtime. It made a sticky sound when I tried to lift it, and I says, "Just—" and stopped short, for I didn't really know what I was trying to say any more.

"He'll be all right," I heard Sister Dinah say to Virgil. "He is just a'working it out." Her hues glittered with purest solicitude.

"Is it fever?" asked Virgil.

"It just is what it is. I suppose every young man goes through it."

I sat up onto my elbows, blinking my eyes, mumbling a half-remembered quote from somewhere. "But tell me, in that time of your sweet sighing, by what signs did you recognize your dubious desires?"

And Sister Dinah, she chuckled to herself, kindly brushing the muck from my hair. She says, "Don't you even think of stepping foot in my cloister."

It was a coal-mining town. Originally, anyhow. That's how Union Fog first came to be settled. A place where youngins shot marbles or tied cans to stray dogs while their mamas hollered threats from the porch. "May now! Amy May Thompson!" Thumping the washtub in warning. "What you doing to that poor hound!" Then those mamas would wipe the damp hair from their brows and return to their wash, their hands bright and puckered in the lye.

Their thoughts would drift. It was early still. No need to get worrying just yet. Those mamas would listen to a milkcow lowing away in the distance, the peal of children's laughter nearby. A wagon full of bricks would creak past the house and a breeze would carry the brimstone smell from the slag heaps up East Mine.

And then it would happen, and every time it was the same, a like scene on every porch in town. Those mamas, they'd feel the deep thump of dynamite and their hands would go still, their reflection all shattered in the tub. They'd close their eyes, and they'd clutch wet shirts to their breasts and pray their husbands returned safe to their arms, then take a deep breath and bend their backs to the wash and pray for the wives of those men who would not.

When the clothes were hung and the youngins were bathed, those mamas would take up with the churning. Or the darning. Or the scrubbing or the sweeping or the scolding or the feeding or anything else to keep rapport with good fortune, for as the saying goes, "It is a lonesome woman, she who's got nothing to mend," and so those mamas, they mended with passion.

But as the sun would go down they'd get to feeling the first knots of panic and abandon all illusions of poise. Pots would clank louder and cupboards would slam. Youngins would grow quiet and watchful. The light in their kitchen would take on a blush and those mamas would pace and wring their hands raw, wearing low-spots in the floorboards before the window.

"May, did you stack that wood like I told you?"

"Yes maam."

Pacing. Pacing. "What about them birch logs out back?"

"You saw me do it."

"Don't you sass back! Your daddy'll be here any minute now. Any minute now and he'll be here."

Then those mamas would halt as if struck, gazing out the window, seeing the first dust of movement down the road. "They're coming! They're coming now! Did you wash up like I said?"

Raccoon-faced and haggard, men walking slow with heads high.

"Amy May, I asked if you—May? Amy May!"

And then it would happen, and every time it was the same, a like scene on every porch in town. A door would slam shut and a little girl would sprint from the house, racing body and soul to meet her daddy in the road. From a distance she'd see one man stop short, one coal-black face among many, and that little girl would leap direct into his arms.

And that man who sweats and bleeds away his life in the earth, he would go down on one knee and hug that girl tight, then a little tighter still, the tendons standing up on his hands. Then he'd swipe something from his cheek and sniff hard like a man and stride home proud with a little girl on his shoulders.

In time, the mines grew deeper and production was high, and the town began to likewise prosper. For every man that died of blacklung, two more strapped lamps to their heads and for every fatal collapse there came another host of inspectors. Officials were pouring in, left and right, and the sheriffs were getting rich off the skimmings. A regular government was in force and living on high when the first of the coal mines began boarding up tunnels. Within the space of six months, three more had dried out, and by year's end there wasn't a solitary mine in production.

It was a blight, folks said. It was the very curse of Jericho, and it's what you get for letting the government in deep. Except now, having nothing to tax, those officials began writing up laws just so people could break them and pay administrative salaries with the fines. Fines for loitering, fines for working, fines for slaughtering hogs on a Sunday. Before long, the mayor and his cabinet were relying so heavily on the money generated from misdemeanors and such, the townsfolk got fed up. Those townsfolk brandished pitchforks and burned effigies in the road, but the sheriffs were in the mayor's pocket and so kept the peace.

That's when Sister Dinah came to the fore. Says she, let's obey every law, follow every edict and decree and thus deny this here government all forms of revenue. It was to be a gentlemen's revolt where for six months, not one soul in town so much as spat on the road. Not one man cursed aloud in a tavern. Model citizens, every one of them, until the red fist of debt squeezed the mayor clean out of town with his officials and sheriffs in fastest pursuit.

On the instant, Sister Dinah became a small town hero for whom authority wafted sweet as perfume. Folks were drunk with it, and naturally began heaping her with the task of command. There was never a vote, nor office allotted her, it was just one of those things that comes about without a word. So long as she managed to keep the fog about town and the Union on the far side of the mountains, the folks in general were proud to have a nun as their mayor, and enjoyed a way of life that afforded freedom from interlopers.

What's more, nobody had to pay a cent in tax. The nunning administration was fully funded by other ventures. The cathouse on the far side of town had ever tithed a good portion of their earnings as a means of compensating the good Lord for their craft. It was compensation so plenty, in fact, Sister Dinah saw to it that nobody bothered those whores, generous-spirited as they were, christening their establishment with the name of Magdalena House of Mercy, declaring those girls to be ministresses of comfort and asking only that they lent shelter to the needy.

<hr />

Never in your life did you see a horse so small. She said it was 'imported', from a little island called Shetland, and didn't stand one inch taller than your hip. Its withers were snarly and brown, and its tail dragged the earth like a rag-mop. In a long holster strapped to its rump was Sister Dinah's shotgun. Double-barrel. Sawed off to the nub.

She finished saddling that creepy little creature while Virgil introduced Jimmy Brown to his stall, asking Sister Dinah if me and him could stay and help with the clipping. She says me and Virgil best not stick around for that. A mule'll remember pain and blame whoever handled him last, so it was best if me and Virgil removed ourselves and let Sister Dinah shoulder the main of his spite. Besides, she says, we couldn't stay here at the abbey. She was happy to hide us, just as we'd asked, but would have to take us other side of town.

"So what is it you two is running from, anyhow?" she asks, throwing a last forkful of hay into Jimmy's stall.

"Welp," says I. "We had us a covenant, me and the devil, but seeing as how I broke it, he's up and taken to tailing me now. Fortunately I got old Virgil here to help me along, but it is a dolorous business." I shook my head. "Very dolorous."

"Good," she says, handing off the pitchfork and rolling up the cuff of one sleeve.

"Did you say good?"

"Or bad. Good or bad. Take it as you like." She started in on the second cuff, looking me dead in the eye. "Have you ever considered the possibility the Lord don't want what you want?"

"Uh... as in actual considered it, you mean?"

"You think the Lord is here to answer your prayers?"

"Well, no."

"Do your bidding? Make you happy because you got a right to be?"

"No. I don't know. Are you saying I'm not supposed to be happy?"

"I'm saying you got a heap of notions in your head. And this dolorous business is the least of it."

She retrieved the pitchfork and placed it with the tools hanging on the wall.

"Do you even know what happiness is?" she says.

I just looked at her.

She says, "It's when the thing you want most in all the world, you realize you already got it."

"But what if you don't got it?"

"Everybody's got it," she says, giving Jimmy a rough pat and starting for the gate.

"What kind of nun are you, anyhow?" I says.

"The irreverent kind. The kind that loves the Lord with all her heart and spits upon a fool's propriety. Now say your farewells to the mule as I got things to do. I need you out my hair and on your way."

Rather brusquely, she swept past me and Virgil, obliging us to follow without further inquiry. So we said a hurried goodbye and left old Jimmy alone in his stall, blindfolded as ever, no doubt pondering his doom the way a condemned man awaits dawn in his cell.

Outside the abbey, folks stopped in the street as we passed them by, Sister Dinah trotting between us as escort. "How do, Sister?" They tipped their hats and she spat streams of tobacco, answering with small-town wit. "Better'n these two."

Jokingly. "Catch them in the cloister, did ya?"

"Don't you know it." She patted the butt of her shotgun and everyone chuckled. Folks loved her, Sister Dinah, champion of their independence, a small woman incapable of smallness. I watched her canter ahead on that stump of a horse, spreading good cheer like the nets of a spell, and I found myself once again flexing my commitment to Madder.

I became disgruntled. What was it, the hold this nun had over me? What Oedipal snares had been sprung in my heart? I was pure fed up with all these trials of faith. On top of venom and blood loss, it was exhausting me to the point where I begun to think it might be better to just—

No.

No, I decided, I could beat this thing. My love was for Madder and her alone. She was my finest hour. My May in December.

Only I had to get away from Sister Dinah. "So where you hiding us?" I asked as she reined up before the last building in town. I was exhausted, as I said. I was drained at heart, just too tired to fight one more battle in my head.

"Safest place I know. And they'll fix up that arm of yours. Give you a nice place to rest."

Good. Whatever. Anywhere would do. I sighed in relief, for at last I would be free of temptation.

<hr/>

From outside, the Magdalena House of Mercy still bore the look of a three-storey courthouse, which it was for a time, with a brick façade and wraparound railings and a commemorative bronze placard on the stele out front. Sister Dinah climbed the double-wide steps, knocked on the door and turned to give me and Virgil a hearty wink. The door opened with a swell of voices, casting a rhombus of supernatural light. I heard boisterous greetings, raucous laughter, and then Sister Dinah disappeared within.

It sounded like a happy place. Looking on from the yard I had the feeling I had stumbled upon the one pure haven in all these mountains. I could be safe here. Virgil's face said so too, for I'd never seen him smile quite so wide.

"We're all right here, aren't we Virgil."

He took off his straw hat and covered his chest. He rubbed the bald spot top of his head. "Oh yessuh," he says, all swelled up with feeling. "I believe this place gonna be all right."

Sister Dinah leaned out to give us the okay, waving us in. Without waiting for me, Virgil shouldered his towsack of bacon and started up those brick steps, whistling a tune pretty enough to make you weep. His hues were so bright they would have thrown shadows back at the sun, for I saw them there, flashing all round his brow like a goddamn chandelier of victory.

———◈———

She had the drawn, hard-drinking look of a woman twenty years older, the unnatural wrinkles crowding the corners of her mouth. Her skin was clay. You could spread it round with a trowel. Each time she coughed I saw her tongue was all swollen and the color of week-old meat. Her name was Christmas O'Doole.

Christmas was the buxom owner of this fine institution, the Magdalena House being her brainchild from the first. She wore an old evening gown, electric blue, so tight at the bust it practically squeaked like leather each time she drew deep on her cigarette.

"Sister says you fellas just arrived," she says, pouring three whiskeys from the parlor bar. After Sister Dinah left, Christmas cleared out the excitement in the parlor with a wave of the hand, girls pouting back to their rooms. I could hear the occasional shriek of feminine laughter, muffled by walls, or a rhythmic cater-wauling from somewhere upstairs. Christmas brought those whiskeys to the stained, overstuffed settee where me and Virgil were sitting, me picking away at the batting that spilled from the arms.

"Just arrived? Oh, yes maam," I says, accepting my glass, hat in my lap. "This here's my first time in perdition."

Christmas blinked at me, swayed on her heels, then released an explosive, chest-rattling smoker's laugh that ended in a violent bout of wet coughing.

"First time, is it? Well then we'll be good to you. Don't you worry, my girls are gentle. And right discreet too, as I hear you both is on the run." She sat down on the ripped arm of the settee. "And how about you?" she says to Virgil, spilling his whiskey as she thrust it at him. "This your first trip as well?"

Virgil took a sip, smacking his lips and giving a little side-wise jerk of his head. "No'm. I believe I've traveled these here lands before."

She gave a baritone guffaw. "I would have thought so." The black on her eyelashes was so thick and tacky that blinking appearing something of a melee. She got back up from the couch arm and threw herself down on the easy chair direct opposite us, slouched way down till her chin near touched her chest, her knees spraddled like a man. She took a long drink from her glass, then carefully rested it on her swollen belly, slowly lifting her hands away to see if it balanced, watching it with child-like concentration, quickly correcting the glass, nudging it this way, then a little bit that way till I wondered if she'd forgotten we were still there.

She coughed unexpectedly and the whole thing spilled. "Shitfire!" she cursed, and without so much as sitting up, hucked the glass across the room where it bounced off the far wall, without breaking, skittered back along the floor and amidst the hush of my rising hysteria, slowly spun to a stop at the bottom of the stairwell.

Furtive-like, I gave old vol Krie an inquiring glance. He nodded back with assurance, having more familiarity with the etiquette of these places.

"Well anyhow," says Christmas, swinging her gaze back to us. "You boys is welcome here. We got weekly rates, if you got the stamina. Gratuity's between you and the girls. And any rough stuff and you'll be out the top window, you hear? But I reckon you two will get along fine. Listen, honey, poor me another drink, will you?"

"Sure," I says, standing quickly. "Same glass?"

"Don't matter." She was busy running her palms across the soaked midriff of her evening gown like she's trying to wipe it off, or spread it out, appearing total baffled by the event. I brought her drink and asked if the doctor makes house calls this time of night. She says the doctor butchers folks, is what he does. His name was Dr. Milton Skandrell, if that wasn't clue enough, and why, did I have an issue needs resolving? I mentioned how I'd been envenomated by a deadly serpent, and then eviscerated up a bit, pointing to the trail of blood leading from her door to the settee. It wasn't her fault she hadn't noticed. I'd grown tired of alarming folks by the grisly sight of my arm and so had taken to tucking it inside my overalls.

She waved her hand dismissively while taking another deep sip. "Mmh," she says into her glass. Sets it in her lap. "I got something better for you. A Chinese. Doctors round here can't do nothing but amputate, but my girl will fix you up suitable."

Virgil asked where he might cook up some bacon. Christmas pointed a languid finger down the hall. Kitchen, what there was of it, was ours to use. Just be sure to use a skillet, and don't pack the woodstove more than half-full or it would go red hot and scorch the flooring. Virgil shouldered his towsack, tipped his straw hat and said he'd see me after a while.

I was famished too, but what I craved most right then was sleep, which is about the most luxurious sensation ever invented. Next time Christmas tipped back her glass—

Glug. Glug.

Glug glug.

—I opened up a little cavity in the cotton batting of the seat and dumped my whiskey in. With a touch of anxiety I watched it darken and swell, then slowly filter down into the bowels of the couch. I stretched my good arm and yawned and says, "I'm about ready to hit the sack. How about showing me to this Chinese wonder of yours?"

"Jezzy!" Christmas shouted from the couch. "Jezzy, come on out here a moment!" A door opened in the hall and a waif of a girl, covering herself with a sheet, ducked her head out. "What Ma?" Then giggling and slapping back something in the room. "Shhh! I told you hold on! Sorry, what you want, Ma?"

Christmas says, "Show this man up to the Chinese, will you? Mama's had a rough night." Swilling her glass, watching the liquor go round.

"Ma!" Hissing, surreptitious-like. "I'm busy!"

"Screw your busy. Just take him upstairs and you can come right back. Mama's had a rough one."

The girl set her jaw. "I bet I won't."

It is refreshing to see healthy rebellion in an adolescent. But Christmas drained that glass with all her might, sat up straight and pitched it hard as she could against the far wall. "Goddammit girl! Take this boy upstairs before I whoop you! You hear? Because if I gotta—oh, thank you Dannon, just set it right there. Because if I gotta—!"

"All right!" The waif gave us a smoldering look and disappeared back into the room. I heard whispering, the gruff protests of a man, more whispering, and then that waif came back out into the hall in a pair of too-big-clogs and a throwed-on dress that hung from her skinny shoulders. "Come on then. Follow me," she says. "Well come on!" She stamped up the stairs without looking back.

"Thanks darling!" Christmas called from the easy chair, then leaned forward in a fit of coughing, cigarette held high above her head.

⟫⟫⟫◆⟪⟪⟪

To remember Mama is to remember a woman like a comma, for even after there weren't any more youngins to tote about on her hip she still thrust it out to one side. You could tell her from a quarter-mile away by the way she stood, like her hip had fixed there for good, or popped out of place. Or if town-chatter be true, like she was still carrying about the ghost of little Maggie.

I have no opinion on the matter. My mama was a fine mama, and she bore us each with a loving hand. She liked to say we youngins were the only good that came of her marriage. Of course if it weren't for us youngins, my eldest sister Sarah at least, there wouldn't have been any nuptials at all, for Pa got Mama into trouble before she even understood how trouble came about, and married her, so the story goes, with grandpappy Woodrow's rifle tip sticking the small of his back.

I've learned there's a bit a good in all folks, and it's only fair I give Pa his due. Somewhere down there in the wind-driven wastes of his soul old Phinny nursed a little flame of self-worth. It was him that taught me to tell it like it is, exclusive of fluff. If folks are fools, they have a right to hear it, and telling them otherwise is a total disservice. Likewise, you have to use your head when sorting through another's lexis. Falling prey to flattery is no better than being robbed.

So when that waif took me up to the third floor of the Magdalena House of Mercy, walked me to the end of the candlelit hall and opened the last door on the left without knocking, the first thing I says to the girl sitting inside is, "For a Chinese, you ain't very Chinese."

And that girl, sitting crosslegged on her cot, she sets her book in her lap and frowns over the top of her spectacles, staring me straight in the eye. Then she reaches up to the shelf and turns up the lantern, saying, "Yeah, well for a fool, you look exactly what you are."

The waif, she calls from the hall, "Ma says he's all yours, Tally Rose. Enjoy." Then clomped back down the hall, clogs too big, pulling her hair back into a ponytail and humming to herself, leaving me and Tally to finish introductions on our own.

She began straightening the cot, avoiding my gaze. Just like that, she was gearing up, making the shift from a nice night reading at home to that of industry. Still standing in the doorway, I says, "So. You live here long?"

She didn't respond, like I hadn't spoken at all. She took the one step from her cot to the only chair in the room and sat down before a hanging-mirror on the wall, putting little pin-thingies in her hair to keep it up. Her movements were brisk, determined. "Not a bad place," I says. "You got you a window at least. Bet it's nice in summer. You like it here in the summer?"

She glanced at me in the mirror, then back to her hair. "Are you asking," she says, "because you truly want to know, or because we happen to be two people alone in a room and silence is too awkward for you to bear?"

Damn. That Tally Rose was a feisty one. "I suppose a little of both. I suppose."

Running her brush through a snarl. "Then don't bother. We don't know each other, you and I, and nor are we like to. So let's not dull our tongues on words not needed. Makes for a sharper point when we speak it." She tossed her chin toward the bed. "Might as well sit yourself down. Or at least close the door."

"Listen," I says, "I'll apologize if I caused you offense. I couldn't care less where you're from. Just that old Christmas down there says you was a Chinaman."

"Yeah, well, I guess that says more about Christmas than it does about me. They said she was looking for a Chinese, and I knew she wouldn't take me in otherwise."

"You mean she don't know the difference?"

"I am proof of that."

"Welp," I says, "you got the dark hair anyhow." Which she did. It was near pine-pitch black, but she bore about as much resemblance to an oriental as I do. Which I don't.

Tally lined them pin-thingies up between her teeth, plucking them out one by one, pinning her hair up high. Business. The look on her face was one of purest resolution, a smart girl resigned to a hard-hitting life. I watched her, thinking she wouldn't be here long. Nope, she had bigger things in store than Magdalena House of Mercy, for you could already see as much coming through her hues. This girl, she had the ice-blue of discouragement all swirling round her head, while bursting right out the top—a crocus poking through snow—you could see the bright yellow of a child when it wakes. I'd give her a week. Two tops, before this girl was on to something better.

For now, looking around the place, I saw it was pretty dismal at best, a tomb just big enough for a cot. There was a standing curtain in the corner to hide her washbasin. Everything else that girl owned was stacked neatly on the floor along one wall. One stack of garments, another of letters, a quilted blanket, and then all the mysterious bottles/salves/perfumes obligatory to a young woman of hygiene. A battered valise was laid out like a card table over a pair of bricks, and set neatly atop it were five-six books of poetry, a palette of dried paints, a couple paint-brushes and a bundle of wildflowers arranged with dried grass in a narrow-neck bottle.

I was dead tired, and clearly imposing without meaning to. My arm had made it this far without rotting clean off the socket and I figured it could wait just fine till after a good sleep. I plunked myself down on the floor and began prying off my boots.

One hand holding her hair up, the other pointing to an ivory clip among her clothes, she says, "Hand me that, will you? I'll just be a minute more."

I passed her the clip and spread the extra quilt on the floor, right between the cot and the wall, saying, "I plan to be asleep and drooling in half that."

Tally stopped, both hands in her hair, staring at me bewildered-like in the mirror. "What do you...you mean..."

This girl, this Tally Rose, I saw a look in her eyes I will never forget. It was like her whole world just screeched to a halt. Then something sparked, a thousand feelings at once and all of it packed into a tear.

I shook my head. "Nah," I says. "It's just boarding I'm here for. I'm sort of on the run, you see, and I'm sorry I got to impose. Looks like you was having a nice night on your own." I lay down and closed my eyes. Immediately, the gravity of sleep began tugging me down, that delicious spiraling into midnight cream. "Don't bother with the lantern on my account."

She went quiet, that girl. I could feel her looking at me a while. And then I actually heard myself begin to snore.

I woke to the smell of bacon. I sat up, scratched my head for a considerable long time, both sides, front and back, and then saw Tally Rose sitting crosslegged on her cot, looking as though she had been watching me all night, just waiting for me to wake.

With a smile that didn't quite reach her lips, she says, "Hello."

"Hello," I says back. She just sat there in her spectacles, her flower-print dress, moonlight coming in through the window. Right off, I noticed the change in her hues. She was nearly yellow entire, like a streetlamp in the mist, with streaks of violet fuzzing the air above her eyes. Even a little round her mouth when she spoke.

"I got you some bacon here," she says, and on a wooden plate before her I'm now looking at the most spectacular mound of belly-fry you've ever seen in your life. It was pile enough to kill a man.

"Actually it was your negro that brought it. But I told him not to wake you."

"That's Virgil vol Krie," I says. "He ain't mine."

"No? Is a free?"

"I reckon he's free as a man gets. My guide too, as he's the only one knows how to get to Valhalla." I sat forward against my knees, tasting my breath, full awake now.

"Oh," she says, picking at the pellets of lint on her blanket. "Well, about before. When you first came in."

"What about it?" I started in on a piece of bacon.

"I just wanted to say, I don't know, thank you."

"Apology accepted." Tender, this stuff. Not crunchy at all.

Tally gave me a crooked grin, still picking at her blanket. "Yeah, well, I guess I wasn't too kind to you at first, but you can imagine most men don't come up here but for one thing only, and I'm not too accustomed to getting respect. I sure appreciate it though. First time in a long while."

I grabbed another piece of bacon from the plate, took a bite. "Listen," I says, pointing it at an unframed painting above her cot. "Did you do that? That's a good picture there."

It was a still-life of wildflowers in a bottle, just like the ones on her valise. It was a good picture, far as I could tell. Course I imagined my Madder could do better. Still, it was a nice picture. Pretty colors.

Appraising it, she nodded. "I don't know, I guess so. But I know I could do better if I had lessons."

"Why don't you get them then?" This bacon was special good. For the first time ever, I started to fathom what Virgil saw in the stuff.

"I will," she says. "I mean I want to, one day. My plan's to save enough money to get to France. I want to go to Paris and walk along the Seine and paint the fountains of Notre Dame. Or Argentina. I don't care really, just about anywhere'll do."

She kept her tone casual, but I saw it was hard, for this wasn't some fleeting notion she spoke of. I reckon the Seine, and her painting its banks, it was one of those load-bearing dreams that holds a life up when all the world's just shoving back down.

I understood. I had my own. "Well what's holding you back?" I says. "Just go right now."

"Cause my Mama, she needs me here. Or my money, anyhow. She can't live on selling wild-honey alone. Oh, there's oranges here too. You like oranges?"

I love oranges.

"Sister Dinah brought them," she says, leaning across her cot and grabbing one off the chair. "Don't know where they come from, but she brings a crate every Sunday."

I ate an orange. "I believe that is the best tasting orange I ever ate. Can I have another?"

I had another.

"Everything's good when you're hungry," she says, "and you look half sta—" She stopped short, staring intent at the orange peel in my lap. "I don't believe I've ever in my life seen a person open an orange like that."

I stood up, turning circles like a dog, looking where I placed my hat. She suddenly grabbed up my orange peel, squinting real hard at it, and says, "Now hold on a minute, how did you do this? There's not one single—"

"You seen my hat? I know I had it."

I couldn't find it anywhere.

"It's drying," she says, still studying the peel. "I washed it while you were asleep."

I stopped dead. I looked at her, then looked away. No one but my Mama, bless her everlasting soul, had ever washed a solitary article of mine for as long as I'd lived. I was near moved to tears. I didn't know what to say. "I thank you," I says, and walked out the door.

<hr />

Having no particular route in mind, I decided to look for Virgil. I started out by knocking the door next to mine. It was the wrong one. I tried another. I knocked every door on the third floor of the Magdalena House of Mercy, meeting all manner of folks in the trying, but Virgil simply wasn't there. I went down to the second floor. Again, I introduced myself a dozen times over but nobody had spent the night with a fella of his description.

Down in the parlor they were doing a brisk business of lying about and smoking, women in nightgowns everywhere just splashed out on the couches and reading catalogs.

"Anyone here seen a friend mine?"

"What's he look like?"

"Oh, stands about this high. Wears a gray ascot round his neck and a great big straw hat. And he wears it like this. He was probable cooking up a whole flitch of bacon not long prior, so I imagine he—"

"The nigra?"

"That's the one."

There was a bit of snickering, women sharing looks. "Down there," they says, three cigarettes pointing down the hall. "Down in Christmas's room, last door before the kitchen."

I went past the drinking bar, down the hall and thwacked on Christmas's door a few times. "Virgil? It's me! I thank you for the bacon! I just wanted to let you know I'm headed—"

The door flew open partway, got caught on something, and then Christmas squeezed in between, blinking at me with cigarette in hand. "*What-in-hell* do you think you're doing? Don't you know how to knock on a woman's door?"

"Not really, no. Listen, is Virgil around? I intend to go locate a surgeon."

"Virgil? Yeah. I mean no, he left about an hour ago." She said this while yanking on the door, three-four good yanks till it wedged tight on the matting of soiled clothes. "Boy, can he make bacon," she says.

"Where'd he go?"

"Up to the abbey." She leaned against the door, took a long, long drag from her cigarette and looked me over. I saw she was in the same evening gown as last night, and her room was a total wreck. I could smell one or the other. Speaking through the exhale, she says, "Said he went to go check on a mule a yours."

"His."

"Whatever. It's a mule. He wouldn't talk about nothing else, so I final told him to quit worrying about the thing and just go on up there himself. Whoa now, what happened to your arm?" It was slipping out of my overalls, the way I had it propped up. Still, we'd had this conversation once already.

"Deadly serpent."

She turned her head to cough. Smoke came out her mouth in a sequence of bursts like a steam engine going up hill. "That right?" she tried to say, only she wasn't quite done with the coughing yet. I waited it out.

"That right?" she says again, sucking so long and deep on her cigarette I could hear the tobacco crackle. Made me a little ill, to tell the truth. She says, "Most folks die from a rattler bite. My brother died from a rattler bite. Was it a rattler?"

"Yeah, well, I must have got lucky."

"Lucky," she pshawed. "You look about lucky as a little blind boy with a square ball. Now if you had any sense in your head, you'd put something on that, or it'll get infected. Now come on in, and let me see what I can find you."

"Welp," says I, lifting my elbow. "I best go see about that surgeon then, as this ain't getting no better."

"That man just kills folks. Here, I got something better." She turned back to her room and began digging through the rubbish, tossing filthy gowns and bloomers left and right. Over her shoulder, she says, "So how was that Chinese for you?"

"Oh, you know."

"Here. Here it is," she says, her feet tripping up on an enormous brassiere. She came to the door and pushed an aluminum tube of something into my hand. It was empty and all curled up, a bit of goop pushing out the corner. "It's gone, I know," she says. "But take yourself down to the apothecary and tell him to fill it up, or give you another."

"I thank you. What is it?" It smelled foul.

"And get yourself some dressings."

"That's why I want a doctor. For to dress up my arm."

"I'm telling you, forget your doctor. Buy yourself some dressings, some clean dressings, and get yourself a tube of that unguent." She tapped her cigarette at it for emphasis, blowing smoke out the corner of her mouth. "That stuff will clear anything up."

I went back out to the parlor. A few heads popped up from catalogs, a few hands paused at their embroidery. "Find your friend?"

"Nah. Listen, you mind if I stoke up that lantern there? Bring it along with me?"

"Where you going?"

"Just out.

"Well what you want the lantern for?"

Darn these women. "For to see with."

There was a short silence, like they were waiting for a punchline. Then someone laughed, condescending-like.

"Forget it," I says, starting for the door, then stopped. "But hey, if my friend Virgil comes back, tell him to wake me next time, will you? Even if I'm asleep. Tell him to wake me up."

But no one said they would. They just stared at me till I walked out the door. From out on the road, looking up, I saw the fog was low as ever. Folks were out and about, just like before, carrying on like all was normal. I realized it was Virgil who had all the money. I'd need some before I bought anything at the apothecary. I went back into the parlor.

"Lost?"

"Sort of." I looked around.

"How about a lantern?" Snickering. All of them snickering.

I says, "You got anything round here might serve as a dressing?"

That waif from before, she was flopped out on the couch, sifting through a magazine, but she lifted her head and says to me, "What did you say? Shut up, Lucy. What did you say?"

"A pillowcase," I says. "You a clean pillowcase around?"

"Not a clean one."

"Well, then, whatever you got I suppose."

She clomped back to her room with enthusiastic apathy, wooden shoes too big, dress hanging off her shoulders, and came back with a wad of cloth in her fist. "Here, take this. He won't come back for it, or expect to find it again if he does."

It was an undershirt, stained yellow under the pits and unnatural gray the rest over, but I figured it would do.

"I thank you."

"Anything else? Hey, did you need anything else?"

I was trying to think. "Nah," I says. "I reckon I'll be all right. I thank you."

I went back out into the street holding that shirt in my hand. Thinking what to do next. It was possible the apothecary would let me work for that unguent. You never know who needs a dowser.

I wandered up the road, looking for the place. Just as I passed the tavern I saw that boy Throckmorton come out, setting a tricorn hat on his head and buttoning his vest.

"Hey there!" he says, lifting a hand. I stopped on the plank sidewalk, far side of the road. He jogged out front of a mule-wagon and came over. "Where did you get off to?" he says. "You just kind of up and left. I was a little worried about you."

"Oh, you know," I says, looking around.

That Throckmorton, he tells me he's headed up top Dustfeather Mountain tomorrow, up above this fog cap, as he planned to be setting off some weathering kites. He invited me along. I said that sounded all right. I asked him where the apothecary was.

"Good. So you going to see a doctor, then?"

"Nah. Ain't got the money. Just going to see about an unguent."

"An unguent, huh? Just an unguent?" He gave my arm another look, cringing a little. "How much are you short?"

"For a doctor? Don't know. How much you reckon a doctor costs round here?"

Right from our first meeting, I was troubled this Throckmorton might be the sort of fella addresses you by name with every sentence, you know, Dannon this and Dannon that, which I cannot stand, but I saw now I had him all wrong. He was a different sort entire. He pulled out a money clip, flipping through the bills. He slipped two out from the middle and pressed them both into my pocket. I didn't see how much. Just go see a doctor, he says. He says, seriously, just go see a doctor. That arm doesn't look good.

"I thank you," I says, giving a little salute. Only I went to the apothecary instead. The bells rang when I walked in, but nobody came out from the back room. You could smell the place right off, dank and earthy. The whole room was wrapped in walls of dark walnut wood drawers, floor to ceiling, with Latin placards on every one, and a few of those sliding library ladders to reach the high places. There were open-mouth horsesacks with herbs busting out top and tinctures galore on the shelves behind the counter.

Then I saw a shingle with Dr. Skandrell's name on it, pointing up the dark stairwell to the right. With Throckmorton's money in my pocket, I figured I might as well give that old Skandrell a try. I am total useless with money anyhow. Don't ask me where it goes. The stuff just disappears in my hand, so I've learned to spend it all quick as I can.

Doc Skandrell's office was the only office upstairs and his door was open wide, blinds pulled on the windows. It was dark. There was a smell here too, only this one was entirely new to me, languorous and heady and spiced-like. The room appeared gutted. There was a tub of saws and hardware soaking in the corner, a cushioned table with buckles and straps. Shoved up against the wall was a ratty old mattress. Plates of half-eaten food and ashtrays were littered all over the floor and the buzz of flies was a steady drone. Apart from the dusty certificates on the wall and an empty desk, the essential feel of the place was that of an abandoned warehouse where bank robbers might peaceably intermingle.

"Low there," I says, kind of quiet, to the man dead asleep on the mattress. That's when I noticed the parrot. "Shut the hell up!" it squawks, tottering side-to-side on its perch, plucking feathers and tossing them in the air. "Shut the hell up!"

Then in a similar voice, only more desperate-like, the doctor screeched the same phrase from the mattress and rolled towards the wall with hands pressed between his knees.

"Uh, low there," I says again, and this time he popped upright, sniffed and looked around in astonishment. "Jesus," he says to himself, blinking at me and rubbing his jaw. He'd been sleeping full-dressed, coat and all. Shuffling around on the mattress with him were crusts of bread and a bits of old cheese, various wrappers and black-tip matches and about anything else you'd expect to find if you took a notion to tip a trashbin over your sheets and give it a shake just to see what falls out. He picked up a long clay pipe from beside his pillow, poked inside the bowl and sucked it once to make sure it was out, then looked dazedly in my general direction.

"I'm almost… is there a problem?" he says to me.

There is something about a doctor in a narcotic haze, surrounded by instruments of agony, staring hungrily out through the dark rings of his eyes at you, a paying customer—it'll give you the chills. Every time.

It's like when you wake in a Mexican infirmary, just after the battle of Monterrey, and find a carpenter taking your head-to-toe measurements. Makes you want to dance around in demonstration of your vitality, declaring there must be some mistake, which is precisely what I said right then.

"Now hold on!" says the doc as I turned for the door. "Just give me a minute here. You came for a reason, now just give me a minute." I watched him go to the basin of soaking tools, splash dark water on his face, shammy his head like a hound and then throw himself down in the chair behind his desk. "Now, what brings you here?" he says with a smile, water dripping down his face.

"Welp," says I, a little reluctantly. "My arm here is giving me some trouble."

I gave him a synopsis of my plight. He took immediate interest, sitting forward and wanting to see the injury right away, only the look in his eyes was pure animal.

I confess I cringed to see him, my blood going thick, for I was developing a powerful distaste for this doc with his hyena's gaze and apocalyptic breath, biting the end of his tongue like a child. "That's quite a wound," he says, poking around in there with the end of a pencil. "Whoever did the fasciotomy saved your arm. What did he use?"

"You mean the slices? Just a cutting knife."

Still digging around, pulling out bits of the Klamathweed, he began shaking his head and mumbling, "No. No. Nope. It's no good." He slipped the pencil back into his coat pocket and sniffed. "Yeah, I'm afraid it's no good. Looks like we can preserve the shoulder, but we'll probably have to take it off about... here." He touched my arm, just above the elbow. Then he bent close again, squinting real hard, one more time for confirmation-like. He shook his head. "Yeah, no good."

He pulled off his coat and tossed it onto the mattress and began rolling up his sleeves as he turned back toward the tub of saws in the corner. "Why don't you take a seat on the table over there. I'll be right with you." He ran a finger around the inside of his collar, pushing through bottles in a cupboard. "So you're not from here, are you?" he calls amiably over his shoulder. Bottles clinking. "Haven't seen you before."

I took a seat like he told me. "Thing is," I tell him, "I was actually hoping to keep the arm entire, as it's little use to me in pieces."

"Yeah, well," he says, holding up a saw, checking the teeth like the hone of a saber, then setting it back in the tub and selecting another. "Problem with that is, your arm's been open to the bone for, what... how long now?"

"I don't know. Week maybe."

"Right, a week. And that's plenty long enough for gangrene to set in. You let that go, and then it's not your arm we're worrying about, it's your life. You ever seen a man rot alive?"

"Actually, yes," I says. "And thing is, I got quite a nose for gangrene, and I don't smell it here. I believe that poultice the Cherokee shoved in there kept it clean or something."

Running his thumb down a saw. "Yeah, well, we won't have to wonder now. Why don't you go ahead and get yourself strapped in there. That buckle on the left gets caught sometimes, but if you knock it on the side it should open right up for you."

I had a look at the buckle. Problem with it was the rust. I rapped it against the side of the table a few times and little flakes tapped off. "Listen," I says. "I got another idea."

"Oh yeah? What's that?"

"How about you just sew it up tight so the, you know, the edges and all stay shut. What do you think of that?"

He gave a dubious sigh, hands on his hips, shaking his head in dismay. "Well, it'll cost you the same," he says, supposing the voice a reason might bring me around.

"Which is how much, exactly?"

"You want that with or without ether? Cause I got ether here."

Generally speaking, it was only officers and above who got the use of ether down in Mexico. The rest of us had to make do with tequila.

"How much with?" I says.

He told me, and I checked the bills that Throckmorton had given me. Then me and Doc Skandrell haggled it for a while

till I had stitches, ether, and a prescription for painkillers downstairs, all of it coming for the cost of five dollars even.

⇒◆◆⇐

I had a powerful headache when I came to again. Doc said that
was customary. Him laying out on his mattress, propped up on
an elbow, he says to me, here, he says, just have a toke on this, as
it will settle most all your troubles. I passed on the smoke, simply pleased to see my arm was stitched and dressed up nice and
neat. But I had to use that old undershirt for a sling as I forgot
to work a fresh one into the original deal. Doc's orders were to
take it easy for a week, no rough traveling, which was fine by me.

I took one of the five-dollar bills from my pocket, unfolded it
nice and neat and passed it over, only it disappeared in my hand.
This disturbed the doctor.

He thought me a charlatan, and accused me as such, but
mid-argument he hit the pipe and few times and appeared to
forget me altogether, nodding absently at the shadow of his coat
rack on the far wall.

Down in the apothecary, I handed in my prescription and
received a silver tin. Sliding the top back I found a black bar of
opium, two-fingers thick.

"I'm not much a smoker," I says. "Don't you got something
I could chaw on? My mama used to get lozenges of this stuff."

The apothecarian, or the chemist, or whatever you call him,
he had one of those classic shopkeeper hairdos, just a fringe of
hair goes around the back of his head, and he's got a great big
mustache and next to no chin whatsoever. He says, "Sorry, prescription reads for it to be unadulterated. See here," he pointed to

the slip of paper. "NO ADMIXTURE. Which it always says. Doctor Skandrell has his preferences. I can give you something to take afterward, make it softer on your stomach, but otherwise you'll have to work it out upstairs with the doc himself."

"Nah, forget it," I says, pocketing the tin. "But what about a pipe? I don't got a pipe."

He said I could pick one up at the general store.

I still had one of the two fivers from old Throckmorton. It would be relatively safe till I touched it. I went to the store, feeling just fine about my arm being all fixed up. No more of folks giving me a leper's wide berth or snatching up youngins from my path. I bought myself a pipe, just a simple little corncob, then with the money left over I got another plug of chaw, a potato, a sack of dried apples and another of feed-grain, thinking of something special for Jimmy, figuring he might need some cheering up when he came back from the Sisters. Then I saw a little rosewood snuffbox that would be perfect for Virgil. And a little music box to give Tally Rose for her troubles. When I'd finished my purchases I had precisely one penny left over, which I told the clerk to give to the youngin that was nosing the counter, hankering for those molasses-twists in a jar.

I went back to the House of Mercy.

Virgil still hadn't returned, so I headed up to my room. Only when I knocked on the door Tally Rose peeked her head out, wincing with regret, saying she was real sorry but she was busy with a customer, and could I hang out down in the parlor for a bit?

That was fine by me. I went down and joined the others slacking about on the couches. I was still a bit groggy from the ether, and my eyes kept closing, but every so often they would snap alert as a man stomped his boots on the veranda, or a whole gang of them even, and then Christmas would come staggering out of that dark hole of a room, lighting one cigarette off the butt of another, pouring drinks all around and assigning boys to girls like a square-dance fiddler.

Of course none of those fellas were old Will Lawson, and each time I saw a new face come in, a face that wasn't his, a surge of relief would spill through my chest. By and by, I commenced to reflect merrily upon the success of our ruse. It began to seem possible Will Lawson would just keep tromping north while we headed east, and never would our two paths convene.

So I drifted off, right there on the couch, waking at some point to find the entire parlor was empty. I had no idea what time it was. I made my way upstairs like I had lead in my boots and knocked on old Tally's door. She'd been asleep. It was the middle of the night, she says, and didn't mean for me to be gone so long, but was glad to see I came back all right.

I lay down immediately on the quilt on the floor while Tally Rose sat up on the cot, crosslegged in her nightshirt, looking sudden wide-awake and rearing to converse like we were a pair of youngins sleeping over in a barn. This was the first time I'd seen her without her spectacles. I was a little surprised to see just how pretty her eyes were, forest-colored, squirrel-bright and nearabout as cheerful. She was bound to make the right man real happy one day.

Problem was, I couldn't hardly keep my eyes open. I lay back on the quilt with hands behind my head.

"Sorry about that," she says. "It's not usually how it works around here, pushing you out like that. But one of our girls, she went to visit her folks and one of her regulars come by."

"No worries."

"You didn't have to take off so long, though. I just meant a few minutes. He was nearly through. Where'd you go, anyhow?"

The stack of letters she kept against the wall, I bumped them when I crossed my legs and they tipped across my shins. "Whoops. Sorry." I sat back up and restacked them. Except I couldn't help but notice they were all from the same person. A woman.

I fanned an envelope. "So who's this?"

"My mama."

There must have been a hundred of them. "Looks like she's got a lot to say."

"Actually, she doesn't. Take a look."

I opened it up and found a blank sheet of paper inside. Nothing else.

Tally says, "Every one of them's like that. Folded neat and tidy without a word upon it." She fussed with a loose string on her nightshirt. "On Mondays I write my mama a letter, every Monday, ask how's she doing, is she keeping warm and all that. And then I send it along with the money. But she's ashamed of me, you see, for what I do to keep us going. So every Friday I get a blank letter come back. It's her way of saying she's still not talking to me."

"But she takes your money. That ain't right."

"Oh, but I want her to. She needs it. She's a widow, you know. My daddy died 'robbing the pillars' down in East Mine."

I found my hat waiting for me on the blanket, nice and clean and dry. I lay back down and placed it over my eyes and says, "What's that? Robbing the pillars."

She says that's when they try and recover the columns of coal that are holding the ceiling up.

"Well no wonder he's dead."

She says, "I know. It's plain stupid, anyone can see that, but it's what they've always done in these mountains and I suppose they'll do it still until a woman finally takes charge of a mine. Anyhow, Daddy's dead. Mama's a widow, making what she can taming bees. For she is a bee-tamer, you know."

I did not know, in fact, and said as much without shame. This is how I came to hear tell of a most unusual heirloom, a bee-horn, made many year ago in a place I'd never heard of, and what's been passed down through Tally's family for generations. When played by a widow it calls in the bees, which can be followed back to their honey.

"Oh yeah," I says, remembering the music box. I sat up and dug it out my bag. "Here you are. For your troubles and all."

A look of quiet came over Tally's face. She wound it up, smiling at the crank going round and round. I don't recall she said a single word right then, but I know she liked it. She liked it plenty, just smiling quiet as can be.

Then she dropped it in her lap. "Oh! Why didn't you tell me about your arm?" she says, seeing me trying to work the sling up over my head. She climbed down from the cot to help me. "I didn't realize it was fresh hurt. My Lord, you never said a word. Here, let me get that." The knot was too tight, even for her who had two hands. She tried to pull it over my head, then paused, palpating my scalp. "What hap—My Lord, what is all this? It's like you got rocks in your head."

"Yeah," I says, "I reckon I've taken a few lumps recent."

"No, what is that?" Palpating still, like she's spreading out dough. "It's like… Jesus, what is all that?"

"Oh, right. Yeah, them's teeth," I says, and she looked at me. "Not my own of course."

Naturally, this led to the questions of how and why I had teeth other than my own in my head, and though I wasn't up for it entirely she pressed and pressed with such enterprising inquiry that I spilled out the whole tale of Monterrey without ever meaning to.

As I've stated, I take no pride in the affair. Of all the crimes I never committed, I regret my failure to desert the Union army most of all. I reckon that's why I've said so little about events so big, even when the marvel of it remains raw in my heart.

Such were my thoughts on the four days of marching from Camargo to Walnut Springs, Mexico, where we of General Taylor's army finally camped on the eve of battle. By that point in my soldiering I had come to know Mexico as a land of church bells and barking dogs, adobe walls and bougainvillea. But also desolation, and places so remote they lacked a name till men died there.

Somehow or another, I'd struck up a friendship with an officer, which was rare among us volunteers who were so poorly regarded—for reasons, I might add, that were wholly valid. Compared to enlistees with boot camp training and discipline, we volunteers were wildcards at best, refusing to wear uniforms and slipping off to drink during battle. Most showed a predilection for murdering each other off over card table disputes before the Mexicans could even take a crack at it. Still, Second Lieutenant Ulysses S. Grant and I, we were different from the most, though akin in our solitude, and on the morning of September 21, 1847, we were sitting together, just sitting on a crate within view of the walls of Monterrey.

The camp was buzzing, for our artillery was in place and the attack was scheduled up for any minute now. Directly before us, across a short stretch of yellow plain was the jumbled tenements of the city, every rooftop sandbagged, every cannon pointed our way. To the left was the tannery, cannons popping out the windows, and to the right was the place we called Black Fort, which we dreaded most of all. From all three directions, every hurtful device the Mexicans possessed was trained upon that hardpan before us.

A charge was suicide, it went without saying, so I said it aloud. And loudly. I believe I profaned.

Lieutenant Grant sighed. He sighed a lot, that man, like the weight of the sky was something felt across his back. And I says, "The way I see it, it ain't the lacking in peace that puts us in straits like these, but our willingness to kill for more." And Grant nodded at this, as he often did, and jotted it down in that little notebook of his.

The main attack that morning was to come from General Worth, who was bivouacked in the hills northwest of Monterrey with the Texas cavalry and two thousand regulars. Everything else taking place, and foremost our lunatic charge, was an organized diversion for Worth's efforts. So when the first assault was ordered and our men geared up for the run on the heavily armed walls of Monterrey, I hadn't a clue what they were so fired up about. We were being asked to run bayonets against bastions for the sole purpose of distraction, but damn those boys were excited to stick something.

I wondered if one man in ten had any notion whatsoever what we were really fighting about. I sure as hell didn't. Not then anyhow. To the best I could make out, it was an American tradition to break all others and now we were finally taking our little act on the road.

I wagered aloud there wasn't a fella among us who knew the truth of this war and could offer proof we weren't dying in vain. Immediately bets commenced flying, left and right, followed by a convoy of spirited arguments. Listening to them, it occurred to me I had bet against myself, for this was a wager I'd gladly pay gold to lose.

An older fella, a Seminole-Indian-killing veteran who was none too pleased with my brand of subversion, he says louder than the rest that I was welcome to shut my mouth, for fate favors the bold if I didn't know it already. I kindly pointed out how it opposes the dead with equal vigor and he spat with contempt, saying I was a disgrace and a dog and furthermore, too green to even know how to die like a man. I says perhaps that is a preferable thing, being green over jaded, and Lieutenant Garland, who was overseeing the first charge, he says they were both goose-shit colored so far as he was concerned and General Twigg's division best load their rifles for the orders were about to go up.

Men retied their boots, fitted bayonets, slapped shoulders with gritty enthusiasm. Problem here wasn't the courage, but the nothing to keep it in check. And then the flags snapped. All down the line our artillery thundered and every man in camp stood hushed, watching, shielding the sun with his palm as talons of light arced over enemy walls. Then we heard it, the distant bump-bump.

Bump.

Bump-bump-bump, that comes up from the earth when death is planted in faraway fields.

Our camp erupted into yells of triumph. On cue-like, a bugle cried out and General Twiggs First Division, of whom we volunteers were not a part, spilled out across the plain like ants kicked from a mound, their war cries instantly muted by enemy shelling. It was mayhem. Mexican cannons pounded the earth, great blooms of it rising twenty feet high. Men were geysering left and right till the very air became bruised with thunder. Before one Union soldier could so much as reply with his rifle or shove his bayonet into the wall, the charge broke and scrambled back in retreat. Mexican cannons halted, their smoke hazing the walls. In the silence that followed, the field slowly came alive, first here, then there, rising to a pitch till it seemed all the maimed wailed with one tongue.

I sat in shock. Of all those men that just dashed out of camp, not moments before, one of every three was departed. More were injured, soon to join the deceased and every ounce of loss undue. I wanted to know why I sat alone with this vision, why nobody else was distressed. But the real madness had yet to come. The real madness was when those flags snapped again, and men began forcing their way to the front like the events of five minutes past were erased. Was it truly glory we sought, or the thrill of going out like a moth? From where I sat I couldn't find a difference.

Again I heard the thunder of artillery, all down the line, and then the second charge cut loose with a yell. They rolled onto the plain like a wave unhitched. Suddenly there was an explosion to my left. One of our own field-pieces was hit. I fell to the ground and covered my head against the rain of dirt and debris. It was close enough I could hear the howl of flame mixed with that of men as they stumbled like incandescent drunkards from the wreckage.

Even as I rolled over and pushed up to my knees, I heard the bugles of retreat, and those men who'd not yet been given time enough to die came sprinting back over the field.

As our camp licked its wounds, huddled and panting, knocked wordless with the shock of exhaustion, the generals reconvened. Word came that General Worth's attack was underway in the northwest and we were to continue amusing the Mexicans in the front. We were ordered to regroup for a third charge. Volunteers this time. But fortunately it was decided we volunteers were to come through the canefields, emerging from behind the tannery. The canefields would offer some cover.

Brigadier General Quitman rounded us up by horseback and herded us volunteers into the cane. We ranked up, eight lines deep, marching through grass that stood taller than our heads. Every now and again a warning yell would go up, ranks would split and a cannonball would go tearing through the cane. Before long the fields were striped with their paths and we were ordered to take up a run. The only sound was the swishing of grass and the panting of breath, men cursing at the slap of leaves, and then all at once we broke free from the cane and were instantly slammed with Mexican shells. Bam, we were dropped in a storm, just like that. And let me tell you, we ran. We ran like rabbits without a why or a where because sometimes it's the body that does the fastest thinking. Up ahead, I saw a fella take a direct hit from a shell and disappear entire, him replaced by the 'crimson mist.' It's what you call it. Just a pink ghost, hovering there on the earth, slapping you wet in the face to run through it.

Suddenly those tannery walls were just ahead, rifles cracking from the roof and the sut-sut of bullets. Somewhere in the moil of it all, I heard another man's yell leap free of my throat and it was chilling, the transformation took place. You just can't understand unless you're there, but something maned and roaring woke up in my breast and my running became a true charge. I couched my rifle like a lance, gritted my teeth and burst forth in feverish abandon. I believe it was my intention to kill everything twice.

The tannery drew closer. I saw the bits of straw in the adobe, the dark mustachioed faces. I saw a cannon pipe recoil from a window. Flash of light. Puff of smoke. Strange though that I never heard it. Not the boom, not the cries, just the slow intake of breath as that cannonball came along, a dark blur skipping through our ranks. It mowed down two fellas, bounced and took another, and then struck old John Morly who was directly in front of me. It ain't necessary I tell you what became of the poor man. But the splinters of his musket nearly crippled two soldiers and I woke with old Morly's teeth in my head.

And Tally Rose, she's still fingering my scalp, only it began to feel a bit more like a massage, and she says, "This one here, you can sort of float it around." She was pressing a tooth back and forth between her thumbs.

I reached back and touched another. "Well see this one here, can you feel that?"

"Oh that's a big one."

"Yeah, well that one started way back here behind my ear, and now look where it's got to. Ow. Ouch!"

"Sorry. You reckon that's a molar?"

"Could be. They took a couple of them molars out already."

"Well why'd they leave the rest in for? Not much sense in that."

"Docs just couldn't get 'em. It's what they told me when I woke."

"But why not? They're all right here."

"Just one them things, you know. Mama used to say life's filled with such quandaries." I chuckled morbidly at the memory of all those lessons she'd given me. "Like trying to end a proper sentence with 'and'."

"What do you mean?"

"Ending a sentence with 'and'. That was one of Mama's favorites. Always saying it can't be done."

Tally looked at me. "But you just did it."

"What?"

"You just did it. Right now."

And I fell quiet, and sort of wondered at that. I lay back down and covered my eyes with my hat and just, you know. Sort of wondered at that.

⬦

Tally Rose, she never learned to swim. She has a little scar on her eyebrow, it's been there long as she knows and one time she saw a bear play with a fox. She doesn't like to sleep late, cause life is too short. She always paints first thing when she wakes. Tally says she's got herself a quart jar near to brimming with buttons, all those trinkets that turn up in her bed. She saves them, Tally Rose, says the jar makes her weep. Says she saves them and she doesn't even know why.

She told me of a time, not long ago, when she was walking along and came upon a fella selling cardinals in a cage. The little door was open and they were climbing about on top, and so she says to him, "How come they don't just fly away?" And that fella, he answers back that he clipped their wings.

I suspect this was the beginning of something, an about-face of sorts, maybe even the first seat-tack in that girl's righteous wrath, for she sprang forward, in a manner of speaking, and says direct to the man, "But why? How could you, clipping a bird's wings? I can't think of another creature on earth better made for freedom."

The man replied simply that he did it because folks don't want to buy a bird that flies away.

"No," says Tally, who's now vibrating like a plucked chord. "You did it because misery loves company." Which she says while scrawling those last three words on the back of a postcard before leaning it, like a placard, against the wicker bars of their coop for all to see.

What it came down to is Tally Rose just couldn't bear to see anything of sovereignty in a cage, which wasn't any wonder once you did the math: just divide the number of buttons in her jar by the blank letters beside it, then multiply by hours of longing. What you came up with is a girl who knows exactly what she's been denied.

It was climbing day. Old Throckmorton had those weather kites strapped to his back as he led the four of us, Tally and Virgil included, on up Dustfeather Mountain. To take the readings, he says, inviting us all along for "the finest view of a lifetime." Old Throckmorton paused on the trail every now and again, studying the ceiling of fog. He'd pull some contraption from his satchel and fuss about with its dials and then squat down to scribble it up in his journal.

Virgil whistled along with that long negro stride of his, those eyes dark blue and twinkling. He'd found himself a nice oaken staff, and it looked good in his hands.

And Tally Rose, she was a different person entire. Get her out of that brothel and she became happy as a schoolgirl, running up that trail with one hand on her bonnet, stopping to fill her pockets with lilies. She'd brought her sketchbook along, which Throckmorton carried in his satchel. She says this was her first furlough in years.

Like me, Jimmy Brown required a good week of convalescence. He stayed in the abbey, enjoying those apples and the grain I bought. I should have stayed down in the valley too but I'd already agreed to come, and besides, Virgil had found me a nice suit coat, I didn't ask where, and suggested a good dose of high air might liven me.

We climbed for an hour solid up through dense pine and laurel, all of it shrouded in gray. The fog muffled our voices and the calls of birds. The trail was worn deep and narrow from the runoff that channeled down the mountain. Then we popped from the fog and discovered we were higher than ever. The trail leveled out. We strolled through the woods, knowing we were at the top of something, but not yet knowing what. Then the woods gave way to rocky ground, a promontory jutting out into sky.

We were way up on a cliff, but with the fog pooled below us you couldn't tell exactly how high. All around, everywhere you looked, just an ocean of smoothest cloud. Here and there in the distance, the peaks of mountains poked through, looking for all the world like moonlit islands. And above it all hung a canvas of stars so bright you could practically read.

Old Throckmorton went straight for his kite. He snapped it together. It was a great big boxy-looking thing made of white linen and pine and he sent it up on a spool of piano wire line. Attached to its frame were knickknacks and barometers and gadgets galore, and then he'd reel it all back in to 'take a reading.' No matter how many times he heard it said, his mind just couldn't allow it was Sister Dinah that brought the fog on. But by and by, he had Tally Rose flying that kite, her laughing all childlike as he guided her hands from behind. To see her standing there, a pretty girl flying a kite, you'd never know what she goes home to each night. It tore me up a little. I wished things could be different. All the same, I was happy to see her now, smiling as she was with old Throckmorton.

I noticed Virgil had taken up on a big slab of granite near the edge of the cliff, that hypnotic line where earth meets sky. He was shucking away at that ball marble of his. Shuck. Shuck. Shucking away. I sat down beside him.

"I got you something."

He gave the ball a few more scuffings, paused, looked it over, scuffed again. "That right?" he says.

"Snuff box," I says. I laid it out on the stone beside him.

"Well thank you, suh. I reckon that'll come in handy." But he didn't pick it up. He just kept going at that old ball marble.

For the first time ever, I took a good look at it, that ball. I'd always figured Virgil would shape it into something, a face or something, but now I saw he was just trying to get it perfectly round. I says, "You keep going at it like that, won't be nothing left."

And he says to me, "Oh, I reckon you right, suh." He says, "This here ball was near big as a melon when I commenced."

And I says, "When was that?"

And he says, "Oh, twenty. Thirty. Maybe forty year ago now. I just shuck away at it. Little by little. You know how it is."

Forty years, I thought. Well goddamn. "That's a powerful stretch a time to be working one item. What you reckon you'll do when it's done?"

"Done?" he says. "Don't know it'll ever be done, suh. A circle that's nice and round and what's got no flaw atall, such a thing's mighty hard to come by. Make just one mistake, take off just a little too much here, and all the rest got to get fixed as well. So I just go at it. You know how it is." He went quiet, so all I could hear was the rhythmic bursts of sandpaper on stone, and further down in the valley, the sounds of a mountain stream rushing through crisp October silence.

Then Virgil spoke up again, his deep voice sort of startling me from my thoughts. I realized he'd been thinking all along, for he blew the dust off that ball and says to me, "But I reckon if I ever finish this here stone, that'll be the day there ain't nothing more for me to do." He blew again, shuck shucking away, then I saw him face down in the dirt. Dead. The blood flowed out back of his head, mixed in a puddle of my own. Our blood, all mixed in the dirt. Then it was just him again shucking that stone.

As so often happened when I felt troubled, I started thinking about my Madder. Sometimes it was like I could see her almost, like we circled the same sun, her face ever obscured by its brilliance. Other times I felt her so strong, so close inside, I knew our coming together was but a fated thing. Like it wasn't even distance that stood between us, but only time, and when that time was behind us and the proper hours elapsed then I would hold my Madder close in my arms. But I had to take a leak, so I got up and brushed the dust from my rear, saying, "So long," to Virgil.

"So long," says he, shuck shucking away. And Tally and Throckmorton, still flying that kite, they waved as I ambled on by, headed back a little ways into the woods. I felt those trees close in behind me like the drawstring on a sack. And that itch you get that's no place on your body, it came up real strong. Something was brewing, though I had no idea what.

I stepped from the trail, ducking beneath the beards of moss that hung from the limbs and reined myself up in a little grove of fir trees. A flock a ravens, which we call a 'murder' back home, well a murder of them took wing all at once. Quite a racket those birds make, little black jackets of feathery grim all caw-ing and crying, troubling the whole forest like it was their work.

I undid my buttons and began my business and even before I knew what I was doing, pissing away there in the grove, I had written out the first three letters of Madder's name in the mulch.

M-A-D.

And then watched with apprehension as my water dribbled to a halt. I buttoned up my overalls, sort of scratching my head over that one, hoping to God I hadn't just forged a curse. I turned abruptly to leave, snapping a twig in my haste, when another raven exploded up from the brush. Just a straggler. Nothing to fret. Nevertheless I jumped half out my skin. That's when something caught my eye, just back there in the wood. I crouched, instinctual-like, studying it up. Then I sighed and slowly stood up.

There's some things in this world a person never likes to see, no matter how many times you see it. But I didn't dawdle, no fussing about. I went right to it, poked once or twice to make sure, then covered the body with fallen boughs and left.

When I came back out from the woods Tally waved me over to join them. She wanted me to have a try at the kite. Throckmorton yelled, "Come on, Dannon! You can do it with one hand!"

I mumbled something, got no clue what, and set myself down there by the cliff to be alone. But before long, here comes that Tally Rose, brushing the grit off the rock and sitting right down beside me. She has that baby-smooth skin with cheeks that glow in a chill, and I can smell the spice of some ointment in her hair. Tally had her sketchpad along. She crossed her legs and set the pad in her lap, commencing to draw up the view with a coal tip.

After a bit of a think, I says, "You know how after you wash a wood bowl, and you dry it out with a rag and the squeak it makes give you the heebie-jeebies?"

"No," she says, describing all the horizon with a broad slash of her coal.

Thinking a bit more, I says, "Listen. Tally. You reckon you'd go to France if you could? If you had the money right now?"

She made three sharp strokes with the tip in her hand, glanced up at the view, then back down to her pad and began furring the lines with her thumb. "You mean right now?" she says. "I couldn't go now. I still got my mama to take care of."

I says, "Yeah, but what if your mama was already taken care of. What if somebody just gave you all the money you need, just plunked it down before you and says, 'Here yar Tally Rose. You are free to go.' What about then, do you think you'd—"

"Yes," she says, hunched over her pad, her coal shushing back and forth. Then she paused, staring at the paper, that black tip pressed hard against it. "Why?"

                            ◆

You ever feel the weight of something, like it's coming straight down, but instead of pushing it away you just let it? And the heavier it gets the stronger that feeling grows until you are set to bust with the thrill of pressure?

Suspense, is what I think you call it. It's like everything inside is at the edge of its seat and hollering at you to stand up and run, so what you do is, you plop right down and let that mood build up until the fireworks go singing through your veins.

I love that feeling.

Just love it.

Pa used to say I have the kind of aspirations that'll keep a fella moving sidewise in this world, never up or down, which is customary. That's because I could sit around for days, literally, without doing a thing, just kicking back on the porch or out on the limb of a tree. And though it may have looked like I was about as ambitious as glue, fact is I was powerful busy. Feeling the speed of the world, is what it was. Watching it whoosh on by, and me like the eye of a storm, just feeling it and feeling it all.

Of course, Pa might have been kindlier on the whole if his only son wasn't such a loiterer and a disgrace. Which I can understand. Had I taken to coon hunting, say, or showed a hand at poetry, well I reckon things might have gone different between us. But me and Gracie, who was my elder sister by a year, one night me and Gracie fed raccoons some pine nuts straight from our palms. Except they didn't just snatch a mouthful and run, like a fox or a squirrel will do. Those coons, they'd reach right in with those tiny little fingers and pick them out careful as a jeweler. After shaking hands, so to speak, with such a clever little animal I couldn't find it in me to shoot one.

What I did instead was, I took to hanging about in the woods, back where no one could see me, and I'd climb a big oak to watch the sun go down. No matter that I'd start midday. The longer you'd wait the more that suspense feeling could grow, so I'd watch the shadows climb up from the crease of the valley, slowly sliding up the side of the mountain. It seemed the narrower the light, the brighter it got until just the top of a mountain would be all lit up like a halo, or a golden crown getting smaller and smaller... and then gone. The day was through. It was time to go home, and that's when the feeling got strongest.

I'd know it was time to rush back or risk getting lost in the dark. I'd know I was many miles from home. But I'd wait it out, letting that excitement fill me up, right to the top of my head till the honey came seeping out my ears. My toes would be vibrating with the buzz of it all, but I'd close my eyes.

And I'd lay back on a limb.

Just waiting.

Waiting for the first chirp of crickets, I'd tell myself each time, just one little chirp. Then I'll hurry home before nightfall.

⸻◈⸻

It was cold in Tally's room and she stoked up the brazier, blowing two-three times on the coals, and then turned the lantern wick up a couple notches. The little room glowed golden.

"Now let's see about your arm," she says. The pain was really coming on. It wasn't too bad atop Dustfeather Mountain, nor even the night after that, but I'd begun to use it a little now and was paying for it.

Tally was fussing with the bandage, trying to get it open. "You're standing right in my light. Scoot over a little. Here, just sit down here, it'll be easier for me."

I sat down on the edge of her straw-tick bed and lifted my arm for her. Still crosslegged, she used her arms to sort of hop-scoot across the cot till she was directly facing me, her head bent down close to my arm.

"Just hold still, will you. It's gonna hurt unless you hold still."

"Sorry."

Her spectacles would slowly slide down her nose, which were sprinkled with a few freckles, and just before those specs reached the very tip of her nose she'd push them back up. "Well darnit," she says, still trying to find where the bandage comes loose. "Where does this thing even begin? I can't even—oh, there you are. Now why's he got it all taped up like that?"

She tugged gently on the tape, but it didn't come loose. She tugged again, but a little bit harder. The third time she yanked it, and I saw a gleam come into her eye like it's goddammit-power that best threads a needle. "Ho, hold wait, hold on!" I stuttered, lifting my arm high with a wince. "I'm thinking maybe we better leave it. You know, just for the time being."

"Oh, but I almost got it!"

Be that as it may, I was coming to learn few things are more dangerous than well-meaning zeal. It was good intentions that'd been snapping hunks out of me like booby-traps.

"Well let me tape it back down at least," she says, total crestfallen. "You can't just leave it like that. But why don't you let me loosen it?"

What the hell, I thought, if it makes her happy. Sometimes you have to just let them do their thing, you know? So I let her tug away at that bandage till she loosened it a bit and began to look satisfied.

"See," she says. "Better now, isn't it?"

"Yup," I says, wiping cold beads of sweat from my quavering lip.

"Listen," I says, "That was powerful thoughtful of you, and I thank you for that, but I have some remedy here, genuine prescription, and I think I may have to give it a twirl."

When we came back down off Dustfeather Mountain, I told Virgil about what I'd seen up there in the wood and me and him went direct to the abbey. He looked in on Jimmy Brown, fed him an apple or two. I told Sister Dinah about the body.

"Let me see what that doc gave you," says Tally Rose. "Cause if it's those pills with the horsey smell you may as well throw them out. They don't do a thing."

I opened the tin with the sticky black bar.

She let out a low whistle, eyebrows arched. "Well that'll do it," she says. "You'll need a pipe though. You got a pipe?"

I had told Sister Dinah exactly where the body was, and what condition she could expect to find it, and asked only that nobody tell Tally Rose for a few days. Tally'd want to see it, of course, and that seemed an awful idea. I thought it better to wait till they could build her mama a proper coffin and seal it up.

"Just go ahead and lie down," says Tally. "No, right here next to me. Lie down on your side. Like that." She lit a candle from the lantern and set it between us on the cot. I lay down on my side and watched her roll a bit of black resin into a little ball and then pack the bowl of the pipe. I says, "Looks like you know what you're doing."

"I am a professional, remember? A minister of comfort." She smiled, ironic-like. "This won't be the first time I helped a man with his poppy."

I looked away. I hated knowing what I knew, and how Tally didn't know yet, and keeping it from her made me feel like a liar. But it was best, I reasoned. She didn't need to see that body. After those ravens had their way, it was only the clothes that could tell you it was a woman. That and the bee-horn I saw laying on the ground, and about a million little ulcers where those bees stung her mama head to toe.

And there was something else too. Something I did.

"You ready?" she says.

Now it wasn't honest, and I won't tell you it was right, but Lord knows where my heart was when I did it. In a little purse of leather, just around her mama's neck, that woman kept a fold a bills. Four-hundred dollars or more, I'd guess. It was all the money Tally worked so hard to send her mama each week. Except that woman was too proud or martyrous, or maybe just too darn spiteful, to put any of Tally's money to use. So I took it, and I put it in my pocket. And after we came down the mountain and I finally found myself alone in Tally's room, I pulled one of those blank letters from the stack against the wall. I slipped out the folded sheet of paper and replaced it with the bills. Then I took up a quill and—again, I won't tell you it was right—but I wrote a mother's last words of forgiveness and love to her daughter. I resealed the envelope and posted it later that day.

From a big rip in the side of her bed-tick, Tally pulled out a long twig of dry straw. She touched its end to the candle and it flared right up, then she handed me the pipe. "Now turn your head to the side and I'll light it for you. No, put it in your mouth first, then I'll light it."

I gave her a look.

"What's that for?" she laughed. "It's just like smoking. Only you hold it in. You know how to smoke right?"

"No."

She shook her head. "You are so funny."

"I'm being serious."

"That's why it's so funny. Look, just suck it in and hold it. Your body'll do the rest."

Which proved out in no time flat. Nobody needs teach you how to cough on poison. My body didn't want that stuff and said so best way it knows how, except Tally Rose was by then total useless to me, tortured with laughter, writhing on her side and patting her chest and clawing for air as though strangled. With ridiculous effort she finally calmed herself just enough to sit up, smoothed her dress, then her features, saying it would get better with time.

Or easier, anyhow.

Then spluttered into a second fit of laughter.

I says, "I don't think I can do this."

It took a moment, but she managed to calm herself again, sniffed real hard, blinking her eyes real wide and wiping them. "Don't be such a baby," she says at last, her lips twitching with the effort of composure. "You just got to keep going at it, or it won't do nothing."

I looked at that big old sticky bar in the tin, about the size of two fingers. I says, "I don't know, Tally. I reckon it's enough there to cough me dead."

She exploded this time. She literally sprayed spittle. "Not the whole thing, you idiot! You don't smoke it all at once!" Then she turned sudden sheepish, wiping her chin with her shoulder. "Sorry. Here, just try once more."

Which I did, and of course she was right. It did get easier. Old Tally Rose packed the pipe, and I did the smoking, and after twelve-thirteen bowls of that stuff I commenced to feel downright warm inside. Suddenly my whole body was marinating in a vat of deep-fried glory and those angels were strumming harps in my head. I could see the appeal. I tried to tell her so.

Problem was, I couldn't tell if I was asleep or awake when I said it. The line between was all blurred up, and the pictures in my head were getting peculiar.

I saw the comb of a beehive with countless little cells, and midget nuns doing ballet in every one. I saw them pirouetting with shotguns and gargling black coffee and galloping about on winged ponies. It frightened me some. My mind had finally gone solo.

But then what happened was, I found myself up top Dustfeather Mountain and I was watching a woman that looked like Tally Rose, only older and sadder with a quilt of lines about her eyes. The detail of my vision was a mind-boggler. This woman, she wore a long skirt brushed the ground and a man's wool coat and she carried a silver trumpet that curled like a ram's horn. It was beautiful, that horn, flawless and silver, wrapping three times about the thin of her wrist. That woman was walking through a grove of fir trees. She climbed atop a boulder, crossing her legs as she sat, and brought the mouthpiece of that horn to her lips. Only something bit her then, something small, and as she turned to swat it away she dropped the end of the horn and it banged against the edge of the boulder. She didn't see the dent. But I did. I saw the little dent in the flaring end.

Then she blew on it, a long wailing moan that made the cool air of the forest seem to warp-like. When she stopped, there was silence. Then the distant droning of bees. She blew again, and leaves twirled down from the trees. She paused a little longer to let the first bees arrive, watching them dance playful about the dark curls of her head. She blew one last time and then the swarm was upon her, and then I couldn't see anything but the horn, dented, among the ferns where it dropped, lonesome and discarded in death.

Then I saw a smile.

Out of nowhere a smile, just rosebud lips hanging in the sky. Eyes so dark they lit like mirrors in the sun, and it was Madder who reached down and stroked my cheek. She'd come to me. Madder Carmine had come, a girl like deep shade in summer.

I threw my arms around her and felt the sweet heat of her skin. I felt the softness of her breasts between us. She pressed her cheek to my chest and my tears silvered her hair and we cried together, because even laughter could not climb this high.

If love in its excess could drop a man dead I would have quit life right there in her arms. Madder pushed her small face to my neck. She tucked promises just under my ear. My lips danced across the smooth white of her cheek, down her neck, reveling in every inch of her skin. I laid my ear on her heart and lost myself to the pulse of many long worlds within her. Everything I had, I wanted Madder to have it. My heart spreading night-sky free. Soon, she said, her dark eyes heavy with love. Soon, and I felt her lips on my brow.

But her voice…

My eyes opened in alarm. I struggled to sit up, half-blind in the dark. I pushed against her, frantic this time, and her silhouette straightened up beside me.

"Shhh… It's only me," Tally whispered in the dark. "It's all right, Dannon. Shhh." She put a finger to her lips. *"It's only me."*

And my heart plummeted to my belly.

I sat there on the cot, staring into the darkness. It was a long, long while before I could relax my grip on the sheets.

"You thought me another," she says, and I saw her silhouette hug itself tight, her features lost entire in the gloom. "You thought I was someone else."

I turned away. I looked out the window. The fog was thick and crept like clouds past her room, wisps of it floating just yonder. And for a moment, for a real good moment there, I could believe we were a ship in the sky, and we'd never come down, and I'd never have to tell Tally the truth. Except a moment ain't nothing but time tied in a knot.

Yup, is what I said when it passed.

I won't lie to you. I was plumb baffled by the event. As I lay there upon that quilt on the floor and listened to Tally snuffling on the cot, it occurred to me that plans, like trust, could be built up over years and then gutted on a profligate whim. I hoped to God this didn't make me an adulterer. I didn't think it did, for in my heart of hearts I had lain in true love with my Madder. I just hoped our Lord wasn't a stickler for detail.

Needless to say, I never touched Tally again, and took a dim view of every class of smoked remedy. And believe me, I felt awful about her. Just awful. Twice that night I got up to retch in the dark, but looking back I can see a simple apology would've been more comprehensive-like.

I spent mealtime down in the kitchen with Virgil, me sitting warm by the stove, distracted and sullen, him cooking up a whole flitch of bacon. The girls there at the House of Mercy couldn't seem to get enough of it. They were back and forth to the kitchen all day, stuffing their pockets and doting on Virgil like moonstruck groupies. One girl in particular trailed him everywhere he went, and I told Virgil he was a regular wizard with hog fat, working some ancestral power over a griddle and flame but in truth my thoughts were elsewhere. Constant ransacked by women, if you need to know it. I was either recollecting Madder and her last words of, "Soon," or else sick with grief over the woe I'd caused Tally. By and by I took my leave of Virgil and tromped up the stairs to see if I couldn't make amends.

Even as I climbed the stairs I could hear the quiet sobs of a girl, for the hall was narrow and the ceiling low and sound echoed around like a covered bridge. When I got to Tally's door, it was half open. I peeked in. Tally Rose sat crying on her bed, her back to me, but in her hands I could see a dented silver horn.

Reluctantly, I knocked, though I knew she heard my steps in the hall. She didn't turn around. She took one great big sniff, which is how womenfolk turn off the crying, then sucked a long wobbly breath. "Well," she says, wiping her nose. "Looks like I'm finally going to France." She twisted over her shoulder and gave me a tight smile, and I saw then she had my letter in her lap.

"Mama wrote me," she says, looking down at the envelope. "Sent me money too, but she wrote me. Finally said everything I ever wanted to hear. And not a moment later, I get this." She fingered the dent in the horn. "To tell the truth, I don't even know how to feel right now. Just confused."

I says, "Yeah, well I'm... I'm real sorry about last night."

She gave a little snort, which was like a laugh and a cry. "I'm a big girl, Dannon." She sniffed. "No offence, but I think I'll get over you just fine." Then she sort of laughed at us both. "Come here," she says. I went and sat down beside her. She gave me a big hug, wiggling her chin into my shoulder, saying, "You're a sweet young man, Dannon, and two years ago I believe I'd have been in love. But right now I got bigger things going on. Besides," she pulled back, gave my hat a yank and placed a little kiss on my nose. "You're sort of funny looking."

Which of course I knew. On account of my mama told me so early on, which is to say I have it on reliable authority. It's my chin, I believe. Either my chin or my lip. My lower lip sort of hangs like it's always packed with chaw, but anyhow Tally Rose, she says, "I think I'd like to be alone now." Dragging a finger over her mama's writing on the envelope. "Do you mind? Can you give me some time? Lucy's out for the weekend if you want to use her room."

So what I did was, I went downstairs and had me a sit on the porch. My arm was feeling good now and I even discarded the sling. I could practically hear cords of gristle snapping as I stretched my arm straight. But it felt good. The fire was gone. Soon as Jimmy Brown On A Rope was mended up, I reckoned we'd be on our way.

Now House of Mercy's got swinging chairs on the porch. Nice swinging chairs. Four of them. So I sat down and had a chaw of tobacco and watched someone's loose hog go snorting around side of the road. He was inspecting the carcass of a dog that was floating in a puddle. The thought crossed my mind that a hog on the fugitive, he wasn't particular safe this side a town, and I felt a tingle of excitement, like a thrill, at the possibility of him escaping notice.

Just lazing away, just ruminating there in the swing, it occurred to me I hadn't yet read that page in my pocket, that page I tore out of Throckmorton's book. I took it out, unfolded it, smoothed it flat on my lap. The title of the book was *The Heimskringla Saga*, though I'm now guessing at the spelling. Written by a fella named Snorre (poor man) Sturluson back about six-hundred year ago. Real old. But the thing is, what surprised me most when I read the page, that Sturluson fella was writing all about Valhalla. I was struck by the coincidence at first, but then quickly lost interest for that saga didn't tell me anything original. Course I'd never heard about Odin or Freya or those banquets for dead heroes, but I already knew Valhalla was a place in heaven.

I folded up that page and stuffed it back into my pocket, saving it for an event I'll get to later, for who should come along at that very moment but Sister Dinah, preceded by that warm breeze that always came down out of nowhere. She came trotting along on that little Eohippus of hers, leading old Jimmy Brown on a rope.

"Low there," I says, tipping my hat. I was over her now. My ardor was quelled.

"And look at that," I says. "No blindfold either. Appears old Jimmy Brown's all fixed up."

"You'll still want to take it easy on him," says Sister Dinah, hopping down from her saddle in a black and white flash and hitching him to the hitching post. She put him alongside an old swayback sorrel that was already standing there, staring into space. She says, "The tar packing held, which is your main concern, but he still seems a bit flighty to me." She spat a stream a tobacco. "Christmas! You're up early!"

Christmas came onto the veranda about then, barefoot and dissolute in her blue gown. I couldn't tell if her hair was mussed or just original styled, but it stood a good foot from the side of her head.

"Low there, Sister." Christmas raised a little leather-bound bible in greeting, a bible, like she totes one everywhere she goes. "Is that Virgil's mule already? Well ain't that som—Virgil!" she called back into the kitchen from the threshold. "Virgil! Sister finally brought that crazy mule you're on about!"

Christmas lit a smoke, then with the sound of a sick engine starting up, she dredged up something from deep in her chest, morning thick, and hacked it into the dust of the road. I saw it roll.

She says, "Why don't you come on in, Sister. Me casa's yer casa. Virgil's back in the kitchen, working up a pile of that voodoo bacon of his but I'm sure he'd appreciate a report."

Sister Dinah stepped over to the verge, pulled out her lower lip and emptied her chaw before kicking dirt over it like a cat.

Then she lifted the hem of her habit with a practiced hand and stumped those little legs up the steps, giving me a manly pat on the shoulder as she passed into the House of Mercy.

Christmas tossed her bible into an empty swingchair, throwing herself down in another. "Whew!" she says, like a day's work is done, lighting another smoke off the last one. She pointed to the hog. "Look a that hog," she says. "I know that hog. That there is Bentley's old sire got loose." Legs spraddled, total undignified-like, she kicked off from the floor and sent her swing swinging.

"Yup," I says, spitting over the railing.

She says, "You know hogs, they's is in fact among the cleanest of animals?"

I wiped my chin.

"Oh yeah. Give them a chance and they'll preen like cats. Seen it myself. It's only cause man keeps them in a sty that they behave as such." She dragged on her cigarette. "Seen it myself."

Thing is, I'd heard something to that effect before. Heard folks in the north were even keeping pigs as pets. Only I couldn't think of another critter that was like to stand knee-deep in a mud puddle, such as this hog was now, to eat the gut-swollen remains of a hound.

"Smart too," she says, snubbing her smoke on a floorboard. "Even if they sunburn like a redhead. Listen, what's going on with you and the Chinese? I can't have her all heart-broke up there."

Careful of my words, not wishing to betray more than I had to, I says, "Oh, she's having a time, I suppose."

"You ain't going to run off with her, are you? Cause I can't allow it. Took me years to find me a good Chinese."

I spat again. "If she walks, it won't be cause of me."

"What's that supposed to mean?"

"Nothing," I says. "I reckon she'll be fine in a day or two."

We sat for a while. Then she says, "Do you love her?"

"Tally Rose?" I says. "Nah. I mean sure, but not how you mean."

"How do you know?"

"Because I know what love is like, that's how."

"I haven't a clue," confessed Christmas. "Not one. I hear people talk about love, and it may as well be the king of Egypt for all I've seen of the stuff."

"Love? Oh, you can't miss it. Falling in love, it's like…" I thought a moment. "It's like getting beaten to death with a dozen roses," I says. "It's the best."

Christmas nodded quietly, gazing at the road. Then a moment later. "Does that mean you and Virgil will be leaving?"

I closed my eyes and pulled my hat down over my face. "Yup," I says, and she didn't say anything for while, just me and Christmas on the porch, just listening to the squeak of her swing.

※

How'd you like a piece of advice, says Christmas, and I realized I'd dozed right off. I sat up in the swing, smelled bacon inside and knew I couldn't have been out for long. Christmas was still sitting there, blurred with smoke, her fat feet kicking off the floor. It was Tally she was talking about. Offering me some counsel on Tally, stating that a woman's tears flow unchecked at man's peril. Christmas tells me to trust her. She knows. She's survived many a year in this business. A cathouse goes plum bonkers every twenty-eight days, and you're like to get hurt unless you know what you're doing.

Christmas, she says women is easy if you're meaning to cheer them up, it's letting them simmer that becomes the pure hazard, and so I kindly invited her to teach me the tricks of the trade, and she says there's ain't no trick at all, just got to always keep this here thing in mind:

If you ever mean to delight a woman, just comment on some small change in her appearance. And if you intend to embarrass a man, do the same. That's all, says Christmas, take it deep as you like, but it's all there in those words. Just got to understand nature and steer clear of the edge. I says, I thank you, and tipped my hat as I stood. I told her next chance I got, I'd go give it a try.

Virgil was standing by the drinking bar in the parlor, casually chatting with a few girls, though I could see he was trying to make his way outside. I says, "Did Sister Dinah ever find you?"

"Oh yessuh. She did. I think she back in the kitchen right now."

Where I was standing, I could sight a direct line to the woodstove, but I couldn't see the Sister. I didn't feel any warm wind either, and it got me wondering.

"You seen old Jimmy?" says Virgil above the natter of his devotees. "How's my buddy doing?"

I says he's doing fine, just fine, but my thoughts were elsewhere for upon that very instant I heard a sound in the kitchen. It was haunting, and distant, like it came from another world entire, though it wasn't anything but the sassy plucking of a banjo.

"Who is that?" I says.

"Who's who, suh?"

"In there," I says, pointing down the hall. "Someone's in the kitchen with Dinah."

The girls fell quiet, Virgil cocked an ear. "I don't hear a thing, suh."

"Nah," I says. "That! You hear that? Someone's in the kitchen, I know. Someone's in the kitchen with Dinah, and they's strumming on the old banjo."

And then it hit me, and I got the shiver-me-ups strong. For ain't nobody in this world can pluck a banjo like the devil. I says, "Get your stuff Virgil, and go load Jimmy Brown. We been found out."

"Found out?" he says, but he's already ducking into Christmas's room, shoving all he's got into a towsack. He knew we had the devil on our trail, and that wasn't any Sister Dinah in the kitchen. So I says, "Just get your stuff, Virgil, and I'll be right back down. I won't be but a minute."

I took the stairs three at a time, my heart pounding when I reached the top. I jogged down the hall to Tally's door, lifted my fist to knock, and then froze. Not because she'd ask for some time alone, but because I heard noises within. The last kind of noises I expected to hear from her room today.

But I couldn't wait. I thumped on the door. A moment later the door cracked open and Tally peeked out, eyes wide. She says, "I thought I told you go!"

I was taken aback. Then I heard a man's voice in her room, him saying, who the hell is it.

"I said git!" she yelled, swatting me away with the back of her hand. "And don't you ever come back!"

A man's voice asked again who it was, and I could hear someone pulling on clothes. Tally looked frantic. I opened my mouth to speak, but she cut me off.

"Just leave!" she screeched. "Just go away and git! I don't never want to see you again!"

Slowly, I turned to go, and then she clutched my arm. The look in her eyes near chilled me to the bone, for they said something else entire.

"*Please*," she whispered.

I got the point. Needle-sharp. I was off like a slingshot down the hall. Just before I reached the stairs I heard Tally yelp and the sound of her door crash open. "Hey!" someone bellowed, and I spun around.

And there he was, standing naked to the waist, belt undone, chest like a curly-haired barrel. Will Lawson's eyes took me in for a good long moment, and then started wide with recognition. He dove back into the room.

I knew what he aimed to get there, and I aimed to be gone when he got it. I jumped full standing from the top of the stairs. I crashed on the landing below, hard, but was too jacked up to feel it. I scrambled to my feet and in my haste practically tumbled down the last flight of stairs, a half-dozen faces staring at me when I came skidding into the parlor.

"Virgil!" I hollered. He was already out front. I saw him cinching up the straps on Jimmy's saddlebags. "Virgil!" I yelled again, running out onto the porch and then covered my head as a gun blast dropped the window beside me. A shower of glass exploded across the veranda and sent a swinging chair somersaulting against the railing.

I stopped. I slowly put up my hands. I saw the bits of glass glittering about my feet. Virgil stood stunned and watching in the road. I heard the hushed whimpering of women in the parlor behind me, and then the distinct click of a shotgun cocked.

Now it is my belief you can take just about anything from a man, right down to the very air he breathes. But choice, that's something too deep for the taking, and as I'm only allowed to do this thing once, I intended to do it right.

I put my hands back down.

I stood up straight, turning slowly around, full ready for my last moment on earth. I saw the girls were flat on the floor, peeking out through their fingers. Will Lawson stood poised before the stairs. Only his hands were stretched high, his musket lying at his feet, Sister Dinah's double-barrel trained at his gut.

⟫⟩◈⟨⟪

There was once a time, I can't say precisely when but it was a ways back, and I was walking down that trail on the backside of Little Partridge, you know the one that branches out from the creek like it's going to old Harlin's place but then fades out into nothing but a deer run? Well anyhow I was walking that trail, the smell of sun-warmed pine needles thick in my nose and those spring squirrels chattering and chucking bark as I passed, when I saw something that stopped me dead in my tracks.

It was hatchet scars in an old sugar maple tree, only those scars were twelve feet up from the earth. It got me thinking, those scars, twelve feet up as they were, and I sat right down to give it a ponder.

Now twelve feet up is quite a distance, and sugar maples aren't known for fast growing. I figured those scars had to be chopped in there, oh, forty-five, fifty. Maybe even sixty year ago. And if I was hearing it right, this here sugar maple was telling me, about loud as it could, that hurts from our past were just too precious to be forgotten, and so remain part of what grows ever higher.

Now I have plenty scars, both inside and out, and as you know, no few of them are recent. But as me and Virgil loaded up old Jimmy Brown, making ready to say our farewells and head on up the mountain and out of Union Fog, I began to wonder if perhaps those scars weren't changing me somehow. For the better, I mean. Every one of them a tribute to some misfortune amended. Or, or even better, you ever notice how a scar will shine in the sun? All silver and gold?

It's like that.

Like maybe our scars are just chinks where the shine gets in.

<hr />

Old Will Lawson landed himself in jail for a spell, though there was little reassurance in that. Sister Dinah expressed a lawman's regret that there is no edict forbids a man pulling his gun on another. Unless he shoots you, there ain't no crime. I mentioned how a man was shot dead, just back up in those mountains, but Sister Dinah had no jurisdiction beyond the fog. She offered to lose the key for a few days but outside that there wasn't much she could do.

Except one thing, a municipal tradition she herself had founded, existing nowhere else but right here in Union Fog. Any man pulls a firearm in the House of Mercy forfeits his horse. No argument, no court hearing or fuss, and seeing as how I was the one most directly aggrieved, that old sorrel gelding of his, the one that was hanging about out front, it went directly to me. I named him Rocinante.

Rocky for short. About the sorriest horse you ever saw in your life. He was swaybacked and mangy with patches of hair falling out, and something of a dead look to his eye. Any man could see he should have been turned to pasture long ago but a horse is a horse, I figured, and all things considered it was better taking him along than leaving him behind.

Old Virgil vol Krie had stocked up on supplies. Bacon mostly. Plenty of bacon, but I saw a few new odds and ends. He divided the loads in half, spreading them even between Rocinante and Jimmy. But old Jimmy Brown looked right put out, mules being what they are, letting us know exactly how he felt about being treated no better than a horse.

Only it was hard to take him serious, you see, for the strangest of things occurred. It so happens when a mule gets snipped, the sound of his bray can change, coming out somewhere between the aw-aw of a donkey and the whinny of a horse. Except old Jimmy Brown had devised something original on his own, and he was right proud of it, ridiculous as it was, coming out like nothing so much as the qua-ha of a circus zebra. Folks were gathering in the road to speculate.

"Quiet, Jimmy," Virgil whispered under his breath as he threw saddlebags over the mule's broad rump. "Quiet now, you shaming youself with that racket." But once Jimmy got started he refused to quit, like he'd finally discovered his voice.

"Give him an apple," said someone from the crowd. Someone else suggested a whip. But old Jimmy just wouldn't shut up. He had lots to say, and he'd finally got the words to say it, and wasn't going anywhere till he'd said them all.

I sat down there on the Mercy's double-wide steps. I packed a chaw. Short of transferring his saddlebags over to Rocky, Virgil tried every way you ever thought of to quiet a mule. Finally Virgil gave up, taking up a seat beside me, saying he reckoned we'd just have sit this one out.

"Yup." I spit off the steps, taking a peek up those mountains. Somewhere over that mist-covered ridge lay Valhalla and the salvation of a girl in red. I says, "You still know the way?"

And Virgil, he says, "No man ever forgets his way home."

And I says, "Is it far then, Valhalla?"

And Virgil says, "Nawsuh. Valhalla wasn't never far off."

Old Jimmy Brown was really putting on a show now, qua-ha'ing away, offering no shortage of amusement to the townsfolk. Rocinante was more apathetic-like, head bowed to the verge where he tugged up mouthfuls of grass. And then the crowd parted as the blacksmith pulled up in his mule-team wagon. Blacksmith turned to the Mercy and whistled once, loud, and then got down from his haystack seat to fuss with the mules' tracings, their bells jingling, when out onto the veranda comes Tally Rose. She was ready to go.

And what a sight to behold, standing there in that white-brimmed hat of hers, a new store-bought traveling dress and a leather satchel over her shoulder, all stuffed to the brim with sketchbooks and whatnot. I saw that quiet look of resolve she first wore when I met her in the mirror, and I knew this girl was headed straight for her dreams.

While the blacksmith, doubling as local transport, crouched to check a few shoes, Tally sat down between us, me and Virgil that is, sort of saying farewell without saying a thing.

"So that's it, huh? You off to go paint the Seine?"

She nodded, an unreadable look in her eyes, old Jimmy still making a fool.

"One thing's certain," she says of a sudden, taking off her hat and setting it in her lap. "Every creature got to find its worth." She had strung roadside daisies through a dozen buttons from her jar and now wore them as a band round her hat—*flower*, *button, flower, button*—which told me more about just how far she'd come than anything else. She slipped the hatband off. She walked direct to Jimmy and set the hatband around his ears like a crown. He tossed his jaw and qua-ha'd again, but like he knew something was different. He paused for a moment, contemplative-like, qua-ha'd one last time and then fell silent, nuzzling his own shoulder while Tally scratched at his neck.

"Well that beats all," says someone in the crowd. "All that, just to get flowers from a girl."

But Tally Rose said nothing. She had crowned a fool and now her work was done, though in a way, I was the fool with flowers. Her flowers, the ones she was giving me all along, the gift of seeing one woman in bloom. It will change a man to see femininity stand, for it is a strength unlike any other. I'll daresay it is sturdier than men's swords for it'll bend without breaking, but'll move straight as an arrow through the dark.

Tally Rose, she climbed into the blacksmith's wagon and without a word of goodbye, clomped on down the road.

<hr/>

I didn't think I'd miss Tally Rose so much till I saw her go. I watched that white-brimmed hat grow smaller and smaller, and then the wagon turned the bend and left town. My heart ached to see it, but it was for goodness sake. My only hope was that Tally was safe. If talk was true, Union Fog was having itself a bandit problem. Bandits this, bandits that, everyone talking bandits. But it was the North Road they prowled, keeping to their mountain redoubt and occasionally dropping down into the swamps beyond, while old Tally Rose was headed east to the sea.

"She'll be fine," says Sister Dinah, squirting tobacco juice from the corner of her mouth. "It is you two that's hopeless. Nobody sensible's riding north these days. You're doomed."

"Well I thank you," I says, climbing up onto Rocinante, "for everything and all. This town's been real good to me and Virgil."

She looked up at me in the saddle. "You know you're like to die, right?"

I says, "Who isn't?"

She looked at me. She says, "I doubt there is a man alive got the power to kill another before his time. The appointment's long set, and every road leads to it. That don't mean you got to race there."

"Welp, I thank you," I says. "Them's kind words, though they ain't yet my own."

Virgil threw a long leg over Jimmy, and Christmas came down from the porch of the Magdalena. She gave Virgil a great big kiss, cigarette held out from them both, and then waved goodbye as Virgil tipped his straw hat.

So me and Virgil and old Jimmy Brown, and Rocinante of course, Rocinante too, we headed out of Union Fog. Virgil's strategy lay in bypassing the North Road entire, climbing back up Dustfeather Mountain, then descending pathless into the lands beyond. "Heading down into the sticks," was the way he put it. He says we could pick up the road again once we were clear of those bandits, and then we'd be smooth sailing all the way to Valhalla.

Except the problems began on the instant. To start with, old Rocky was pure worthless. If I had set out on a sawhorse I would have been better off, for though the two were equal enough in wits I would have saved myself a whole bushel of disappointment. If I intended to go left, Rocky's intentions went right. He couldn't pass a clump of grass without grazing. And if I gave him my heels he'd simply stop dead, obstinate as a stick in the mud. Halfway up the mountain I dismounted, flustered-like, and led him by the reins up the switchbacks. Near the top we came up against a roaring creek that poured over our trail and Virgil and Jimmy, they splashed on through, water coming up the mule's knees. I climbed saddle to do the same, only when we got midway across the creek Rocinante commenced to turn back around. I sawed on his reins but he took no notice. When I gave him the heels he froze, cud-chewing-dumb, right there in the middle of the creek.

So there we stood, me and Rocinante, him appearing quite satisfied to remain there. I resorted to cursing, but it left no impression. By and by I climbed down and tugged him on by hand. In the end we summitted Dustfeather Mountain, with horse, in twice the time it took us on foot with Throckmorton.

And then there was the view again, that view from the top. Enough to make misery itself forget its woes. With that silvery ocean of fog below, I was once again lost in affection for a girl on the far side of night.

After a brief repast of cornbread and cold bacon we descended the other side of old Dustfeather, Virgil leading the way by smell. He tells me freedom's got a scent. A fragrance all it own. He tells me he can follow freedom through thick and thin with no better than his nose for compass. And he smelled it strongest when he first came across me.

"Oh yessuh," he says. "I knowed it right off. The moment I seen you I says to myself, I says, that boy is headed for Valhalla. And you don't fetch him along vol Krie, you may as well not get there atall."

"That true?"

"True as can be, suh. For even if you'd not licked old Mista Lawson with them fists of yours, I'd a'joined your company all the same. I'd have found a way, for a Miss Odessa said as much when I left. She said I might be bringing a body along."

As ever, when I inquired further into this Miss Odessa of his, Virgil would go sudden tight-lipped and vague. She was good to him, and that's about all I knew. She was good to him, and so far as his freedom was concerned, Virgil was likely to choose his Miss Odessa over a pair of wings.

If such a thing is possible, the backside of Dustfeather Mountain was bigger than the front, for we seemed to be dropping down much farther than we'd climbed. We came out in a valley so deep and wide you might have thought we were down in a Louisiana bayou. The sounds of the forest were different, louder, harder to place. Same could be said of the smells. The mud got so thick it threatened to swallow your boots so we were slow going, trying to keep to high ground until even that gave away to pure water. It was like the woods were flooded entire, leaving the trees to grow straight from the mire with wild buttresses and orchids and lichens hanging low from the limbs.

"Virgil vol Krie," I says. "I believe we's in a swamp."

And he says back, "Swamp is what you call it."

We pressed deeper into that quagmire of flatulent despair, and I says, "So it's for real then, ain't it. This here's the Styx."

And he says back, "Oh yessuh, we's in the sticks for real now."

There you have it, I thought. The mightiest of crossings.

"Virgil," I says, "I swear you are a genius among men." Goddamn that Virgil was good. "I daresay you are a guide without equal." I gave him a slap on the back but he played it off humble, as he often did, letting on like he doesn't know what I'm talking about.

I says, "I mean it Virgil. You are a good man."

"Well I thank you, suh." Only he seemed a bit distracted right then. One arm resting across Jimmy Brown's saddle, he stood looking out on the bog. His attention was fully honed upon the myrrh of freedom, I suspected, for it was thin as tincture in a land foul as this, and powerful hard to trace through the vapors.

"Something tells me," he says, sniffing at the air. "Something tells me we ought to go thisaway, suh."

"You're the boss."

There was a mist in the trees that whispered like dank spirits. It twisted and curled over water that was blacker than coffee with evil little bubbles that stunk like a bean-eater's wind. The mere thought of wading in there got me shuddering with heebie-jeebies, so I was plenty happy when I saw Virgil skirt the water entire. Under his omniscient guidance we trudged round the edge of that fen, swatting through foliage, getting trapped in the mud and constantly digging out the mounts.

And the skeeters. Let me tell you. You couldn't come out that swamp but half a man for all those skeeters left behind. Clouds of them were ever buzzing your ears and clotting your eyes, and just excited as all hell to go pouring into your mouth when you opened it.

"See there," says Virgil when I least expected it. "I told you I got me a bloodhound nose. What's that sign say there?"

Nailed to a tree was a piece of rotten plank. Scratched into it were the words, 'Port ahead. Boteman.'

"I believe you found us the boatman, Virgil! Now all our problems is solved."

Boatman's shack came right out onto the water, just skimming the top on pilings. But one of those stilts was all kicked askew so a whole corner of the cabin sagged into the water. The entire thing was so old and decrepit, so overgrown with weeds that you had to look twice to know it wasn't a thing of nature. Only the door hinted at some earlier alliance with man, being all strung up with decorative jugs.

On the backside of the shack was another door opening direct onto the water. Leading off it was a dock of sorts, two planks laid in a line and balanced precarious as all hell upon rotten pilings. But I didn't see any boat.

When we came upon Boatman he was sitting on a stump out front, skinning a possum with a little whittling knife. He was skeleton-lean. He had on his overalls and a battered felt hat, and his bare feet were all crusted with mud.

"Howdy," says Virgil as we came along through the muck, but old Boatman didn't so much as look up. The yard was all stumps and mud and scraps of ate fish. And then in a lazy voice, a voice made for yawning, the old Boatman he says, "Sick 'em, boy."

A hound dog exploded out from the shack and came tearing across the yard like lightning. Me and Virgil both jumped into the saddle and that hound came barking and snapping till we lifted our feet and our mounts spooked and danced all around. Old Jimmy Brown commenced to qua-ha.

"S'nuff," says Boatman, yanking down on a fistful of fur till the skin came clean of the possum, and that hound dog crouched flat on the earth and began to whine. Boatman tossed the skin in the mud. The hound dog pounced on it, growling while he ate it whole.

"Damn," I says. "That's a hungry dog."

Boatman turned to me and Virgil. He says, "So's you know it, you ain't welcome here."

And I says, "Sign says you are the boatman."

Boatman held up the possum by the tail, inspecting the wet corpse as it twisted in the air.

"Wuz." He spat in the mud. Then cocked a thumb back at the dock and I noticed, just barely, the prow of a sunken skiff poking up through the water. "My old lady got fed up with the outings. Done took a shotgun to the keel."

And if that just ain't our luck, I thought. Sunk. Who would've thought to even worry about such things when planning an excursion through Styx?

"Bir-*dy*!" he hollered suddenly, like a train conductor calling out stops. Then he whistled the way Pa would when calling us in for a beating, and a tremendous and beefy woman heaved out from the shack, the whole thing rising slightly as she stepped free. Boatman held up the possum for her to see. Birdy stamped barefoot through the mud, her apron bespattered in God-knows-what, and fetched that possum by the tail, saying, "I ain't cooking fer four, you know."

And Boatman, total wore out and exasperated-like, he says, "Hwell goddangit woman, I guess you are if I tell you to!"

And that Birdy of his gave me and Virgil a hard look and then stamped back into the shack with that bloody possum across her shoulder.

"Women," says Boatman and then spat in the mud. And if I wasn't mistaken, I sensed the fuzzy pangs of camaraderie. Had a woman like that ever stomped into my life and taken a shotgun to my only paying enterprise, well I reckon I'd get to feeling blue myself.

I says, "Boatman, my friend. I think I see your troubles. Perhaps what you need is a vacation."

"A hwut?"

"A holiday. Look at you, your face is gaunt. You're all wore out. I suspect you've known better days, but me and Virgil here, we're headed to Valhalla. Why don't you come on along?"

And Boatman, who's got dull, dark eyes sunk back deep in his head, he says, "Hwell," he says. "I ain't sure what you just said." He spat in the mud. "But whether I like it or not, I spect you two just been invited for stew."

<hr>

Varmint stew! There is nothing in this world beats a good bowl of varmint. I have to say I was looking forward to the offer, lonesome as I was for homecooking.

Course it was nothing like I expected. Round these parts, stew was a grayish mucous of crunchy tendons and tails and the odd crawdad for texture. I got a bite or two in, grinding it up with my teeth, but lacked the fortitude to see the thing through.

"Mmm," I says. "You try this Virgil? You should try this."

"Oh yessuh," he says. He had nearly finished his bowl, which meant if I was sly enough I could fill it with my own. But before you know it, Boatman's wife ladled Virgil up a second helping, an act equal in threat to a knife at the back.

"Oh, thank you maam," says Virgil. "Yeah that's plenty there, maam, that's—" But she filled it up, daring either one of us to voice a complaint. Fact that woman was pure crackling with hostility, making me jump from my skin every time she lifted a spoon. Then old Boatman, who never looked up from his stew, he would make some sideways request and she'd slam bowls and splash ladles till the chore was done, her eyes just brimming with bayou-bitch-wrath.

But old Boatman didn't care, or was too busy eating to notice. He had a fungal little beard wouldn't quite come in, giving him a face sort of rat-like and scrawny. But that man could eat stew like he's got holes in both feet. Bowl after bowl he hunched over that spoon, both elbows on the table, going at it like a piece of hard work. The only sound in that shack was the slurping of spoons and the throb of insects outside in the swamp.

Eventually, old Boatman, he pushed his bowl forward and says, "Hwell, I guess I'll have to get up myself. If no one's gonna fetch out that bread." He didn't get up.

After a glance like log-sparks, his wife screeched back her chair and stamped to the shelf. She pulled down a basket of rolls and slammed them down center of the table.

"Oh, hwell thank you," he says, leaning forward to select himself a roll.

For myself, thinking old Birdy was just as likely to offer me bread as beat me about the head with it, I helped myself to a roll before she decided.

"I suggest you scrape off the blue," says Boatman, doing that very thing.

Problem was, after scraping the blue there was nothing left but weevils. "Oh but that part there is good," he says to me, noticing my little pile of blue fuzz on the table. "Yeah that mold's fine, once it goes to hair it won't hurt you none. Jis give it a try."

"Otis," says his wife to him. "Otis, you keep eating that mold hair and I won't even have to poison you."

"Hwell darnit woman, you're killing me one way or another. Now shut you're squirly mouth and git my jug."

And she says, "I swear, Otis, I swear to you, if you didn't already own this place outright I believe I'd leave you."

And he says, "That right? And if you weren't my only uncle's daughter I'd have left you twice over! Now do I got to get up from this goddarn chair, or are you gonna fetch me my jug?"

He crossed his arms, sulking there at the end of the table. Birdy stamped over to the back door, which opened onto the swamp proper, and pulled up what looked like a bait line. Only it was a jug that came up from the water, slick with slime but cooler, I reckon, than anything else in that shack.

"Thank you!" he says when she slammed it down before him. "And for my friends here?"

From the shelf, she took down a crockpot covered with cheesecloth. She poured out two cups from the crockpot, setting them before me and Virgil. I drank mine down. It was clammy and thick. And spicy. I didn't like it.

"What is it?"

"Sausage water," she says. She poured me another, and I saw the links bobbing about in the crockpot. "You're wanting something else and you got to discuss it with your fine host here," she says, indicating Otis and his jug. But old Otis just stared at her, like he'd make her eat those words, by God, make her eat them raw if she didn't happen to be twice the man he was. He began patting his pockets, his sunken dark eyes searching round the room.

"Now what?' says Birdy.

"Why, I'm looking where my knife is at."

"No," she says. "You are looking where it ain't, and that is the problem."

Then old Otis, he reached deep into the chest pocket of his overalls, squinting real hard at Birdy. "Oh. *Here it is*," he says with slow and unmistakable intent, and then took out his whittling knife to shave himself a toothpick from the table, watching her all the while.

Now by this point in the evening, all my expectations regards to swamp love were total shattered. Folks down here in bogs were just as petty as those above. My concerns, however, ran along the lines of me and Madder. Having been giving this glimpse into the complexities of matrimonial life, I began to fear we too might one day find ourselves scrawny and fat, blowing holes in boats and hating life in general among the slime-dwellers.

Course it'd be different, her and me. She was an artist for one, a painter, and wouldn't ever hold with any swamp shack. And me, I reckoned I'd die before I bickered over mold-hair and liquor. I'd be too busy loving her to even think of it. Fact it seemed to me the only difference between 'marital' and 'martial' is where you place the 'I', which is to say it's every one of us selecting the way of things.

"Welp, I thank you for the supper," I says to our hosts, choking back the last of my beverage. "And your place here, it sure is... well it's very..." I scanned the moldering walls of the shanty, looking for something to compliment.

Defeated, I raised my cup. "It couldn't have happened to a better couple."

I hoped not, anyhow.

"Boys," says Otis, having whittled down his toothpick. "Hows about we retire to the yard."

Me and Virgil said that sounded fine. Privately, I figured the sooner Otis and his wife were apart, the better. I feared a slaying coming on, and had already speculated on the method. I reckoned old Otis kept his knife handy for a reason, and made sure his woman knew it. She however, being taciturn by nature, gave me more to think upon. On the one hand, I could see her ripping a leg clean off the table and battering old Otis for fun. But then she'd spoken vaguely of poison and had proven access to firearms. It was a real gamble. I'd not bet on an outcome.

The men of us went out to the yard and rolled three stumps down to the water. We sat real quiet-like, listening to the swamp, which gave me the creeps like nothing else prior. The mist clung to my skin like a fever-sweat. I kept turning to the sound of kerplops.

"The hell is that?" I says. "What is them things, keeps ker-plopping about?"

"Jis critters," says Otis, picking his teeth. Washing it down with his jug. As he made no move to share his liquor, and me and Virgil were equal in our enjoyment of a drop after supper, Virgil came right out and says, "So that the good stuff you got there? Some real white lightning?"

Sniff.

"Hyup."

Tips it back.

Wipes his mouth on an arm.

"Mm hmm. Mm hmm," says Virgil. "And you make it you self?"

And old Otis, he spat in the mud and says, "Let's just say it'll put a little sun in your belly." And you could see he had some proud in him after all.

But not so much as to offer it around, you see, so old Virgil vol Krie, he gave me a wink on the sly and then says to Otis, "Hows about we play us a game?"

Otis gave him a suspicious look, sucking his toothpick. "Hwut kind a game?"

And Virgil says, "It be called 'Drink The Fish.' You ever play it? Nah? I'll show you how it goes. See I got a fish right here, right here in my pocket. Now hand me that jug." Virgil held out his hand, and old Otis, squinting with mistrust, he was downright begrudging in passing that jug over. Best he could do was give it a slow, halting—and painful, by the look of it—slide from his thigh to the end of his knee before his willpower petered out entire. So Virgil met him halfway and snatched it.

"Now I got me a fish right here in my pocket, but you can't see it, you see." Virgil turned sideways a little to block the view, and moved about till you couldn't tell what he was up to. "There. Now I just put my fish in the jug. He be swimming about, and each of us got to try and drink it down, you see? Who wants to go first?"

Otis looked right put out. "Did you just put a fish in my liquor?" I reckon the notion hit him harder than most. I just kept my trap shut, thinking to see how it goes.

Virgil says, "It be the winner what drinks him out. Now watch close now, and I show you how it's done." Virgil tipped that jug, and I have to say I was impressed. I'd no idea he could ship water like that.

"Gimme that," says Otis, wrestling the jug back. And by the look of it, he aimed to get that fish in one go.

Naturally I took a pull or two, and by the time we got to the bottom of that jug no one thought to ask what became of the fish. Old Otis lay snoring spread-eagle in the mud, his bare feet soaking in the swampwater. Virgil, with a slur to his words, he says he reckons we're on our own now, and may as well get to it.

But much as I hate boats, I discovered I hate swampwater more and was total uninspired to go wading around in it. Rocinante made it clear he would have to be led by the reins, and even Jimmy Brown was out of sorts. And to top it all off, I felt a storm coming on.

"How about we sleep it off in the shack," I says, "and set out when the rain lets up."

"What rain?" says Virgil. He says there's no weather coming, and the sooner we set off the better. But sensing rain was just something goes along with dowsing, I suspect. Can't say how, but I generally know rain before the clouds do. There was once a time, just after the war, and we were coming back up the coast, up the Gulf of Mexico, and I says, "There is weather a'coming," though there wasn't a cloud in the sky. I says to the lieutenant, "We best take cover," and before the hour was up we saw the leading edge of a hurricane blowing whitecaps off the sea. By evening we were hit, hard, but to our good fortune we were already holed up in the adobe grain-houses of a little inland village while 200 mph chickens pelted the walls.

I says to Virgil, "You know your business, but there is weather brewing. We wade out there now and we'll get drowned."

Reluctantly, Virgil agreed to the delay, and we picked up old Otis by the shoulders and dragged him back to the shack.

"You want him in the bed?" I says from the door. And Birdy says, "What bed?" So me and Virgil dumped him there on the floorboards and went back out to make sure the mounts were tied up good. When we came back, we lay out beside Otis, saddles for pillows, and fell asleep right there on the floor.

At some point in the night I woke to the sound of a rain. But not just any old rain. It was a regular Baptist downpour out there, sounding like rakes and shovels pounding down on the roof. I says, "Virgil!" just to see if he was awake, but I couldn't even hear my own voice over the din of it.

Sleep took me. Next time I woke it was absolutely silent, except for the creak of the shack for it was slowly listing to one side. And my back was all wet. I sat up, real quick, and saw the floor of the shack was under water. Just the touch of that stuff gave me the jitters, and I jumped up onto the table. "Hey," I says, hoping to wake whoever would wake. "Hey. I believe this here shanty is sinking."

"Hyup," says old Otis from the floor. He was laying there in the water, apparently half-awake, arms crossed behind his head. "Happens from time to time."

"Well, what you plan to do about it?"

"Oh, nothing much."

Assuming we weren't afloat somewhere, pulled clean off our moorings and doing the Noah thing, I reckoned things would dry out when the swamp drained. "Virgil," I says. "Virgil, wake up. We got to go check on the mounts."

Peeking out the door I saw them, still hitched to a cypress limb. The water out there came right up to Jimmy's withers, which meant it was chest high for myself.

"Well suh," says Virgil vol Krie at my side. "Ain't no point in waiting around."

Letting himself over the edge of the porch, he slipped down into that evil jambalaya, mighty guide that he was, waded across and took up Jimmy by the rope. "Ain't so bad," he says from the trees. "It's just like—" He broke off, staring warily down the bridge of his nose.

"What is it?"

Holding real still, he says, "Something just brushed gainst my legs."

"Was it big?"

"Weren't no bait."

Dammitohell. "So now what?" That water stunk worse than ever. Even the rain wasn't strong enough to break up the skin of slime on the surface.

"Now nothing," he says. "We got to foot it, or else stand here in this batter."

Slowly, very slowly, I sat down on the threshold of the door and let both legs slide down into the water, my flesh crawling at the first touch of it. I let a shiver run through me. Then shoved off, slipping in right up to my chest.

No exaggeration: Sinking nipple-deep into a pool of raw sewage could be no less pleasant. I plodded along, cringing and gagging, absolutely terrified of slipping and going under. The mere thought of taking in a mouthful of swamp sent me shuddering and dancing in my skin.

"What you doing there, suh? You can't just stand there. Come on over here and get old Rocky so we can go."

I says, "I don't know I can do this, Virgil."

"What you talking about? You already standing in the muck. Now just get you self walking."

At the best of times I got a weak stomach. But after a night on the jug, followed by a dip in pure slime, the fell rumblings in my gut commenced to clench right up.

"All right, I'm coming! Just don't push me, all right? I'm coming!" I took a deep breath. "I just want to ask you something."

"What?"

"How about we go tomorrow?"

"You stop that now. It just water. Now come on. If you was in the desert you'd be dying for this."

I wiped my brow with my hat, then pointed it vaguely at the extant water. "But there's animals in there."

"Oh, come on now. They's all friendly-like."

I tried to argue that one when Virgil took Jimmy by the reins and started off without me, then turned over his shoulder and gave me a look.

"All right!" I says, "You don't got to give me no look! I already said I'm coming, just don't push me is all. I got to go slow."

I closed my eyes and took a good breath. "All right, see there, I'm coming now. I'm walking." I'm walking, and I can taste my gizzard in my throat cause it keeps trying to jump out and my eyes keep rolling back in my head, and all I can see back there is higher ground. Higher ground. Arable levies and islands, colossal hummocks of loam, bridges. Dry Bridges. Wrought-iron railings beneath a searing blue sky, my hair sun-hot to the touch. The air tastes bright. The bridges are dry. Hot dry bridges in the sun.

⸺◈⸺

Except for the use of a mirror, I don't suppose anyone has actually and directly seen head nor tail of himself, and yet it's reasonable to assume both exist. The man that says he has no head, just because he cannot see it, is likely to find convincing in the Pain of All Saints.

Likewise, I hadn't yet seen one critter in this swamp worth my fear and disgust, yet I knew they were out there. I suspected they were amassing in secret, churning the water with their numbers, just waiting to get me all at once.

"I believe I'd hire them bandits," I says, wading into the mist, "if they'd agree to rob me somewheres dry and clean."

"Ain't so bad," says Virgil, who'd been leading the way. "Won't be in this swamp forever, you know."

That was only true if you didn't die here. But I was expecting something foul and tentacled to be dragging me under any moment. I'd already shrieked like a girl when something squirmed up my leg, only to find out it was a bubble coming up from the mud.

"These mounts is wore out," I says. "Rocinante here is about to do his standing thing. I'd like to get him on hard soil before he gets overly obdurate."

"Yessuh," says Virgil. "I keep my eye out."

The sound of bugs was a dull screech in my ears, but loud as they were, you only heard them when they stopped. We plowed through the muck, and my gut got tighter and tighter like someone was slowly winding my bowels round a spindle. I began to wish I'd never drank any sausage water. Not that second cup, anyhow.

"There you go, suh," says Virgil at last. Up ahead, among a thicket of cypress, a little hump of mud lifted free of the water. "I reckon that's good as it gets." We sloshed up onto it, the mounts bogging down in the mud.

I looked around. "This is the sorriest island I ever seen in my life." The hump was barely big enough for all of us standing, but I was already sticky and foul and couldn't imagine a sleep in this sludge could worsen things any.

Virgil waded back out and broke off limbs for a fire while I got Rocinante and Jimmy going on feed. You could tell how deep the swamp was by the highwater marks on their coats, which left a ring of dark slime. I didn't even bother to stake them down, knowing horses weren't like to go wandering from land. As I was eyeing our mound, trying to figure if there was room enough to sleep, I saw the slide marks where gators went skidding into the water.

Virgil came back with a couple sticks and rubbed a fire. Before you know it, he had two-three pounds of bacon sizzling over the coals and the smell of it went straight to my gut. "Oh God," I says, doubling over in pain. Virgil poked at the bacon with a stick. He says, "You got the runs too?"

"Oh God," I says. It was like someone driving a railroad-tie into my belly. "I got to go."

"Best not dally."

I broke out in a sweat. "Where'd you go when you went?"

"Right there in the water," says Virgil. "Didn't even stop walking."

"Oh God." I clutched at my side. The pain was jagged and screeched like a hawk. I couldn't breathe, let alone break for the water. I froze there like a statue of someone shot in the gut, waiting for the pain to slip past.

"Oh Lord," I panted when my breath came back, wiping the sweat from my eyes. "I believe that woman done poisoned us. That poor Otis must have—Oh!" The next wave was upon me. I threw back my overalls and charged down to the water.

"You got to shush all that hollerin', suh," says Virgil from the fire. "You gonna set old Jimmy Brown off for the night."

As I squatted there in that cesspool of putrefaction and rot, I swear my insides near to dropped from my body. At one point I clenched right up, afraid I'd lose something vital if I kept on.

I crawled back to the fire on my hands and knees. "Feel better?" says Virgil.

"No." I flopped onto my back like a puppet clipped from the strings. The detergent effect of that evil beverage near to scoured me out, and now a cramping emptiness was opening up inside, elbowing for room. Virgil held out a piece of bacon on a stick, the grease still leaping and popping. "Here you are, then. Try you some this. This here hog fat'll cure bout anything."

For the first time ever, I refused Virgil's bacon. I lay curled about the fire, my head pillowed on a lump of mud, pondering the countless inroads of misfortune. I wondered if there was a limit to it all, a point where a fella just breaks and says he cannot endure any more. I had to be close. I had plumbed the depths of damnation, taking all manner of thumps and couldn't imagine the devil had much left to throw at me.

"Here you go. Just lay you head on this." Virgil passed me his towsack of raw bacon. It was clumpy and greasy, but better than mud. I nuzzled into it with a passionate groan, felt its contours mold to my face. And goddammit all if a man's only rest doesn't lay in the hairsbreadth between what is sacred and profane.

But as I lay there on my side, firelight flickering about the swamp, I saw something coming towards me through the mud. It was a leech. He came inching along, right straight towards me like he could smell the warm blood in my veins.

Now I'm looking at this leech, and I am thinking to myself, I'm thinking: I am now officially estranged from the Lord's good favor. And I know this because I am seeing par with a slug. Or a worm, or a vermin or whatever it is. I'm on a level with the lowest form of creation. And in my mind I can locate a voice so far gone it says, "You know, Dannon, so far as pets go, leeches ain't half bad."

Sure, says my reasoning, making a quick sketch of their virtues: Leeches are affectionate, loyal, and generally cheap to feed. They won't buck you from saddles or piss on the bed. They are hypoallergenic. It's only a horde that'll give you trouble, and that's what I saw when I grabbed a torch from the fire.

Me and Virgil stood right up, watching a ring of leeches close in on our camp. "Sweet Jesus," I says. "It's a goddamn exodus."

"I ain't never..." says Virgil, shaking his head. "Never in my life. Nuh uh. Where they all come from like that? We got to— no! You see that! That one just looked at me! You see that? Look at him, that one there is a' following my voice!"

"Oh it just looks that way," I explained, "for because we is beleaguered."

"What you mean?" he says. "You saying they can't see us?"

And I says, "I mean leeches ain't got no heads, is what I mean. I thought everyone knew that."

"No heads?"

"Nah. No heads. They's freaks of nature, you know. Just teeth is all. And little bellies that say *Squaw-Squaw-Squick* when they don't get enough blood to eat."

"That sounds mighty awful, suh. Mighty awful."

"Yes it is."

Virgil began casting wary looks above, anywhere that hinted of safety. He says, "You reckon them leeches can climb trees?"

"Like goddamn monkeys, my friend. Trust me."

Back at the Pain of All Saints there was a young fella, name of Tobias Quick—seventeen years old with a head of gray hair— who got himself dragged in for eating four-hundred-seventeen dollars paper money and a half box of cigars. His issues aside, he wasn't a bad fella. He fancied himself an archangel of the Lord and liked preaching to us on a Sunday noon, which we mostly enjoyed, for his interpretations of scripture were boldly new-fangled. But at some point in the sermon he'd generally lose focus and commence eating the passages, and then we'd all shuffle back to our cells to pick at the fossils in our walls and chew our calluses in uninterrupted rapture. Nevertheless it was Tobias Quick who taught me all about leeches. He knew all about those things. He says what you got to do is, when you are beleaguered by leeches, you just stuff your socks full of tobacco. If you stuff your socks with tobacco the leeches will leave you alone.

Course neither me nor Virgil had socks of any kind, but we shredded up my plug of chaw and split it between us. We wetted it down and filled up our boots till tobacco burst out the tops and then watched to see what class of good it brought on.

The leeches clustered around till they were just a carpet of squirm. They climbed right up our boots and over the backs of each other, and then stopped. They just stopped right there, never going any higher.

"Well I'll be," says Virgil in purest astonishment. "If that ain't the trick of all tricks." And this was a fine thing while we stood. A very fine thing. A fella can stand around a fire all night. Only that's not what happened.

I was so battered and worn I don't even recall sitting down. I certainly don't recall laying out. But when I woke, it was to find a carnivorous slug clinging fast to my eyelid. I pried him off, then found another on my lip. "Oh Lord."

They were everywhere. I began flipping them out my ears and from back of my neck, from every nook and fold in my skin, and when I stood up I found my whole body was slicked and sticky with blood. Thinking it was a booger, I even blew a little one right out my nose and then emitted a silent shriek of horror, biting hold of my knuckle as I watched it inch slowly away.

"Virgil, wake up," I says. He was lying other side of the fire. "Hey Virgil. *Virgil!*"

"Wuh?" he mumbled.

"We's been feasted upon."

"Whusat?" I saw him pop straight up. His face was a mask of leeches. "Good God!" screamed his lips, while he clawed at leeches with both hands. We spent the next little while ripping critters from our flesh, and then another while just shuddering by the fire. Some things are easy to blot from your memory, and others are made of pure stamina. I reckon my nerves won't ever come back to center after that one, and to this day I got me a little nervous tick, just back here beneath the ear.

"Where's Rocinante!" I suddenly cried out.

Virgil and me spun about, searching the mound. He was gone.

"They *ate him!*" I says, and Virgil began shaking his head and whispering nuh uh, no lord, this cannot be, over and again, until I found Rocinante staring at me from another mound of mud not thirty feet away.

And poor Rocinante. He looked like he had black stockings on, all four legs and right up to his shoulders. The leeches were so thick on him I feared they'd hollow him out and leave me nothing but skin and a saddle. But for reasons unknown, old Jimmy Brown didn't suffer a bite. He still wore that crown of buttons and flowers, withered as it was, and Virgil claimed it was fraught with voodoo. He said such things were common as cotton back where he came from. Yessir, he'd seen practical hundreds of crowns just like it, knew all about them, and we could rest assured its powers would get stronger and stronger the mangier it looked, till it got so damn potent the daisies would snap clean from his head and leave old Jimmy Brown shining and Godlike.

I said I'd like to see that.

I said that is one thing I'd stick around to see.

PART III

REDEMPTION

M Y MAMA, SHE USED TO TELL IT LIKE THIS: There was once a boy. He didn't like the big things in life. His interests ran such that it was only the little things that mattered, and most of all that boy loved sand. Had him a collection, just a few jars on a shelf, and every day he'd take one down, get his magnifying glass from the drawer and set one granule of sand in the palm of his hand. That boy would study it up, real close, just to see how pretty it was. And when he turned that speck over it was always different. Each granule was a little diamond in his hands and so he burned up most all his youth just fawning over bits of sand.

But along came a day when his mind got to thinking, and he thought, now how about if I got some more sand? If a little is just right, wouldn't a little more be righter? Perhaps one or two more jars would do, and they'd look mighty nice there on the shelf.

So he went and got more. Next thing you know he was bringing it in by the barrel. When that wasn't enough he filled wagons. Soon that boy had collected sand from every desert on earth, having pillaged every beach and sandbank. He had so much of that stuff he filled all the land around him for miles and miles till the horizons were nothing but dunes. And you can probably guess what happened next.

One morning, as a man full-grown, he goes out for a walk through his sand, only to discover he's no longer among those beautiful granules he'd loved so much as a boy, but lost in a desert of his own creation. Drum roll, cymbal splash, the end.

Sometimes I look at this world and see folks grabbing and grabbing like there ain't enough to go around, and next thing you know they're poisoned by it all. Poisoned by needs that ain't really needs. Mama liked to say, "Just a bunch ants, a'drowning in a bowl of honey with bit more sophistication we are."

And when you think you've gotten away from it all, think you're so far beyond the reach of the world and its honeybowl greed, then along come the ants, marching all in a line, ready to carry you back in.

"Hey there!" calls a voice through the mist. Me and Virgil, still standing there on that hump of mud, we peered into the night but were too fire-blind to see a thing. Then I heard the haunting song of a calliope, coming closer, and the creak of several caravans on the move. A whole string of them.

"Jesus, Virgil, we camped right beside the road. Look there, it's not a hundred foot away."

"Well I'll be," says Virgil. The swamp water had risen so high with the rains that the road sat nearly flush with it. It was nothing but a flat serpent of mud slithering through the water, half-invisible till you ran up against it.

"Hey!" came the voice again, and the mist twirled so I could now see a couple fellas on horseback. "What you boys doing down there in the mud?"

"Oh, you know," I says, sharing a look with Virgil. "Just doing our thing."

"Well how come you ain't doing it on the road?"

The fools. "For because of bandits, of course."

I heard one of them chuckle. "Then why'd you go and build a beacon fire?"

The string of caravans creaked to a halt behind those fellas, and on the sideboards of one car I read the words *Plutus Bros. Menagerie and Circus Extraordinaire!* The caravans sat quiet, so quiet I could feel it, but that calliope carried on, and to hear such cheerful piping come floating through that mournful mist was wrong somehow. May as well have been the moaning of ghosts for all the jeebies it gave me.

Suddenly, some trick of the fog brought their whisperings right to us. We could hear them talking like they'd joined our fire.

"Yeah, fodder. But not much else. I doubt their mule is even worth it," says the one.

"Well, what you want to do then? You want to wake Jemester, or just take care 'em ourselves?"

I heard the sound of a peacock, a cry that hung in the air, and then something like a lion's growl lifted from one of the cars.

"They ain't no stagecoach, I'll tell you that. But look at the lip on that one. Jemester's been looking for sideshow material. Hey!" he called down. "You boys stuck or something?"

"I already told you," I says. "We're hiding from bandits."

The two glanced at each other without speaking. Then one of them, he calls out, "Why don't you boys come on over. Introduce you to Jemester Plutus, ringleader of this outfit. I reckon this road's safe to you, long as you're in with Jem."

They smiled, and there wasn't a full head of teeth between them.

Well Jemester Plutus, he was short and stout like a stump of muscle, and bald, but in a way that reminds you of a walrus, bushy mustache and all. He's got wagon-crash laughter and a belly that thumps like a melon, and his eyes sparkled with a showman's zeal. But then he's got this little roll of fat just back of his bald head.

Not a huge problem per se, not a big deal, but Mama, she always said you got to wonder about those folks. Didn't say you couldn't trust them, what's got a roll of fat back of the head. Just that you got to wonder, you know. For caution's sake.

So I was pretty much on my guard when me and Virgil went to meet Jemester back there at the end of the wagon train. He had a caravan all to himself, mighty plush-like. Locked away among the other cars was said to be a lion, one camel, a biddy elephant, a pair ostriches and a peacock, a tiger, a parrot, and a toothless monkey on a leash, but old Jemester's private quarters were lavish with carpets and cushions and pretty pictures on the walls, shelves of knickknacks and artifacts and a good many empty bottles. I saw a buffalo rifle above the door.

"Well hello boys. You two any good at cards?"

Old Jemester sat across a poker table, cozied in a purple overstuffed chair, holding a fan of cards to his breast while he surveyed us with a winning smile and the hues of a falcon just before it goes into a dive. At the table with him was a fella he introduced as Garupti, the world famous snake charmer of Jukharihod. Garupti was a long, skinny-looking fella near as dark-skinned as Virgil, with consumptive bright eyes and cheeks like empty bowls. The bones of his face stretched the skin so tight, you already knew what he was going to look like a year in the grave. But he wasn't dressed like any swami I ever heard of. That Garupti, he wore a gentleman's wool coat with hair oiled back, a holstered Colt at his hip and an empty shot glass on the table before him.

"So?" says Jem. "You two players or what?"

"What can I say?" I answered. "E Pluribus Yoonum."

There was a moment of silence whereupon all eyes narrowed in astonishment at my superior intellect.

"E *what*?" says Jemester.

I thumbed an itch in my nose. "Pluribus Yoonum."

You wouldn't believe how long I'd been waiting to use that one. Got it from the back of a coin. Back of a dime, I believe. Long was the time I'd spent toying with the idea of salting my rhetoric with superfluous languages. *But my dear Monsieur Rudelaire! Certainly you don't mean to imply 'annuit coeptis covus ordo seclorum!' Oh ho ho! Oh ho ho ho ho!* Stringing together all manner of nonsense I'd memorized from the backside of money so's to make myself sound more cosmopolitan-like. Bedazzle my peers. Demoralize my enemies. That kind of thing.

Problem was I can't barely speak English, let alone prattle in jabberwocky.

"E Pluribus…?" he repeated one more time, cocking his head to the side.

"Yoonum," I says again, nodding gravely. "Just means I'm up for about anything."

"Does it now!" And suddenly his mood shifted. With a sly grin, Jem picked a dime from his betting stack, glanced at the backside, then at me again, his grin broadening as he slid it to the center of the table. "What you waiting for then?" he says with a wink. "Ante up! Take a seat!"

So I pretty much blew that one. Me and Virgil, we sat down, but with the disquieting sense that in so doing we were now formally committed to disaster. It was just one those knowings that starts deep down in your belly and then wriggles—*wet tail flapping, blind bulbous head*—up and under your skin. I stole another glance at that rifle on the wall, then at the pistol on Garupti's hip. Jem saw me looking, and his demeanor darkened.

He says, "So. My boys out there think you might be something special, might make sideshow material. But to be honest, I just don't see it. You, there ain't nothing wrong with you," he says to Virgil. Then indicating me, he says, "And plenty folks got a lip hangs worse than yours. I mean, sure it's…" He leaned forward, taking a closer look. "Well. Actually…"

He sat back in his chair. "Are you natural deformed, son?"

"Pardon?"

"Were you born that way, or did you just catch one too many fists in the lip?"

"What, my lip? Nah, it's just from chawing is all. Stuffed it too full as youngin, so's it grew kind of funny."

The meaning of this conversation was somehow eluding me. I turned to Virgil, hoping for his guidance in this matter.

One elbow on the table, a finger pointing lazily in my direction, Jemester says, "Well can you at least put something in it? Like something unusual? If you could, say, pour a whole cup of dice in there, or stuff a rat, I could see folks paying for that. Or if you could stretch it real far, you understand."

"Like how far?"

"Can't say, but at least past your chin. If people are gonna pay, it'll have to be special. Let's just see what you can do."

I pulled my lip down until Virgil yelped like a dog and tried slapping my hand away. Even Jem was cringing back into his seat like he's trying to curl himself into oblivion, for I was trying my best, me figuring if we could just hitch a ride with these folks then we could travel the North Road with impunity, and that was certain to speed us along to Valhalla.

When I finally let go my lip, massaging it back into place, old Jem gave a little clench of the shoulders like he's trying to shake off what he just saw. Then he leaned forward in his seat and pressed his cards flat to the table. "I don't know." He sighed, one hand spreading his brows. "I don't know, Garupti, what do you think? Hey, Garup. Garupti!" But that Garupti fella was passed out cold. His head was flung back in the chair, mouth open and drooling. "God da—Garupti!" Jemester tossed a glass of whiskey in his face but the swami didn't so much as twitch.

"That man," says Jemester in disgust. "He weren't so good at losing cards I'd never pour him a glass. But here's the deal, boys. I can't use you." He leaned back in his chair, which groaned in response, and began counting on his fingers.

"Right now I got me a Siamese twin, a body-twister, a certified cannibal, a fire eater. Let's see, a voodoo princess. A Martian. The oldest woman in the world and a mermaid from the Black Sea. And that's not mentioning my trusty snake charmer here. I just don't see where you two would fit in. I mean you're ugly enough, the both of you is, but unless you got some tragic misfortune I can profit from…" He gave an apologetic grimace, hands open in appeal. "If Garupti here could find his head, I'd ask him what to do with you. But as it is, you're about worthless to me. Ain't nothing left but to rob you blind and leave you stranded in the mud."

He smiled, a heartily robust and gleeful smile.

Still looking me in the eye, he called out loud enough for those fellas outside to hear, "All right boys! Silas! You can come on in!" He opened his mouth to call out again, and then went slack with horror. The blood drained from his face. He stared in convulsive anguish at a woven basket on the empty chair beside Garupti. The rope that held the lid down had worked itself loose, and now a snake came slipping on out.

To be honest, I don't quite know what came over poor Jem. It wasn't a rattler, that snake. Wasn't a copperhead either. What it looked like was just a big old black pinesnake, which is total harmless, excepting this one's neck was all puffed out like an umbrella. So I picked him up and put him back in the basket.

"There now," I says, "The fright is over. There you are." I patted old Jem on the back till he regained his color. Some folks lose total control at the sight of a serpent.

"Just take a few deep breaths now. That's right," I says, and Virgil smirked and pulled his straw hat down tight on his head, saying, "Good old Dannon take care of you, suh. There ain't another boy like him."

And Jemester Plutus looked back and forth between us, the strangest look you ever saw in his eye. I guess he put ample stock in that little rescue for he stood right up and declared from this day forth, me and Virgil were under his personal protection.

———⊰·◈·⊱———

But me and Virgil, we still had to work, is the thing. There wasn't any free ride with the circus. As hired hands we got our own hay-tick bunks in the ostrich/peacock car, got two meals a day and best of all, guaranteed passage up the North Road and out of the Styx. Our duties weren't entirely clear.

"Can you boys work a pistol?"

"Yup," I says, and Virgil nodded in agreement.

"How about a crowd?" says Jem, fingering the roll of fat back of his head. "You know how to work a crowd?"

"Shore," I says. "We can do most anything. And Virgil here can whistle. And fry bacon like a banshee. And I can dowse a well and... yeah, we can do most anything."

"That's what I like to hear," says Jem. "I need men with spirit. We lost one on our last job. Good man. But if we'd had some real brawn along I think we could've handled the situation, you know what I mean?"

"Not too much, no."

He gave me a hearty slap on the back. "Garupti will fill you in," he said. Shouted, actually. He had quite a voice, that Jem. "Garupti knows the ropes. When it comes time, just do exactly what he says and we'll all get along fine. In the meantime," he says, putting an arm around Virgil's shoulders. "I'd like to try a little of this bacon I been hearing about."

Old Jimmy Brown got hitched to a tracing team and spent most his time hauling the tiger's car. Sometimes the performers', but mostly the tiger's car. Except his spirits were up, I'd say, looking mighty pleased to be in the company of other mules. Old Rocky was another story.

"You are hiding your horse?" says Garupti one night when we were all sitting round a fire eating supper.

I says, "Are you asking me, or telling me?" Because I couldn't ever tell, what with that singsong of his, that swami's intonation total throwing me off.

"I am asking you where is your horse at."

"Oh," I says. I had a feeling this might come up. "My horse you mean."

"Yes. The horse."

We always camped in the road there in the swamp, for it was the firmest ground and we seemed about the only ones upon it. We generally had two fires going, for not everyone in the outfit wished to mix. That is to say the performers preferred their own company, though Jem and Garupti sometimes joined in, while the roustabouts and handlers and freaks and such all took their leisure around a second fire, by far the more boisterous of the two.

But old Rocky. Darn that horse. You never met a dumber horse in your life. Nor one more fixed in his ways.

"So where is he?" Garupti asked again, clearly losing patience.

"What, you mean Rocinante?"

"I am talking about your horse!" says Garupti. "Mister Jemester is wanting to know where your horse is!"

"Right, that one," I says, spooning up split peas from my plate. "Welp, that horse and me, we disagreed considerable as to which direction to go. In the end we parted ways."

"You abandoned your horse?" Garupti looked around in alarm, like old Rocky might be waiting in ambuscade. "You left your horse? Here in a swamp?"

I took another mouthful of peas, tipping my head back so they wouldn't fall out when I spoke. "More like he left me." I swallowed. "But on good terms, I'd say. There weren't never much love between us."

Garupti was at a total loss. He checked his pocketwatch. He was always doing that, like he had somewhere to be and had been checking watches all his life, but there was too much novelty in the performance. And he had a way of clicking his jaw when he checked the thing. Grinding his teeth-like, over and over. I wondered if he really knew how to read it.

"Hey Garup!" one of the roustabouts called over. The man was fussing about with the caravan ties. "The wagon tongue's busted on the feed-car again! You want me to move it up front?"

Garupti yammered some pert little orders, his voice high and petulant. The roustabout gave Garupti a casual salute before crawling back under the car with his wrench.

"Mister Jemester will be very displeased," he says in that lilting accent of his, winding his watch with irritation. And I says, "You mean about the wagon tongue, or that horse I turned loose?"

I didn't realize how tall he was, old Garup, and he was even skinnier up close with one of those ugly purple worm-veins that throbbed at his temple. I privately speculated as to whether he charmed serpents in his frockcoat, or sported a turban at the last moment.

He says, "I am meaning, *sir*, even useless animals have a use in this business."

"You figure?" I says. "I can't see how. What's your thoughts on the matter, Virgil?"

"Oh, I reckon Mista Garupti got a point there." Virgil sucked his spoon clean and slipped it back into his pocket. "Why, best thing about a willful horse is they is made of meat. I spect that matters when you got a whole mess of beasts to feed."

There was some laughter round the fire as Eliza, the one-armed and supposed "surviving half" of a Siamese twinship, dumped her plate of peas over the coals. Like most in this outfit, she was tired of Winston's cooking. Despite headlining as a cannibal from the jungles of Borneo, Winston cooked up nothing but plant matter. Boiled roots and tubers, wild-harvest salads. He insisted such cuisine was invigorating for the heart, a fact he'd been researching before dropping out of medical school in Boston due to finances.

Virgil was sitting right beside me on the log, taking up with that ball marble of his. He says to Garupti, shuck shucking away, he says, "Mista Garupti, why don't you set you self down for a spell. You appear mighty worked up over nothing. Here, have you self a good snuff of this." Patting his vest pockets till he found his rosewood box, then sharing it around.

I believe what rankled that swami most was that his serpent had escaped from right under his nose, and it was us that had to rescue Jemester Plutus. But Garupti balanced his ignominy by smoking his little clove cigarettes—cloves, you will recall, being one of the two smells that makes me retch like a swillbelly. I was just sitting there beside the fire, touching at the shiny skin around the scab on my arm when I first caught a whiff of the stuff.

On the instant, I leaned forward and heaved between my knees. I spat like a drunkard, wiped my mouth on a wagon rag, sat up straight, and before I could speak, was thrown forward and heaved again.

Head still down, I waved that smoke away. Which was a mistake, I see now, for soon as that swami saw it, he gave me a wicked little grin.

From that moment on we were foes.

<hr />

How anyone could encounter so much swamp amidst so much mountains, I do not know. The bogs seemed to go on for days. I began to suspect we were just going back and forth, searching for stragglers to entertain. Then at last it happened. The earth firmed up, the waters gave way and we found ourselves working our way east, up the East Road now, same way Tally would be headed. Looking out my window, I saw hills to either side. Then genuine mountains.

"Gear 'em up!" came the call, then again, further away. "Gear 'em up!" I lay in my bunk, listening to someone walk down the line and pounding the side of each caravan. "Town approaching! All hands to!"

Me and Virgil, we rarely caught much sleep. The bunks were an amenity, but an ostrich is a rather large animal far as quartermates go, and two of them in a tight space will keep you vigilant. Furthermore, they were like to peck you when they took the mood, and unless you've been hit in the forehead by a beak of those proportions you just cannot appreciate the disconcertment it will cause, especially when you are trying to slumber. Imagine yourself laying there, eyes closed, just waiting for the next knock on the head. They hit like a shovel, case you are wondering.

And that damn peacock. He could cry for hours. Just soon as I'd fall asleep I'd hear one of those ostriches get to rapping at the planks, looking for whatever, rapping and rapping, and then that peacock would get so excited he'd shoot his fan, slapping you in the face with it because quarters were so packed. He couldn't turn around without smacking you twice, and then those ostriches would get to knocking their heads around under the bunk till you felt about ready to do the same. It was a madhouse, I tell you, with birdcalls and feathers and everything climbing onto the bed, and me and Virgil just trying to catch a few winks.

Socially, however, we were doing considerably better. Ever since Virgil took to the cooking, folks were treating us mighty respectable. Course he never cooked anything but bacon, but we lived off it like manna and the outfit's morale took wings.

"What I want to know," says Eliza one night as she gazed philosophically at the bacon in her fist, "is how he gives it that oak-barrel taste. And how come it falls apart in your mouth like stew meat."

Someone else declared Virgil's bacon tasted just like learning to swim, whereas Winston, the vegetarian cannibal, he argued it wasn't swimming they tasted, as such, but rather the intrinsically transcendent drive of the human condition.

But getting back to our travels, I daresay I was looking forward to the prospect of labor if it meant escaping this bayou and getting that much closer to Valhalla. The East Road got drier as we climbed up into that valley. Most the trees were balding. Their leaves scaled the road. At the mouth of a hollow, the East Road branched off and we trundled up a little path till we were creaking right into a village. That evil calliope took up and townsfolk stood hushed in the street, the odd child crying in arms. We were a creepy troupe if the looks of townsfolk spoke true. Not one of them so much as waved. But then Jemester set the tumblers loose and a crier climbed atop the lead caravan. From a scroll that hung to his feet, the crier announced 'the atypical and stupendous arrival of The Plutus Bros. Menagerie and Circus Extraordinaire!' That little elephant trumpeted from somewhere back of the train and suddenly the townsfolk were cheering, spellbound, rearing for the thrill of a circus come to town.

To the accompaniment of the calliope we looped around in the cul-de-sac at the end of the hollow, which was a sight and chore given the train we were hauling. Then we creaked right back through town, just as we'd come, waving and tumbling till we spilled onto the East Road again. In like manner we visited two more coves, both nearby, making our dubious appearance in their villages before creaking our way up to the valley's terminus where the East Road opened onto a meadow, all of it frosted by a crescent moon.

Here in the meadow Jemester ordered a halt, and instantly every caravan door flung wide and every hand piled out, throwing tents up fast as you can. While they hammered in stakes and hoisted huge canvases the performers climbed into costume, shouldering each other before the mirrors fitted to the sidewalls of their caravans. Buffoons were sent back to lead the townsfolk like herds while the handlers began unloading the beasts.

Lacking direction of any kind, me and Virgil had us a nice set on the steps of the ostrich car, more or less stunned with fascination. Within an hour's time, that meadow was transformed into a carnival. There was a menagerie tent twice as big as a meeting house, concession stands, house of freaks, a gypsy gazebo and then a curious pavilion, 'The Big Top', they called it, that had a single, narrow entrance at the front.

Just last night, Elmer, a temperate fella with watery eyes who was always looking after the livestock, he got sent to our car to discuss a business deal that interested old Jem. Seems Jemester had heard Jimmy Brown qua-ha'ing in his traces and figured with a few stripes of paint he could have himself a genuine zebra. By the sound of it, Jem had spent a considerable amount of time, all alone in his caravan, yearning and plotting for such a thing. And so Elmer, who's not the shrewdest of hagglers, he came over and says, "I got me instructions to offer you ten dollars for your mule there. If you won't take that, then I'm to offer twelve and then twelve-fifty. But under no circumstances am I to pay you more'n fifteen."

Virgil gave it a think, and then pointed out the daisy-button crown upon the mule's head, explaining to the man that Jimmy

Brown here was likely to become a supernatural deity before long. We were just waiting for the hex to take full effect. And once that happened, there just wasn't any call for vending as the very notion was sure to offend nature.

Good old Elmer saw the logic immediate. He agreed that tampering with nature, not to mention hexes, was a sticky business at best and tipped his hat before bidding us good night. But now old Jimmy had set up a considerable qua-ha, and Jemester came over on his own, wanting to know if Jimmy could be borrowed for a time.

"How long?" I says, exchanging glances with Virgil.

"I want him in the Big Top," says Jem, "when we lead everyone in. He's too much an attraction to leave him loitering around out here. It's challenging enough getting all the folks into the tent at once. Can I count on him? Is he dependable?"

"Well, sometimes."

Jemester had come marching out of his caravan in a red-velvet vest, a battered old top hat and jodhpurs that fit tight as socks. Suddenly distracted, he cried out, "Garupti!" He waved the man over. "Garupti! What are you doing? Why aren't you dressed? I need you to get these two gentlemen going! Come on, come on!"

Why he chose Garupti as his right-hand man was a constant source of mystery. It is true that having a petulant, sniveling puppet at your side makes you look all the more competent in a crowd, but even the roustabouts deferred to Garupti with lip-trembling smiles.

"I am dressed, sir," he says in his indignant singsong, touching a hand to his pocketwatch for reassurance.

"No, no, no, no. No! We've been through this before!" Jem stabbed at the man's chest with his snubbed cigar. "How many times do I got to tell you, Garup? People don't want to see no aristocrat taming snakes! They want a swami, for God's sake! A genuine Hindoo!"

"But I am agnostic."

"I don't care what you are! Folks are coming to see you in your natural habitat. Now go get into costume before I give these two your job. Go on!"

"Damn he's stubborn," says Jem when he left, casually pinching at that little roll back of his head. I believe he adored it. "Listen. I don't have much time. Folks are already piling in here like cattle, so here's what I need you to do. First of all, you got to go find Elmer. Tell him he's got to fit you out with a couple pistols. Get yourselves some pistols, but here's the thing. Once we get everyone on site, you're gonna start to see the roust-abouts guiding everyone into the Big Top. That's your cue. Once everyone's inside, I'll be requiring you two gentlemen to guard the door."

"Guard for what?" I says.

And old Jem, he relights his cigar and flicks the match. "Bandits, of course. Can't have bandits despoiling our customers now, can we? Now I'll expect you to pop your heads inside the tent once or twice, just to let the folks see you're there. And let them see your guns, of course, so they understand they're protected. Makes them feel safe, you understand. So its pop your heads in. Show them your guns. You got that?"

"Yessuh," says Virgil. "Just show 'em our guns." And old Jemester Plutus gave us a proud wink before turning to bark orders at a couple handlers. They were trying to lead a camel that didn't want to be led, so that beast kept sitting down, folding his knees in a way that was total unnatural. And for some reason seeing it, those legs just doing it all wrong, it gave me a powerfully dose of what you call a 'foreboding.' A sinister pre-sentiment, is what it was.

I turned to Virgil, more than a little uneasy. As if to convince myself, I says aloud, "Boy, I guess this one's simple."

I just couldn't bear one more blow. One more trainwreck to the soul.

"Yes sir, Virgil, I don't reckon there's an easier job in this here outfit."

And to my momentary relief, Virgil was good enough to agree. "You might be right, suh," he says, scratching the white fuzz at his jaw. "And you know what else? I do believe Valhalla is just over them hills. Over them hills and a little ways, but mighty close, suh. We getting mighty close, as I can smell it."

And that exact thing, that thing right there, I believe that was the core of my troubles. For I could not smell it. Valhalla felt further than ever. It was like I couldn't hardly see it any more, just this tiny light in my mind, a light at the end of a tunnel, a coin of light receding into dark. It gave me this restless, melancholy, saber-edged angst like I might never catch up with my Madder.

Me and Virgil, we walked down the train, calling out for Elmer, my bearing that of a man who knows his days are numbered.

"I don't know, Virgil. I don't want to wake up some morning and… and find out my past is bigger than my future. And I got nothing to show for it."

"Then don't."

I turned to him. "But how? How Virgil?"

He didn't say nothing.

I clucked my tongue and rubbed my brow. "Something's coming down," I mumbled. "I just know it. I can feel it."

I felt like a man walking to the gallows. Like my point of return was somewhere three years back on a document co-signed by the devil, and now, just like this caravan on a single-wide path, there was nowhere left to go but forward.

"Well, screw it," I says aloud. "Just screw it all."

"Yessuh, I hear that."

We called out for Elmer a few times, knocked on a few doors. Reached the last car and doubled back. I was on my tippy-toes, peeking through the window of a caravan, Virgil doing the same beside me, when I heard someone say, "Psst!" It came from the shadows between two cars. When I turned to look, I saw someone hiding there, sort of swaying side to side.

"Psst!" I heard again, and me and Virgil crept closer to inspect. Just then, that someone stepped full in the moonlight, and I saw it was none other than Levi Such-and-Such, sodden bane of my days.

———◆———

I barely had time to get over my shock at seeing the old fool when that Levi comes right out and warns us, "Welp, I hope you boys is got your danger pants on."

He stood there, staring at us, wretched as ever, like something blown out from the nostril of doom.

He says, "You boys got no idea atall what you're into. No idea. I suggest you two skedaddle before the real trouble hits. Shhh! Quiet, don't let no one see us a'talking. I was a part of this here troupe once, before I took to the Lord. They see me here and they'll shoot all three of us standing."

I asked what in hell he was talking about, showing him no more tolerance than he was owed, and he says me and Virgil were in with thieves. Said this here outfit was known to clean a town out in a single showing, luring them in all at once and then burgling them blind. "You got to understand," he continued. "The life of an itinerant showman is chockfull of deprivations. It's only natural that a circus should turn to piracy in hard times."

So I says, I told that old tosspot with his bloodshot eyes, I says, "You ain't nothing but a turncoat and a sot. You deceived us once already, and we got no reason to trust you now. Why'd you come here atall even?"

"Well boys, I won't lie to you," says Levi. "The congregation, they've about had it with my benders. They never was too partial to my drinking, failing to appreciate the God given benefits of corn-liquor-acumen and how by its grace alone I have penetrated the deepest mysteries of our universe! Sons a bitches. Anyhow, bottomline, I'm on my own now and a little short on funds, so's I got to put in favors wherever I can."

"Still working that karma racket then, are you? Helping folks out in hopes of reimbursement from heaven?" He shrugged in a way that says, *What can you do? Every man got to work.*

But I just couldn't see how a man could go staggering through this world belly-first and dissipated and rightly expect compensation. And so I says, because I really wanted to know, I says to him, "Ain't you worried about your eternal soul?"

That Levi lifted a finger, which quavered a little, and he says, "So happens I've given—"

Brought a fist to his chest, stupendous belch.

"—so happens I've given some thought to that topic, that very topic, phosopher that I am. And I figures it like this. Seeing as how eternity ain't just around the bend, so to speak, or even likely to get here atall, how can you rightly compare it to those pleasures what's immediate? You see what I'm saying? It's a question of now against never. Take that there swami, for a sample." He indicated Garupti, who was now standing before a mirror and wrapping a strip of white cloth about his head. And Levi, he says, "Now in Indya, your average Indyan, he goes to town ever Sunday to get his head shaved, not like this fella here. No sir, he shaves his head *now* for to have beautiful locks when he gets to heaven, you see what I'm saying?

"All of 'em?" I says. "What about the women?"

"The women?" he says. "Oh them too, I suppose. Yeah. Yeah, even them! Fact ever one of them is bald! The whole damn country. And ever body wears skirts so's the men and women look the same exact and you can't tell the difference between them."

"There is a way."

"Course there is! But you see my point, right?"

"I sort of forget."

"Huh. All right then. All right, well lets take your cow," says Levi, forcing the point. "Or even better a goat. Now a goat, you must have noticed how goats, if you're looking at them real close, how their eyes is *square*. And why do you suppose *that* is?"

"I got no idea."

Levi didn't seem to either, falling into a distracted quiet, stumped-like, scratching his head as though he'd lost his line of thinking. "Anyhow, you boys best skedaddle. That's my word to you. I done my part, which karma can't dispute. What you choose to do with it is your business. So long to you all." He turned to go, but I spun him back around by the shoulder.

"Where is he?" I says.

"Where is who?" I saw the spinning about was a bit much for old Levi. I steadied him with a hand and says, "Will Lawson. Where's Will? You led him to us last time. I won't have you do it again."

"Oh you don't have to worry about that one," he says with a chuckle, the way you might if old Will Lawson were already dead and the joke was on me for asking. So I says, "Why? You kill him?"

"Oh no," says Levi. "But I hear he was seen down in the swamp aways back. Tromping through muck with some nag of a horse. I'd stake my gizzard he's turned back around already, a'headed home the way he come."

And I'd have taken that bet if I thought Levi would pay. For I knew old Will Lawson would not turn around. That man was much aggrieved, and had come too far already to quail before a stretch of mud.

"Enough chatter. I've said my piece. You two is on your own."

Levi turned to go, and I let him this time. As he slunk back into the shadows, I says to Virgil, "You reckon he's telling the truth this time?"

Virgil clicked his tongue and shook his head real slow. "Don't like it, but I believe he is."

"Me too," I says. "And that means we best quit this place and get on up to Valhalla before we're dubbed and hung for highwaymen."

Virgil set his jaw, which was a new look for him. "Oh, I am in agreement, suh. I'm in agreement, but we ain't going nowhere without old Jimmy."

"Course!" I says. "Yeah, of course." Though I'm ashamed to say now, I had forgotten about Jimmy.

"He is fixing for old Valhalla much as you and me," says Virgil. "We got to bust him out the Big Top."

"Certainly," I says. But folks were already piling in. Hundreds of them, looked like, roustabouts herding them through the tentflaps. "Yeah, sure," I says. "We'll get old Jimmy, only we got to hurry, is all. And we'll be needing some sort of stratagem."

"Stratagem, suh?"

I was afraid of that. I felt my face go a little flush, for stratagem happens to be another of those words, like bourgeois and communiqué, that I know only from books and secretly suspect I'm mispronouncing it.

"You know, like a plan, Virgil. We'll need a plan. For Jem'll get suspicious on us if we just go and ask for old Jimmy back. We got to think this thing through, you know. Like, we got to think it through."

"I see what you mean."

"Yeah. Yeah, so we'll need a plan."

"Yessuh. A plan."

"Yes. Exactly." Fingering my beard. "Exactly what we need."

"So what you got in mind, suh?"

"Yeah, nothing actually. Nothing's coming, how about you?"

"Well suh…" Virgil dug round in his coat till he found his pocketknife. It was practically rusted shut. He opened it up, working the hinge, greasing it with his own spittle while laying out the closest thing he had to a stratagem.

"That's a fine stratagem," I says, pronouncing it different this time and watching Virgil's face for confirmation. "Yes, that's a right fine plan. You're good at this Virgil. Only let *me* sneak into the tent, and you stay at the door. For I am haloed."

"You what, suh?"

I was still working out the kinks, but I had a new theory. "I'm haloed, you know. Protected? Yeah, you see, a fella can only get hit with so much calamity in a lifetime, so my quota's all filled up. I'm safe now."

Virgil winced with uncertainty. "I don't know, suh. I always thought of you more like a, like a bank of it, you know?" He chewed his lip with regret. "I mean, ain't none of my business bringing you down, suh, but I already been wondering..."

A bank. A whole bank of it. I hadn't considered that. I wasn't entirely certain I should. After all those bumps and bruises and general crashing about, not to mention the endless lamentations of my soul, well you could say I'd grown a bit fragile in my plight, a cracked porcelain bowl. You wouldn't want to handle me too rough about now. In fact, one more hard tap on the rim and odds were I'd go straight to pieces.

<hr />

Even over the crescendos of wave-crash-applause, I swear I could hear Jemester's voice from outside the Big Top, filling the place up, practically bulging the tent sides with the bulk of sound. Me and Virgil, we never located any pistols, but we poked our heads in through the doorflaps like we were supposed to. I saw folks packed shoulder to shoulder, heads tipped back to watch the trapeze girl. Somewhere in the middle of the crowd would be old Jem, still hollering away with that battered top hat held high, his showman's voice bigger than life.

"Can you see Jimmy?" Virgil whispered.

"Nope. I think I hear him though. You hear that? He's on the far side of the tent."

No one paid me any notice as I slipped inside, skirting around the edge of the tent. There were multiple acts happening at once. A small crowd was gathered around a fella that guzzled fire, and another was gawking at Winston, who now had a bone through his nose as he grunted like an animal and rattled the bars of his cage. Finally I saw Garupti, sitting crosslegged in his turban, no shirt, dot of paint on his forehead and goddammit if he didn't look total cryptic and terrifying. He played on a little gourd-flute while that hooded pinesnake perched up on an elbow and swayed to the movement of it. Folks were enthralled. I crept right past till I came to another crowd, decidedly smaller, this one standing around looking confounded as all hell while old Jimmy Brown qua-ha'd from the end of his tether.

"What you reckon he is?" someone asked, chewing a piece of straw. Poor old Jimmy had been painted with stripes.

"Why he's a, he's a horse of some kind, ain't he?"

A third fella, he says around the stem of his corncob pipe, "Got more a mule's look to him. If you was to ask me. But what in tarnation's wrong with the thing?"

I shouldered right in, saying, "Hidy there, hidy there folks. Your pardon please." Old Jimmy still wore his crown. I crouched down by the stake and tried to work his tether loose when suddenly I felt something like an icy finger dragging down my spine. It was the cold brush of doom. It was finally here.

"What's wrong with your horse?" says a little girl, still holding her daddy's hand.

"Oh, he's had himself a time," I says without looking up. The knot wasn't coming loose, so I tried yanking up the stake.

"Is he sick?"

Nearby, I heard a final round of applause and then Garupti's crowd began breaking up. His act finished, folks were already drifting over. "No," I says to the girl, trying my damdest to hurry. "No, he is just daunted is all."

"Well what's he do then? I mean, how come you got him in a circus if he can't do nothing but bark?"

It was about this time things went bad.

I turned to the girl, gearing up to reply, when all of the sudden I smelled something. Something familiar. Before my mind even had time to name it, I'd doubled forward and retched.

All across that poor little girl's dress. She screeched. Her daddy gasped and swelled up like a balloon of wrath. From down on my knees, heaving up my guts, I caught a glimpse of Garupti standing in the crowd, smoking on his clove cigarette. He gave me that wicked little grin before turning to the girl's father, who was verging purple with violence contained, and says to him in his singsong accent, "I apologize for this man's behavior. He is doing this all the time to the little children." He dragged on his cloves, blew the smoke my way. "I only wish he would stop following them around." And as I crumpled forward to empty my guts once again, I heard someone growl 'damn ya', and then a great ringing silence as a giant fist cudgeled me upside the ear.

And so I lay there for a good while on that bed of straw and dung, just listening to the ringing of bells. I pondered the nature of love and salvation, the elusive temperament of red, all of those phantoms that flounced at my periphery.

This wasn't the first time I'd found myself laid out in the muck, and a good part of me was inclined to stay put. For I was beaten, you see. I was finally down for the count. I'd hit rock-bottom and didn't want to climb up, for experience showed I'd only get knocked back down.

But the other part, there was another part of me that always knew this was coming. Had been waiting, even. Except that part didn't want to get up either.

Old Jimmy qua-ha'd for my attention, on and on, till I threw a fistful of straw and opened my eyes. I sat up with a grunt and curried the straw from my hair. Then my beard. Found my hat.

Which was flattened. My left ear was so hot it near scalded my hand. I looked around and saw the girl and her father were gone, but didn't truly care one way or another. It's all the same when you're dead, which is what I was inside.

Just dead. Nothing. Black. Blah. I sat there, evaluating my reasons to stand.

The crowd began to roar and I heard Jem's voice rising to a pitch like he was cranking them up for a finale. Then Garupti crouched down before me, a smug grin on his face. "You were not wise to be causing me trouble."

I nodded, spit between my knees.

"Now go back to the door," he says. "Before I tell Mister Plutus you have been shirking."

I shook my head, staring numbly at the straw that was dung-glued to the tread of my boots. "Can't."

"What do you mean?"

"I mean I can't," I says. "I quit."

Garupti scowled. "It is too late for that. Look." He pointed to the roustabouts, each of them armed, taking up positions around the audience. "The final act is about to begin."

"Nah," I says, standing up, slapping the dust from my hat and putting it on. "I quit. Ever thing. Me and this here mule is going solo." I pulled a wagon rag from my pocket. Looking Garupti in the eye, I blew my nose so hard my ears squeaked.

Garupti's face tightened into an ugly grimace, cheekbones jutting. One eye quivered creepily with indignation. "Wait here," he hissed, and then waded back into the crowd, a good foot taller than the rest, his turban bobbing and bobbing away.

When he turned around I went back for Jimmy's tethers. I gave them another yank but that stake still wouldn't budge. I was done playing around. I popped open Virgil's pocketknife and cut the rope short, and then slashed a long tear in the tent behind us, which was close enough to our original plan.

"Hold it! Git back here!" someone shouted. I turned around, but they weren't git-backing at me. I heard a pistol shot somewhere, then another. Screams and hollering.

"NOBODY MOVE!" Jemester's voice rose up like a thunderous genie, and everybody in that tent fell silent. Not one soul shifted as Jem laid down the law. Except me, for I squeezed through that slash and yanked Jimmy's rope till he came stumbling on through.

"What took you so long!" whispers Virgil, good old Virgil, who was already there and waiting. He smiled those big white teeth and swatted Jimmy with his straw hat. And then me and him and Jimmy Brown On A Rope, we snuck back up into those mountains.

⊰•◦✦◦•⊱

But something had changed. I believe a lightness began working its way into my step as we blazed up into that stand of mountain sumac. Once you hit bottom, there's nowhere left to go but up. The moon was low and gave me a sidewise grin. A little breeze chuckled the leaves in our path.

"Virgil?"

"Yessuh."

I paused. "How come you're always doing that?"

"Doing what, suh?"

"Calling me *sir*. How come you call me that? You know I ain't your sir."

"I call everybody suh, suh."

"Yeah," I says. "Yeah, but you're laughing at them when you do it."

And he says, "Ain't laughing at you."

Through a break in the trees the moonlight hit Virgil full in the face, and it seemed to me that all along, through every step of our journey, there was something he was trying hard to tell me. And for a moment there, I believe I understood what it was. I believe I saw it in the way his broad face glowed up, the way his blue eyes came alive in the moon, and then we were sunk deep in the shade of trees again. "That still don't answer my question," I says.

And he says, "Maybe you question don't need no answering."

Virgil sighed and let himself down on a log beside the path. I sat beside him, marveling at just how much racket a mule can make trying to masticate a mouthful of grass. You'd think it was apples and sand by the sound of it.

I picked at the peeling bark on the log. "So what you gonna do about old Jimmy here?" I says, for we'd already splashed through a stream and those stripes of paint didn't want to come off. "You reckon he's a zebra for real now?"

Virgil had taken to whistling again, close as we were to Valhalla. The higher notes echoed back from the woods, eerie-like, but familiar too, like that chandelier that still hung above his brow. And I have to say watching Virgil right then, just whistling peacefully away, was about the closest I ever came to understanding why a wolf sings to the moon.

"Oh, can't say for sure," says Virgil after a moment's deep thought. "Can't say as I know what it is, what makes a thing real. Only that it got nothing to do with the wishing for it."

And I realized what it was, this thing that was changing. I was no longer struggling to get free of damnation. It's like when Mama used to say, "Leave all them weeds alone, Dannon. For you know a weed, left alone, turns to gold with the sun."

Looking back I can see that giving up hope, a fella can set aside all his reasons for fighting and running and general miserabling about. Fact he can just sit right down, simple as a child, and finally enjoy all the pretty colors of hellfire.

———◆———

That night, me and Virgil camped on a hill. I believe I heard Rascal far off in the distance. We built up a fire and roasted two squirrel on a spit, flames popping and licking the sky. And we were quiet, for I believe both of us had some sense of the events soon to come, but neither of us knew quite what to say. So we said little, just feeding the fire. Then Virgil, after I thought he'd fallen asleep, he shifted about, dipping into that rosewood snuffbox I gave him. We were so close now, he says, if we was to fire a gun, folks in Valhalla was sure to hear it.

"How close?" I says, for that meant little to me. The strange carriage of sound in these mountains was ever a cause for my bafflement.

So Virgil, he snorts the snuff from his thumbnail, gives an inaudible 'ah', and then says for answer, "See that down there, suh?" He pointed down into the misty glen below. "You can't see it now, for all them trees and fog, but that's where we is headed. That is good old Valhalla right under you nose."

"Right there?" I says, sitting up straight. "You mean right out there, just below us?" I couldn't believe it. "Well what are we doing up here then? We ought to a keep on!"

Virgil fell back on his elbows, and I saw that old gleam in his eye. "Cause I want you to see it all in the morning," he says. "Ain't nothing like coming on to Valhalla, first thing in the morn, sighting it from atop these here hills."

Then he got right in under that hat of his so you couldn't see his eyes, and went to shuck shucking away at that ball marble. Myself, I stretched out beside the fire, thinking about as hard as one can without injury.

Now of all my childhood memories, I reckon my fondest is of being abandoned in the woods. I spent two days hungry and wandering, cold and tired, but otherwise soaked in a tranquility like I've never known. For two whole days I lived in a world forged of cotton. Goodness converged upon whatever I touched. It danced a jig in the hollow of my footprints. Ironic then, that it is the only event Pa ever apologized for.

When he came home from fishing without me, Mama asked what in hell he was doing, leaving his only son unaided in the woods? Pa said in all his life he'd never known of a boy so whiny and indolent as the one reared right here in this cabin, and I couldn't go on forever expecting to be taken care of. It was high time I learned some accountability.

And Mama says, "Phineas Lereaux, that boy is just turned four. What is it you expect him to account for?"

And Pa says, "Welp, I am sorry, but he got to learn sometime. And I expect he'll—"

"Excuse me?"

"What?"

"*Say it again…*" says Mama, who's got that look in her eye. "I want to hear you say it one-more-time."

And Pa, he shifted in his seat, for he knew that look well, then leaned forward to pick at the birds-eye grain in our table. "I am just saying I'm sorry but—"

"But? Did you say *but?*" Mama threw a finger in his face. "It got a heart for feeling and hands to make amends, but there ain't no *but* in 'I'm sorry!' You got that Phineas? You certain now? Good! Now go find that boy and tell him so."

So Pa, he went searching all through the Blue Honey Mountains. And I watched him searching, watched him from high in a tree. But it didn't occur to me to say anything on it, for in the spirit of misadventure, I didn't know I needed any finding.

It was evening when Pa finally caught me unaware as I lay flush on a boulder in the middle of a stream, overlooking the ledge of a little waterfall. For hours I had lain there upon that cool stone, my belly rushing and leaping and wandering free like the water droplets pouring from my eyes.

Next thing I know Pa had me by the scruff of the neck, his eyes throbbing with rage. Then he set me down on my feet, collected himself on a breath, and says to me, "There ain't no but in I'm sorry."

For many years I thought that's what you said to a person when you caught them unsuspecting in the woods. Except now I know different. Now I understand every person alive is in some way searching for redemption. For forgiveness. Except forgiveness isn't something you can give, or get. It's just something you are. And once you are, everything else is just words, is all.

Just a bunch words.

When I woke and sat up beside the smoking coals of our fire, I saw Virgil was still shucking away like he'd been at it all night, still leaning back against Jimmy's saddle. But he stopped at that moment and turned the ball marble in his hand, looking it over all thoughtful and peace-like. A profound hush crept across the features of his face, and I understood he was finally finished.

It was done.

After forty some years, his craft was complete, a perfect thing in an imperfect world. And as he held that ball up, his face caught the light of the sun for it was just peeking up over the rim of the mountains.

⟫━◆━⟪

It was dawn that spilled, gathering up the peaks in a pool of violet light. I felt my heart fill my throat. I turned to Virgil, my guide. I was breathless.

"What's it mean?"

"Means the night all over," he says, standing up and stretching, giving nary a hint that this wasn't just any old dawn. But then he took the few steps to my side, squatting down before me. He turned that ball marble slowly in his hand, looking it over one last time. It appeared he was searching for the words to give it to me.

But then he says, "I want you to give this my Miss Odessa."

I was stunned. "All right, Virgil," I says, trying not to show my unease. "I'll give it to her like you says. But where is it you're gonna be, that you can't do it yourself?"

He took off his straw hat and scratched the bald spot on his head. "All goes well," he says, "I be right there beside you. Right there in old Valhalla." He set that ball marble in my hand and then put on his hat as he stood, and I swear his hues were pure spattered with a whole opera of light, and I hadn't the first clue how to respond.

So I sat there numbed, holding that ball in my lap, staring after him as he commenced lugging Jimmy's saddle. Feeling the dead weight of it, I finally looked down at that ball. I could see at a glance it was flawless. I guarantee in all your life, you have never seen anything like it. No matter which way you turned it, its curves were exactly the same with only the marbling swirls of the stone to tell you different. I turned it over and over, listening to the soft creak of leather as Virgil got those saddlebags over Jimmy. I heard the sound Jimmy makes when he's real pleased with a treat, then I heard the nicker of another horse blowing its lips.

I looked up. Virgil was gone, having hidden himself with uncanny stealth. Will Lawson sat upon a skinny old roan, rifle laying across the leather chaps on his lap. He was chewing something as he watched me from his saddle, chewing a seed or something, which he spat loudly as he gave me a grin. "Ah ah. Nope. Don't bother getting up." He slung himself down from his mount, slow and sure. "I'll just be shooting you back down as it is."

So I sat there. I watched him stroll over to our fire and casually kick through the coals, poke at the dark pile of Virgil's coat with his rifle tip. "Well I'm real pleased to see what you done to my mule there. Turning him into a clown and all. Brings pure joy to my heart, but what I want to know is, where's my nigra got to?"

"Gone."

"Uh huh." He spat another seed. "Gone where?"

He looked me dead in the eye, knowing I had nowhere to run, and I says, "Give me one of your guns."

He gave me a baleful look. "Now why in hell would I do that?"

And I says, "Because you got two there, counting the one at your hip. Not much sense in that, is there?"

His eyes went hard. He turned his head, spat a whole mouthful of seeds and then jerked the rifle-butt to his shoulder and drew a bead.

Before he could pull the trigger, I says, "I'd do the same for you, if you was in a position."

"I ain't in no position," he says, squinting one eye down the barrel. Appeared he was aiming for my mouth.

"No, you ain't in a position," I says, "toting them two guns to my none."

He hesitated for a breath, then dropped the rifle to his hip and snarled, "What, are you like appealing to my honor? I'm here to hunt you! You got that? Now shut your mouth and prepare to die."

"All right," I says. "Have it your way."

"By God I will." He lifted the rifle to take another bead on my face, and then dropped it just as quick. "Sonuva—" he cursed, kicking the grass in frustration. "All right, here." He stamped over to me, holding out his pistol. "Here. Now get up goddammit so I can shoot you proper."

I stood up, took the pistol. Turned it over. I should of known I'd get the pepperbox. "Is it loaded?" I pulled back the hammer, checked the action. Which was about bad as I expected.

"It's a gun, and that's all you need to know." For the third time, old Will Lawson drew up that rifle and took his aim. He says, "Now turn your back. And walk ten paces."

I started out, but after two-three steps I stopped and says over my shoulder, "Ain't really a duel if you got that rifle a'trained upon me already."

"Walk."

"Well, are you going to even allow me turn around?"

"I said walk."

I walked. But before I reached ten, I heard the distinct ruckus of someone charging through bushes. I turned just in time to see Virgil rush out, leap for Will Lawson, and Will's rifle swing round like a club. It caught Virgil direct in the head.

And it broke my heart, the sound it made. The kind of sound that left nothing in the way of hope.

A groan came up from the floor of my soul as Virgil, my guide to the end, crumpled bonelessly to the ground with a whump. Will Lawson stood over the body a moment, still panting with surprise. So I took aim and fired, which was a misfire of course. And then old Will Lawson shot me down.

⟾◆⟻

First thing I did when I came-to and realized I wasn't dead was, I lifted my head to look for Virgil. Only he was right there, right there beside me. Will had dragged his body beside mine.

So there he was, my friend, face down in the dirt. The blood had flowed right out back of his head and mixed in a puddle of my own. Our blood, all mixed together in the dirt. Now it was just me and that ball marble he carved.

I do not know how long I lay there on that hill, waiting for my wound to staunch. I grew powerful thirsty, and my tongue swelled up big as a gopher with my waterskin nowhere in sight. But I was alive. The musketball had passed straight through my shoulder, leaving me permeable but otherwise in a piece.

At some point, I looked over and saw Jimmy standing there, snagging up grass with those lips, just waiting for me and Virgil to wake. I had a vague recollection of Will leaving him behind. Happened just before I passed out. Old Will had tried to bring Jimmy under a rope, but the rifle crack had spooked him, not to mention the smell of our blood. Jimmy Brown was about consolable as a storm, bucking out like a mule turned bronco. In the end, Will threw down his rope with a froth of curses, stole the boots from my feet and rode out of camp, leaving me and Virgil vol Krie for dead.

And now the morning mist had cleared, sucked back into the mountains, and Valhalla lay shining below. I could see it, just as Virgil had promised. That glorious home he was ever after.

I dug his grave right there on the hill. Took a while, as I had nothing but my hands and a stick. And I had nothing to wrap him in, no shroud at all, which troubled me more than you might expect. I didn't have it in me to throw dirt on his face, so in the end I covered it with his hat, that beautiful straw hat, before shoving the soil back over him with both hands. Then I piled it with rocks to keep the varmints away. His own boots I set atop the grave.

But before I did all that, I did one last thing. Something I expect you might have guessed already. I took out that folded page from my pocket, the one from old Throckmorton's book, the one telling about dead heroes going to meet Odin in Valhalla, well I took it out and read it aloud. I read it to Virgil vol Krie, messenger and guide, then placed it in the breast pocket of his coat.

To this day I don't know just how much he knew, or whether he ever considered himself the man that I did. But in the end he found Valhalla, if at the end of a rifle, just as I found it on the backside of night.

⟫◆⟪

I kept a vigil over his grave that night, if sleeping beside it could be called such a thing. I owed Virgil the respect, but was too weak from the gunshot to stay awake. I know he would've understood.

It rained just before dawn. I woke up to the smell of wet woods in my nose, the sound of water drip-dripping from boughs. The sun peaked up, though the sky stayed dark, and the mist refused to burn off. I cooked up the last of Virgil's bacon, eating it while overlooking Valhalla. And it tasted like your common bacon, just salt and crunch, making it the worst and last bacon I ever ate.

The shot wound through my shoulder was surprisingly clean and mostly unproblematic, just a spicy ache when I moved my arm up or down. And there was the big old bruise on my chest, which I figured would match another on my back where the bullet exited just above my wingbone. More than anything I was just tired. I drank lots of water. Sometimes the sun peeked through and I napped in its shaft. I ate up its warmth like food.

You might think I'd have been feeling powerful anxious, having arrived at last, thinking I'd be in a hurry go down and find Madder. Truth is, I was quite satisfied to sit there beside Virgil's grave. I felt no hurry at all, like I could still see the smile on his face and hear the eerie echo of his whistle, and then I'd catch myself staring direct at the sun. But I'd promised Virgil I would deliver that ball marble, so late that afternoon, after a splash bath in a stream, I saddled up Jimmy Brown On A Rope and headed down the switchback path that wound its way into town.

On the road leading in, a wagon passed me by. The driver yah'd his mules and raised his hand in greeting, and I believe there were tears in my eyes when I waved back. There was a melancholy in the air, and it had nothing to do with Virgil's death. I felt it strongest as I came into town. It's like the sadness you feel when you realize you ain't what you thought, and the world just doesn't square up with your dreams. It was like that, only it was good, somehow. Like a sadness too sweet to push away.

At first glance, Valhalla was like any other mountain village. Feed store. Livery. Dry goods and a tavern. All of them crooked and crowded together. The buildings were millboard and in some places dark brick. Rainwater still dripped from the eaves. The road was narrow and mainly mud, climbing up through town at a slant. If you were to set a dozen beads on a piece of paper and fold that paper in half, those beads would be Valhalla in the mountains. That's how tall they stood, or how deep the village. Back among the misty slopes to either side of town I saw the woodsmoke of cabins, folks tucked away in their coves, living their mountain lives unseen. I heard thunder, but it was far away.

I climbed down from Jimmy, just walking him now, when some youngins rolled a barrel hoop over my foot.

"Hey," I says, for I saw them hiding behind a bunch barrels against a wall, peeking out and giggling at Jimmy's stripes. "Hey, you know where I can find a Miss Odessa?"

The moment I spoke, one of them squealed with laughter and they all broke and scattered like geese.

The village was quiet mostly, like even the sounds were too soggy to get all the way to their feet. The autumn air was chilly and damp. The smell of woodsmoke strong. And though the sky was gray and slung low like a sheet, it appeared so lacquered with sentiment that everything took on a vague glow. I was dizzy with affection.

The blacksmith I passed had left both the broad doors to his shop wide open. Inside was dark but for the blush of his forge. I heard the rhythmic tink-tink of his hammer, which stopped when I looked in, then started again when I led Jimmy up the road.

I passed the barber. I passed the dentist. I passed the general store, pausing to peer through the window, and then walked on a few steps, and then halted. Scratching my jaw. I walked a few more steps, finally swiveling in the road. That was Tally Rose in there. Inside the store...Tally Rose was in Valhalla.

She was wearing the same white-brimmed hat, the satchel at her side. Through the shop's window, I saw her speaking with the storeman, pointing to some item on the shelf behind the counter. Then I noticed the wagon parked out front, the same one that had passed me. The driver waved out a match as he lit his pipe, most likely waiting for Tally to return with her purchases.

It was no great wonder, after all, that we should brush shoulders again, as we were both traveling the same road east. Still, there is nothing more desperately erroneous than a second goodbye. I stood there in the road, uncertain what to do.

I was struck by the image of two tightrope walkers, high in the sky, coming upon each other on a solitary cable in the clouds. Once the improbability of it has brought you both to a standstill, there's only one conversation left, and that's which one of you will be turning around, and which will be following the other.

I glanced up the road, at the glistening mountains beyond. I glanced back at the storefront—fairly certain she hadn't seen me.

"Moment of truth, Jimmy?"

He gave his tail a swish-swish. He lowered his head and I gave him a good long scratch.

"Alright boy. Let's get moving. Come on."

Near the top of the road we came upon a craggy-faced old woman churning butter on her porch. She was wrapped in a dark wool shawl. A little stream of water cut a groove down the road between us. Distant thunder again.

"I'll beg your pardon. Where am I to find a Miss Odessa? An Odessa vol Krie?"

She directed me to the mouth of Byron Hollow, up yonder mountain. It'd be steep going, she says, slippery too, but I was to follow Whitlers Creek which would be so swoled up about now I'd either find it or fall in trying. Just follow Whitlers Creek up the hollow, past the old watermill, continue for the time it would take to smoke you one deep pipe and then start looking for the bridge. Once I crossed the bridge I was to leave the creek behind and bear west through the woods on whatever trail I found, for all of them's like to lead to the vol Kries.

This I did. And it was steep as she promised, and slippery too, but I barely noticed for the rushing sounds of Whitlers Creek were near to hypnotizing. The hollow was lush and vibrant, soft with moss and the tender white of mushrooms blistering up through the earth. They hummed brightly as I crept past their clusters.

I heard the old watermill before we reached it. I knew it by that watery sound, too rhythmic for nature, that creaky sloosh-sloosh over rocks. The little millhouse itself was built right into the bank and so old it was furred with moss. That paddle just went round and round, sloosh and sloosh, and when we neared I could hear the millstones grinding within, a rough gritty sound you could feel at the base of your spine. This little place had probably been grinding flour since before the Revolutionary War.

As I stated, the wood-sounds were nice, the hollow lush. The air was spiced with the wet of leafy things and mulch. I took out Virgil's ball marble and thumbed it awhile, watching Jimmy Brown endeavor to bite a fly.

But soon my shoulder got sore, for you know how chilly it gets when you sit beside moving water. I asked Jimmy if he might be about ready to go.

"What do you say, Jimmy? You set to go find this Miss Odessa?" I scratched him below the eyes, which he seemed to like. It occurred to me he was now mine official. By all accounts old Will had left his mule behind, and someone had to look after Jimmy.

"There ain't but one Virgil in all these mountains. Ain't that right, Jimmy."

I scratched between his ears, and my finger snagged on his crown. It snapped free and suddenly little buttons and dried daisies lay scattered about my feet. I jumped back. I bit the tip of a thumb. My eyes went wide with angst and foreboding as I waited to behold Jimmy's transformation.

But if Jimmy Brown was turned godlike, it was in some detail I couldn't see. He twitched his ears and gave his chin a little jerk, and then resumed the indispensable chore of chomping flies.

When I continued on, it was in a more reflective manner. The path charged right up the east side of the creek, just as that old woman assured me, then came to the most interesting bridge you ever saw in your life.

Someone, Lord knows how long ago, must have tied a rope to a little cottonwood sapling on this side of the creek, tugged it toward the other, and then tied the rope to the far bank. In this way, the tree grew sidewise instead of up, bridging over the water like a deadfall, and then rerooted itself upon the opposite bank. Presently, the cottonwood was so ancient, and the topside so flat and shiny from tread, that two or maybe even three folks could walk side-by-side across it.

Which I did, Jimmy Brown traversing the creek on his own. The woods on the other side were storybook dark with granddaddy cedars and nothing but the narrowest footpath slipping through. I entered with a feeling not unlike stepping indoors, going from full noontide light into shadow. I heard birds but did not see a one. The forest mulch lay thick and black and I saw the tracks of pawed critters in the mud. Next thing you know, I smelled woodsmoke. It was cedar, as you might expect, which'll give off perfume and heat in about equal measure. Then I came to a pile of woodchips, freshly hacked, where someone had recent chopped a tree. The chips lay bright and glistening with moisture.

All at once the path opened onto a clearing, with a little stone cottage all alone in the clearing, firewood stacked neatly along the south side. This was it. The vol Krie's place at last.

Between us and the cottage was a stone-rimmed well, mossy with age, a warped leather bucket balanced on the edge. I saw the margin of a garden as it crept around from the back, herb plants grown big as bushes. There was a stable too, at least I think it was, with gabled roofs and hay spilling out the entry. In no part of the clearing was the turf level, high up the slope as we were, but the clearing was old, with no sign of the stumps and stones that must have once been. I left old Jimmy right there at the mouth of the woods, hanging his reins on a limb. You could still hear the rushing of Whitlers Creek back in the woods.

"You stay," I says, giving him a good scratch. "I'll be back in a minute." Dark stoles of smoke chugged up from the chimney, so I knew someone was home. I crossed to the porch, climbed the four steps and knocked on the pine-slat door.

"Hello?" I called. I took off my hat. I held it with both hands, but that made me feel like a beggar. So I tucked it under one arm, which I found too casual. I glanced briefly around and then slung it like a disk in the direction of Jimmy Brown. "Hello?" I knocked again. Eight quick raps of my knuckle, which struck me immediate as a peculiar rhythm. Five knocks works just fine on a door. Seven works. Even three has something natural to it, but eight? Eight does not work. In fact it's an abhorrence, is what it is. Makes your ears clench up. How could I possibly have made it this far in life without comprehending the taboo of the eight knocks? And why was I so damn nervous?

Thunder rolled down from the mountain again, and then I heard something like a chirp, or a child's squeal within. A feminine voice. Footsteps. Soft. The lifting of a latch. A young woman opened the door. She wore a long homespun dress tied at the front with an apron, into which she wiped one hand and then the other. She just looked up at me, waiting for me to speak. She had that look about her, the one you yourself might affect if you opened your door and found the likes of me shadowing your porch, standing stiff as a rod, staring back at you with eyes of wonder. For that girl was Madder Carmine.

"Can I help you?" she says, maybe a little bit guarded, and leaned against the door to block the view inside. And even before I could answer she sort of jumped back, reached down and picked up the littlun that was tugging at her skirts.

"Shush now. No. I told you no," she scolded, her voice even lovelier than I remember. "Sorry, just hang on," she says to me. "I'll be right back." She perched the child on her hip and disappeared into the recesses of her cottage. I peeked my head inside and saw her squatting down on the flagstones of her kitchen, setting the child up with a spoon and some couple pots to bang on.

I believe I choked. "Are you...uh..." I cleared my throat. "Are you..."

Coming back to the door, she says, "If you're looking for Enoch he's still down in town. Won't be back till evening, but you can leave any message with me."

"No, I just...uh...I'm sorry." Shaking my head. "I'm sorry, are you... are you Miss Odessa?"

Her eyes so dark, chips of glass in the sun. "I am," she says, "But not the 'Miss' part. Only the nigras call me Miss."

My mind just slumped. It went blank entire. "But, you have a child."

"Two. Why?" She became nervous all the sudden, leaning her head back from the door and calling to the kitchen. "Shush now. Mama's right here, hun. Just play your pots a minute. Sorry, why? Is it little Johnny Ray? What's he done this—"

"No," I says. "No, it's just that, well I was looking for a Miss Odessa. On account Virgil vol Krie."

"Virgil?" She straightened, quickly pushed a dark lock behind her ear. "You know about Virgil? How is he, where is he?" She stepped forward despite herself.

"Oh. Virgil." All the air whooshed out of me like a bellows. "Yeah. Well he is dead."

She just stared at me, like she's still waiting for me to speak, like my words were just circling and circling but couldn't find a place to land. Then little by little, a mist came over her eyes. She brushed once at her cheek and then put her fingers to her mouth. She turned away from me and walked inside.

⬅◆➡

I had every intention of whirling on my heels and running away from that place forever. My knees were jelly, my arms floated up from my sides. My mind was tumbled bricks. I had no more understanding of how to behave in that moment than if I'd been asked to build a ship to the sun.

Only one thing was certain. I lacked the courage to converse further with this woman. It was entirely out of the question. Although Madder, or Odessa, or whoever she was, showed not the slightest recollection of our ever meeting, she had been my whole world till today, my life entire, had governed the foaming tides of my blood. How could I sit down with her now, knowing I was nothing to her but an awkward stranger with news?

Suddenly it was settled in my mind. I made the decision to leave and then watched helplessly, forlornly, like a man chained to his horse, as my feet carried me inside the cottage.

Odessa vol Krie was beautiful. Beautiful as ever, if maybe a little heavier round the chin. And devastated, naturally, by the report of Virgil's death. She sat down beside the fire and cried without shame, telling me Virgil was like kin, she'd known him all her life, him practical raising her up as a girl. She never would have let Enoch sell him if times weren't so hard, and she always bore the intention of bringing him back. She had pawned Virgil in her mind. Just pawned him is all, and even maintained some fancy that he'd get himself married over in Nuckton and come back to Valhalla with a little wife on his arm.

She blew her nose. "I always told him he'd be bringing somebody along."

But now Virgil was dead of events she could not change, nor fully acquit herself from in her mind. She was mighty hard on herself, I'll give her that. Only I'm not sure how that honored Virgil's memory. Odessa asked questions, details, as if only to feel the sting of each answer, punishing herself with my stumbling narration.

And I obliged her, I believe, because I was too fearful to stop. If I wasn't talking about Virgil, then what? A part of me remained stunned, total awed by her presence and the fact we were finally sitting together in a room. The rest of me knew I'd spent my life lost in a fiction.

As you may well know, there is nothing in this life like getting total sobered all at once. Losing Mama was about closest I ever came before. Dropping a brick on my toe was a running second. And now here was this girl who had lived a whole life in my head, a secret life she knew nothing about it. She had a husband of her own. And kids and a home and...

Where in Lord's hell had I been?

When Odessa was done crying and her questions were all quenched, I recalled what had brought me to her home. I dug that beautiful ball marble from the bulging pocket of my coat, and I gave it to her.

"He wanted you to have it."

She gave me a dubious look.

"It's a perfect ball," I says. "Perfect round. See there? See how every bit is smooth? He worked awful hard. Harder than you can imagine."

"Hmph," she says before standing up, turning it over once in her hand, and then setting it beside a vase on the mantle. She squatted back down and poked at the logs till they rolled and the jumped to life with fire.

There was a loud clang in the kitchen and her boy started to cry. She went and picked him up and shushed him, walking him around the house, murmuring in his ear. With her free hand she hooked a black kettle over the fire for coffee.

When she sat down to suckle him, I didn't know what to do with myself. I felt buried alive, trapped in my skin. Even though she'd thrown a shawl over her shoulder I stared into the flames, reluctant to move or scratch or shift at all until I could be certain she'd put herself away. By and by she buttoned her dress, wiping the sheen of milk drool from her littlun's cheeks. She asked if I might stay for supper, but I could see she was only being polite. I gave her my thanks, saying I best be on.

"At least finish your coffee."

So we sat across from each other at that huge oak slab table, just sat there in silence, nervously sipping our coffee without a single thing to say between us. You'd think we were actually interested if you saw how attentively we watched her little boy scribble on the blade of a shovel with a coal-shard.

"So where's this Johnny Ray?" I says when I couldn't stand the tension any longer.

"School. Why are you here?" Her look was pointed, pushed me back against the wall.

"I told you. I made a promise to Virgil."

"Not till he died you didn't. Or just before," she says. "I'm asking what brought you here. What are you doing here, in Valhalla?"

My heart began to beat. I no longer knew the answer myself. Madder Carmine was nothing but an apparition of the heart, yet that spark, that fire that burned through me and stood me up when I fell. That stuff was for real. I know that now. I didn't before, but I know that now, just as I know the difference between wanting a thing so bad it hurts, and just loving it simple and true.

"Can I ask you something?" I says.

"Will it answer my question?"

"No," I says. "Not particular. But I'm fairly certain that's a question you don't want me answering."

She looked at me a moment. Suddenly it was the Madder I remembered, the one who could read me at a glance. It occurred to me I might not be the first fool of a man to lose the balance of his mind and intrude upon her life with his fantasies. She turned back to her child. He was sitting spraddled on the floor, clinking on her empty coffee cup with the spoon. She finally nodded. "Go on then. Ask what you like."

"Do you paint? You know, like paint pictures and such?"

"Some. Why?" She glanced at me, then back to her child. "I mean how'd you know?"

I couldn't conceive of a single answer that wouldn't pull us off track. "Welp, I was just thinking, if you don't mind and all, it might be nice to see one of your paintings. Before I go."

She took the coffee cup from her child, pulling him up onto her lap. She kissed the top of his head, resting her lips in his hair. "I can do that."

Odessa led me out to the rear porch. She hung back in the door's threshold, her child propped on one hip while I advanced to the railing where an easel overlooked a small garden. The garden was lush, overgrown, not yet pruned back for winter, and it was this recklessness of growth which she had replicated in paint. I looked long at the canvas, bending closer in examination, but even then I could not believe my eyes. After many moments of silence she says, "It's not yet finished," and I realized I was being prompted, and probably should have made some comment. But what could I say? The painting was terrible. Of all my expectations that failed to come true, none seemed more significant than this.

We exchanged a few words, Odessa and I, all of them meaningless, awkward, rife with weirdness and strain, and I took leave shortly after with a remarkably unremarkable farewell.

Beneath a sullen gray sky I walked to the edge of the clearing. I unhitched Jimmy Brown from the trees. From somewhere down in the valley came the rhythmic echo of a hammer on wood, or maybe an ax, and I dug an apple from the bottom of my saddlebag. I turned it over in my hands, just looking, looking, but red or green I still couldn't tell. Until I stopped looking and took a bite.

It mattered not that among the many paint jars I'd seen lining the edge of Odessa's easel, one had been labeled 'Madder Carmine.' No magical epiphany. No fireworks of the soul. I had stared at that jar like some fabulous artifact, unable to comprehend, until it all came together with a thump.

And I could philosophize to you about all the lessons I'd learned, or suddenly understood, and why such a road was needed to get here. But after so much yearning and toil, so many mountains and miles, all I understood was this: The searching was done, and in the done was my rest. Even if I found myself more alone than ever.

You could say it means something different, being alone at eight, at eighteen, at eighty. Same could be said of heartache, and the things we long for and don't find. That's why home can never mean the same thing twice. But when you have seen the ridgelines of October, the trails stinging with leaves, when you have walked one last time down a certain path through the woods, never to return, never pausing in stride, then you may recall love in the vague outline of your thoughts.

ACKNOWLEDGMENTS

The first draft of *Madder Carmine* was written nine years ago. Since then, many people helped shape this story into its present form, and I'm indebted to each. In particular, I thank Anika Enfield, Erik Hanzen, Debbie Hanzen, and Azure James, for their early readings.

I thank my wife Leala for never insisting I get a real job, and being a wellspring of support, no matter how rough the draft. Same is true of my mother, Susan Enfield. Both women are pillars of encouragement, and I could not have written this story without them.

I thank my grandmother, Fonda Spooner, for the fantastical tales she told me in her matter-of-fact voice, encouraging my love of magic-realism. And also my grandfather, Elmer Wagner, whose colorful life and language inspired the dialects of this novel.

Sincere thanks to *Existere Journal*, and also *Gargoyle*, both for publishing early chapters.

And I am sincerely grateful for fellow author Gail Sidonie Sobat, who held the door open, and then shoved me through.

Lastly, a huge thanks to everyone at Great Plains Publications for bringing this story to life. Gregg Shilliday, Catharina de Bakker, and Mel Marginet—you have my gratitude and respect. Well done.

Shelfie

A **free** eBook edition is available
with the purchase of this print book.

CLEARLY PRINT YOUR NAME ABOVE IN UPPER CASE

Instructions to claim your free eBook edition:
1. Download the Shelfie app for Android or iOS
2. Write your name in **UPPER CASE** above
3. Use the Shelfie app to submit a photo
4. Download your eBook to any device